WEST TO THE SUN

T.G. GOOD

Outskirts Press, Inc.
Denver, Colorado

This is a work of fiction. The events and characters described herein are imaginary and are not intended to refer to specific places or living persons. The opinions expressed in this manuscript are solely the opinions of the author and do not represent the opinions or thoughts of the publisher. The author has represented and warranted full ownership and/or legal right to publish all the materials in this book.

West to the Sun
All Rights Reserved.
Copyright © 2010 T.G. Good
v3.0

Cover Illustration © 2010 Outskirts Press. All rights reserved - used with permission.

This book may not be reproduced, transmitted, or stored in whole or in part by any means, including graphic, electronic, or mechanical without the express written consent of the publisher except in the case of brief quotations embodied in critical articles and reviews.

Outskirts Press, Inc.
http://www.outskirtspress.com

ISBN: 978-1-4327-5162-3

Outskirts Press and the "OP" logo are trademarks belonging to Outskirts Press, Inc.

PRINTED IN THE UNITED STATES OF AMERICA

To Daniel, who inspired the book,

To Chris, who made me write the book,

To Gopher, who is on every page of the book

CHAPTER 1
UNCLE PETER

When Uncle Peter arrived at our house, it was as exciting as Christmas, Declaration Day, and the fall harvest festival combined. The sun was brighter, the water fresher, and the apples crisper and juicier in our mouths. For a ten-year-old boy, life when Uncle Peter was around was a picture of excitement.

Uncle Peter was everything my father was not. His laughter was loud, showing his teeth underneath the beard that he always sported. He knew the games of boys and was never too important or busy to play them. He told stories of the things that he had seen in a way that made you dream of these previously unseen wonders. While his clothes were never stylish in a modern sense, the buckskin that he favored always spoke of daily adventure. The dirt was not that of the sweat in a field, rather it was the dust of the trail taken and not forsaken, the uncertainty of life beyond the horizon. While Father worked hard and provided daily sustenance for us, the life he offered was life focused on eternity beyond the grave.

Uncle Peter was not a big man. Yet his frame spoke of strength and toughness that would be ignored only by those who would make the error of underestimating him only at their own risk and only once. His hair and beard were a sandy brown. I once asked him why he always kept his beard so carefully trimmed. He told me that he never knew when he would meet his lady fair and he would not want to scare her if he met her with a scruffy beard.

Father lived his life behind the plow, making the most of the Tennessee bottomland that was dependent for its fertility on the rains of the region. I always wondered, as he followed the plow if he dreamt of the life of his younger brother, of going west, climbing mountains larger than the mind could imagine, of speaking with wild natives, and seeing herds of bison that went on as far as the eye could see. Yet, if he ever had these thoughts, they disappeared as he drove our mule to make a crop to survive another year on the land.

For Father laboring to support his family was a religious rite and his sweat was its holy water. He lived a disciplined life, willing to shove fun to the end of a long day, as long as there was no more work that he needed to complete. As a father, he was a man to be admired and feared, but never embraced.

This is why when the gate opened and I saw Uncle Peter's figure ride through on the tall horse my heart leapt inside of me. I was swinging on the tree swing outside our cabin, trying to avoid, again, the call of the hoe and the field of weeds that occupied my life.

I leapt off the swing when he shouted, "What does a stranger have to do to have a cool drink of water?"

"Just show me what you brought me, Uncle Peter. Show me something new and you can have all the water that you want."

"Are you telling me that a man can die of thirst around here if he doesn't have lumps of Spanish gold to trade for cool water?"

As I was about to reply, my mother came walking out of the cabin onto the front porch. Like every boy in the world, I always thought my mother was the most beautiful woman on earth. The sound of her singing in the cabin, as she was tending to food or Bitsy, my three-year-old sister, was more beautiful than any of the songbirds that God placed in the trees around our home. Those times when she dropped her work and listened to me talk about my day, my hopes for tomorrow and my frustrations with yesterday were times in my life when the world opened to me and all its possibilities were real and attainable.

My mother was taller than most of the women I knew, with beautiful chestnut hair. I know, because I saw her when she did not think I was able to see her moments of vanity that she loved to brush out her hair and shake it over her shoulders. Once when I was talking to her in a quiet time, when her work was approaching completion, she told me of the suitors she had when she was younger. While Father had a good piece of bottom country land, her people were townsfolk. Grandpa Buttron was a lawyer and a leader of the community; his people had brick houses and house slaves and money. Why my mother chose this life with the bottomland instead of the town, I never fully understood. Yet, when I questioned her, she told me that at first sight she knew my father was a better man than any of the handsome dandies from town with their fine airs and empty conversation. When she saw him from a distance at the county fair, both from his looks and from the way, he responded to other people, she knew that this was a man who had inner strength that she admired. I never fully understood this comment, because when I looked at my father I saw hard work, hard words, and a hard life.

"Jeremiah, who are you talking to?"

I never had a chance to answer, because my Uncle Peter swung off his horse and bounced lightly across the dirt yard and swung his hat down in front of him in a large, dramatic bow, and announced in his laughing voice, "Why it's Peter Symons, at your service milady. Do you have any dragons that need slaying? Has my brother already slain them at your bidding? Where is that little Bitsy that I have come from afar to tickle?"

Then he lifted Mother off the ground and swung her around, laughing all the time. The laughter infected the scene and caused my mother to join with a laugh that set my heart free.

"Jeremiah, bring your father home. The plow will wait another day. Your Uncle Peter is back from Timbuktu or wherever he has spent the last two years. While you are doing that, we will wake little Bitsy from her nap to greet her uncle properly."

With those words, I ran, as I could only run when my heart was running, across the yard and into the field, looking for my father. The day was hot, but the sweat of the run felt good, because the news was good. "Father, come quick, Mama wants you."

My father dropped the reins, exasperated that his day of labor was interrupted by any outside influence and turned around to me. "What is it Jeremy, what does she need that you cannot do for her."

I stopped and I looked at him and said in a quieter voice "Your brother is here and she said the plowing can wait one more day."

"Will she say that when there is no food on the table one day and Little Bitsy is crying? I need to finish this job and then I can go visiting. God has given me this family to protect and as much as I want to see him, I would not be doing His labor if I were to avoid it for the fun of your uncle's company." Then my father turned and moved on with his plow.

I felt my shoulders slump as I heard his harsh words. There were times when work was a substitute for living for my father.

I always thought that to Father it was easier to understand those mules than his family and sometimes that plow was just too easy an escape for him. As I watched him move into the distance, I felt a hand touch me on the shoulder, guiding me to one side. Uncle Peter breezed past me, seized one side of the handles of the plow, and started walking with Father down the row of corn. Father turned and smiled at Uncle Peter, who simply nodded and called out to the mule, urging him to move forward. In that moment, without a word being passed between them, I learned that there is a bond of brothers extending far beyond geography, temperament, and experience.

I stood and watched this odd scene of two men plowing. I heard from the long row the sound of men laughing. I realized that there was no place in this scene for me. I was watching something that did not include me and I turned and returned to my world of chores and boyish games which were brightened by the arrival of the always fun Uncle Peter.

Later that afternoon, Father and Uncle Peter returned to the house, full of the dirt of the field and laughing the laugh of men whose labor has been productive and is now complete. My mother greeted them at the door of our cabin, barring the way of entry as if her frame would be a sufficient barrier against these two strong men. She used a wooden spoon to point to the wash bucket and, her voice full of authority, she scolded these two strong men:

"Jedediah Symons. Peter Symons. You will wash yourselves before coming into my clean home. We have company and I will not have a couple of dirty field hands eating off of my best dishes."

Father nudged my uncle, laughed his laugh rarely heard around our home, and told him, "We better do what she says because she is too fierce for me. You can take a town girl down to a farm but when she brings out her good dishes, we all need to act like dandies."

My uncle laughed and slapped my father hard on his back. My mother just scowled the look of a woman who wants her fake anger to be intimidating. She silently pointed with the wooden spoon to the water. There was not enough power in the biceps of my father that would let him enter that home without obeying the words of that strong, lovely woman.

Supper, when there was company at our home, was a festival of tastes and sounds that added joy to my heart and stomach. Gone were our usually silent simple meals of beans and cornbread and in their place were sumptuous flavors. The dinners with guests always began with the prayer of my father that called the blessings of the good Lord on the guest. Once the blessing was complete, Mother would bring to the table heaping amounts of chicken fried in her iron skillet with the right amount of lard which left a light brown crispy skin and the inside white meat that was perfectly juicy and tasty. The beans were strong and cooked with crumbles of bacon, which added a flavor that masked the fact that I was a boy eating his vegetables. The cornbread tasted differently when surrounded by my mothers chicken. When my belly felt like it could not contain any more, Mother brought out the peach cobbler that she baked from the fruit I picked off the trees growing just outside our home. This fruit had been stored in the cellar that my father dug into the side of the hill next to our home. The crust of the cobbler was golden brown and the peaches had the perfect mixture of sugar and tartness. When we left the table from a meal with a guest, we were sure that God had blessed us with the bounty of heaven.

I helped Mother clear the dishes from the table and brought the water to clean them. Father and Uncle Peter sat on the front porch, watching the sun slip past the gray rugged bark of our tall locust trees and listening to the sounds of the birds as they bedded their little chicks down for the evening. Bitsy worked at delaying her impending bedtime through trying to impress Uncle Peter with her young jokes and games. Mother hummed a tune to herself as she did the dishes, a happy tune sung by the girls of her age who dreamt of romance, adventure and a beautiful life.

Once the dishes were done, Bitsy reluctantly gave in to my mother and allowed herself to be put to bed in a corner of the main room. She giggled as Mother kissed her and told her to fall asleep. Then, it was my turn, as I went upstairs into my loft and put my head down on my bed.

One of the many things I loved about our cabin was that my windows extended over the front porch of the cabin. That meant if I was interested, I could listen to any conversation occurring on the front porch. If ever there was an adult conversation that I wanted to hear, it was any conversation involving Uncle Peter's life. To hear better, once my mother went down the stairs of my loft, I crawled to the wrong end of my bed and listened carefully to the grown-ups, propping up my chin with my hands.

Uncle Peter strummed a guitar that he always carried with him on his travels. Mother was humming some of her tunes and Father was silently rocking in his chair, with the chair making a gentle and predictable squeak. Then Father cleared his throat and asked the question that I know he had been thinking since he first saw his brother at the plow:

"So, Peter, what brings you this way after two years away from us? Have you come home for good or are you just resting up for another adventure?"

Uncle Peter replied and I could hear the smile in his voice. "It has been a long time, and I have seen amazing things. I have made it all the way to the Pacific Ocean and seen mountains the like of which I never even dreamt. The land is good brother and the world is an amazing place. I will not say that I am here to stay. I aim to see many more things in my life but I want to see them with you, Mary, and the children. I would love to take you, Mary, and the children away from this place and show you some of the world outside of the fence rails of this farm."

"Now, Peter," my father began, "you know that we are much different people. I work the land and am bound to the labor that it has. The Lord has given me this family to support and this bottomland to make fertile in His service. I do not have the time, the means, or the freedom to travel the world."

"Ah, Mary, it never used to be this way." Peter laughed as he ignored my father's interruption. "I remember Jeddie as a boy was going to go to sea, to battle the Barbary pirates and steal the hearts of wild exotic women in all corners of the world. This Tennessee land was never going to see him once he had a chance to leave it behind. I was going to be the man on the land, planting, hoeing, and harvesting. We never would have believed the way it turned out with me being the man of the road and him being the man of the land and of the responsibilities it brings."

Mother laughed the laugh of a woman who imagines the boy who has became the man she married. "I cannot see either you being the man of the land Peter nor Jeddie being the man who dreamt of pirates. I am glad, because my husband is a good man, a man of substance and support. If he were a silly dreamer, then he would never have convinced this town girl to marry him."

Uncle Peter's voice became serious for a moment, as he turned his chair and spoke directly to Father. "Let me talk to that man of substance, then, Jeddie. This Tennessee bottomland is no place for you to raise the family. You know that there is no room for you to grow here and you know what you see in this Tennessee world is not what you believe. You never have been a man to let another man do your work while you ride around on a horse watching him sweat. Do you want your boy living and learning how to treat people in this community? What will you give him other than the portion of bottomland and neighbors who treat God's created people in a harsher way than they would treat a good piece of bottomland? And what of the little Bitsy, who can you trust with her?"

My father's voice was sharp. "Peter, there are good people here. This is our home and this is where we should stay."

"Jeddie, I'm not saying that there are not good people in this community. I am saying that you can have good neighbors in other places, without the evil of things that you do not believe are right. You tell me of good bottomland and I can tell you that I have seen land that is better than any land of which you have dreamt. I can tell you that I have seen land where trees will bend over and nearly break with the weight of the fruit they bear.

"Beyond the land, there are things I have seen that you could never imagine. I have seen running herds of buffalo, beasts so large and so mobile it astounds you. They have horns that make them look like the fiercest of animals and they are so fast, large, and numerous that when the herd runs the whole earth shakes under their feet. Yet, to watch them with their calves is to know that they are the most wonderfully gentle of beasts.

"The mountains are so large. They must be miles high and they astound you. The carving of the rocks must have been the handiwork of a master sculptor. I cannot describe what I felt like the first time I saw them. I felt like both laughing and crying at the same time. They reached beyond the sky and their very tops were covered with snow even on the warmest of summer days. It does something to one's heart to be sweating in the furnace of the lowlands, look up, and see snow-covered peaks reaching to God's heaven. The skies are so blue they leave you breathless. Clouds are things you remember, but never see. Some of the other beasts, the elk who I have heard bugling in their high-pitched voice for their lady love, and the fierce bears, the wild sheep, and the haunting coyote; these are things you would see on the way to this land."

"Peter, you always did spin a tall tale," Mother began before he interrupted.

"But it is no trappers' tale. It is a way to a new life that will let you, Jeddie, Jeremiah, and little Bitsy live life in a way that will please you. There is plenty of hard work, but Jeddie will not have to work himself to an early grave before the next crop comes up. Jeddie, I am surprised at how you look. You are getting old before your time and if you do not care about that, look at your beloved Mary. I still believe she is the belle of the ball and the most beautiful lady in seven counties, but I do see some lines growing in her face. Are you willing to let her get old just for this piece of bottomland?

"Jeddie, the local government gives you the land just for being a married couple who will work it. The land is so lush and green. If God took the time to create such wonders and the government is willing to give it to you, it seems ungrateful not to go and take it. Jeddie, I know it is time for me to settle down. If you will come to Oregon, then I will come with you, buy the farm down the lane, and we can live the life our parents always wanted."

"But, Peter," my dad said in his low quiet voice, "how would we get to Oregon? You can decide to go one day and the next day you mount your horse and go. We have a farm and a family who cannot just mount a horse and go because someone says that beyond the sun is a better place. There are things that keep us here and people we love who cause us to remain."

"Jeddie, I know it is hard, but you know that old man Lucas has been looking at this land as long as he has been around here and he would pay you a good price. I know there are people and places you will leave behind, but you can never see new places and people until you move forward. As far as how to get there, every spring there are wagons heading from Missouri to Oregon and we can join one of these groups. I am here to help you and I know that next spring we can head for a better life there than the life we both have today. If you do not come, then I will forever miss you, because I am going and I will never venture here again."

"Peter," my father said, in the voice that always precluded answer, "we will speak of this some more, but not tonight."

With that, silence descended on our farm. I could hear the light playing of the guitar from my uncle on the breeze. Uncle Peter played the guitar with the style of the rovers he had met while he was on the Santa Fe Trail. I moved back to the head of my bed and fell asleep listening to the songs of the crickets and dreaming of herds of buffalo shaking the ground under my feet and of mountains that reached forever into the sky of brightest blue.

CHAPTER 2
TOWN DAYS

Peter stayed with us throughout the rest of that spring and into the summer. Hard work continued around the farm, but it was more pleasant than in the past since Uncle Peter was more helpful around the farm than I would have thought possible. Somehow, I had always thought of his life as an adventurer and not the boy who grew up on farms working for his father. There was no more talk of Oregon, at least within my hearing, but still I occasionally saw snowcapped mountains extending miles into my dreamland heavens.

During the early spring, after the planting, I attended the school that was just a few miles down the lane. Miss Spencer taught the school. She was a young woman of maybe seventeen years old. She stood the same size as some of the older boy students. Through her stories, she opened the eyes of her farm students to a world of adventure outside of the rural community. For this and for her many kindnesses, we loved her. Any student, though, who thought he could bully Miss Spencer because of her youth was quickly proven wrong.

The spring days turned naturally to summer. School ended as the days became warm and the corn and sorghum started to grow tall and well rooted in the bottomland. I no longer spent my days studying the heroes of the past, but instead I hoed in the fields, mended fences, and dealt with the needs of the milk cows and chickens. Sometimes, my uncle and I slipped away after the morning milking and tried to catch the catfish that lived in the Stones River just down the trail from our farm. I studied Uncle Peter, observed the way he approached the fishing, the preparation and the quiet study as he tried to decide where the fish were most likely to seize his bait.

The crops grew well that year. With Uncle Peter working alongside me the daily chores felt less oppressive. Even Father was less stern and more like a man who enjoyed life. Every night, Uncle Peter pulled out his guitar and played the haunting tunes he had learned from the traders on the Santa Fe Trail. With this music drifting to my room and the tunes the trees played as the breezes flowed through their upper branches, sleep always came easily to me as the day ended.

Sundays were always special to us. The chores were limited to those that we needed to do for the safety of the animals. The weeds had a daylong respite from our very personal war. Bitsy and I gathered in the back of our wagon, with Mother and Father sitting up front. Mother was always dressed in her finest dress, which made me so proud of having the most beautiful mother in the whole world, or at least in the county. Even Father, who rarely showed emotion, glanced at her on these occasions where the summer sun danced through the hair showing under her bonnet and played games with the light with a look that was pure love mixed with sinless pride. While my parents rode on the wagon, Uncle Peter rode alongside on his horse, looking far more like a country gentleman than a wilderness adventurer.

From time to time, Father would take his turn preaching. He always told Old Testament stories of the prophets and patriarchs. His voice seemed surer in the pulpit than it did in the field when he was directing my labor. He spoke about God as if He were an intimate friend. When he preached, I understood my father in a way that I never did when we worked side by side in the fields. The distant father showed a more expansive personality when he spoke of God. Flashes of humor appeared more frequently when discussing the larger issues of God and eternity than they did when he spoke of the yield of the bottomland. Sadly, I realized that I learned more about the man I loved from his sermons than from the time spent battling the weeds in our mutual combat.

After the Sunday meetings, we would stand outside the little church. While the adults socialized, I would try to find my best friend, Billy Hollis. The two of us would climb the trees and tell each other of the fish caught or almost caught that week. From our high perch, we would watch as the younger boys pulled the ponytails of the younger girls and then run away when they squealed. A few years ago, we had been the boys who were pulling and running, but now we had moved onto more mature pursuits that did not involve tormenting squealing girls in any way.

One summer Sunday, following a lengthy sermon, Billy and I ran to the tree and climbed to the top of the thick branches, which, were able to support us. "Look at that, Jeremy."

I looked down and saw Uncle Peter walking down the lane talking quietly with our very own Miss Spencer. Why would Miss Spencer ever speak to anyone who was older than we were? We had frozen her in time always speaking to students and telling us of faraway places. To see my uncle laughing with her and telling her of the places he had seen seemed beyond our ability to comprehend.

She was only our teacher: What interest could he have in her or her in him?

Billy and I clambered down from the tree and started to stalk Uncle Peter and my teacher. We could not come close enough to hear the words that were being said, but we could hear her laughing lightly as the young girls did when they spoke about knights in shining armor. Billy and I practiced our silent walking, as if we were natives who would walk in the woods as they were trying to sneak up on some deer who would become their supper. From tree to tree we would walk, silently trying to move closer to the couple. Finally, as we were just about to move close enough to hear them, I saw my uncle turn around and say aloud, "Sarah, it has been so long since I scalped a couple of boys and I am really out of practice."

"Peter, I think you should do whatever you need to do to make you happy. But, if you need to scalp some boys, then could I at least have one of the scalps?"

"Certainly, Sarah, I would love to give you one of those scalps. Maybe I should give you the scalp of a relative to make it more special."

"Please do so. A relative's scalp would be a most lovely present."

Uncle Peter pulled his knife out of its sheath, turned towards the tree behind which Billy and I were hiding and made a yell that sounded like what I imagined how the scream of wild banshees from faraway jungles would sound. We ran down the road without looking back while hearing my uncle chasing and laughing behind us. Finally, when we reached the churchyard we turned around and saw that he had stopped running half way down the road. He and Miss Spencer were bent over at the waist from laughter.

Throughout the summer, we protected the corn and beans from

the birds and weeds and waited for the day when the crops were mature enough to harvest. The rains were kind that year, arriving neither too early nor too late and in amounts that neither flooded the fields nor parched the ground. Before we knew it, it was time for us to be in the fields, laboring from the early morning until it was very dark. The work was hard, but essential. Father said that the Good Lord had given us this bounty and it would be insufficiently grateful for us not to work to bring it into our storage.

So the four of us worked: Mother, Father, Uncle Peter and me. Bitsy ran in the fields, responsible for nothing but herself. To make herself feel more involved, she would occasionally grab low ears of corn, but mostly, she just chattered to us with any observation that struck her three-year-old heart. Her enjoyment of the time made our work less laborious since her childish laughter led to our constant smiles.

At night, following the day's labor, food was an afterthought to me. I would sit by the fire and let the thoughts of the day and aches of my muscles descend upon me as my eyes became heavier and heavier until I would feel myself being lifted to my loft. My next real conscious act would be to wake up in my bed the next morning.

The days went on like this for most of the week. Then, as suddenly as the labor began, the labor concluded. The crops were out of the ground and stored away in our cellars and bins. I prepared for winter, which, was always a more relaxed season on our farm. The constant battle with the weeds would enter into a truce that would resume with renewed ferocity upon planting.

The evening we finished the harvest, Father turned his attention to a corncob that he had secreted away from the corncrib. With his hard hands, he carefully removed all of the corn kernels into a bowl. Then, he gently but firmly poked the sticks that he had been carefully whittling into the corncob. Next, he went to Mother's sewing box and removed a small portion of the wool yarn she had been hoarding. With his quick fingers, he wrapped the yarn around the cob, loop after loop until it became apparent that the naked corncob was becoming a little doll. Then, he took scraps of fabric that lacked any apparent value and wrapped the little scrap dress with a ribbon that my mother used to wear in her hair when the ribbon was fresh and new. Silently, he slipped the little doll into Bitsy's bed, returned to his chair, and renewed whittling. My sleeping sister stirred, rolled over, and reached her sleeping arm over her doll and on her dream-ridden face, I saw a tired and innocent smile.

The Saturday after the final corncob was in the corncrib we loaded our wagon and headed into town. During this busy time of year, town visits were passed over due to the press of urgent work. This made this visit all the more festive because the labor of the season was done and the crop was successfully in storage. Neighbors who we ordinarily did not see except in the confines of church were in town also, gathering supplies and sharing the gossip of the day. Teenagers, freed from daily constraints of life on the farm, engaged in the careful looks and shy rites of courtship. Mother traded in Mr. Cressley's store, Father visited with the other farmers to compare crop yields and tell stories, mostly true, of the fertility of the ground, and the growth of that seasons calves and horses. Being a ten-year-old boy with a world of curiosity and five cents to spend, I naturally drifted between the emporium of sights and smells in Cressley's store and the conversation of the men just outside of the door.

Around the corner of Main Street, I noticed Vernon Lucas riding his horse, too fast, as usual. Mr. Lucas, who most people simply referred to as Old Man Lucas, was the most successful farmer in our area. He rarely left his own farm. On Sundays, when we did our visiting and attending church, Mr. Lucas was checking his fields. He was one of the rare people in our farm community who owned slaves, but he worked alongside his slaves and sometimes worked harder than they did. His slaves were poor; ill fed and mistreated. A man who loved money as much as he did was not disposed to spend money foolishly on his property, even if that property took human form.

He pulled his horse roughly to a stop. He swung his leg over the horse and slapped the reins into my face. The leather stung my face and a well of tears involuntarily filled my eyes. Blood trickled moist and hot from where the hard reins hit me. I felt my fists clench but then unclench as I realized who I was about to hit.

"Hold my reins, boy; I need to talk to that father of yours. Now!" The cruelty of his voice cut through me much as the reins had sliced through my skin.

Father and Uncle Peter had been standing with a group of men. They were listening to the stories but Father missed nothing with his eyes and jerked his head around as if he had been the one hit in the face with the reins. He strode with a quickness that was foreign to the father I saw on a daily basis and said in a tone of voice that while not raised in volume commanded respect:

"Vernon, don't do my boy that way. If you had the manners that your mother taught you, then there is no way you would have struck my boy. Hold your own horse and I will speak with you later. Maybe."

Uncle Peter sprang from behind Father. Making a guttural noise of anger, he swung his right fist right into Old Man Lucas' jaw and knocked him to the dirt street. He stood over the fallen man and pointed his finger down at him.

"My brother is too much of a Christian gentleman to do that to you. Where I am from, we handle things differently than with just words. If you get up, I have more for you. Now, Jeremiah, hand this man's reins back to him and let him hold his own horse."

With that, Uncle Peter and my father each put an arm around me and moved me away from the scene. Despite the blood that trickled down my cheek, the wound did not hurt anymore since the attention from these two good men relieved a good portion of the pain. Uncle Peter spoke first:

"That man would not survive long in the west. We may be rougher there, but we do not learn our manners in eastern schools. Instead we treat boys more like men; not like beasts of the fields."

My father replied, "Peter, he is to be pitied and avoided. He has money but nothing else. No one loves him; no one even regards him well. At night, he counts his money and his cold gold is all he has to keep him warm. When death finally comes to him he will be alone and only his money will mourn him."

"Still, with all of his money, you would think that he could buy some manners."

Father nodded his head sadly, examined my face to ensure that I was injured none too badly, turned, and strode over to Mr. Lucas, who was still sitting in the dust of the street. He had an unaccustomed look of bewilderment on his face. Father extended his hand and lifted him to his feet. Old Man Lucas tied up his horse. Then Father and my adversary walked down the street, chatting like men of acquaintance, but clearly not like friends. This left me alone with my Uncle Peter, which is exactly what I wanted since I had a question for him.

"Do you miss the frontier, Uncle Peter?"

"I miss it every day, Jeremy. The distances of the west make you feel free and yet so small simultaneously. The mountains and the canyons are immense; you see them for days before you are actually there and when you finally reach them, they are even bigger than you had the nerve to dream. Sometimes, when I was in the dry lands headed to Santa Fe and then beyond on my way to California, it might rain just a sprinkle. Thee drops of water caused the world to come alive with noises, sights, and smells. The flowers turn from brown into any number of colors; the animals that have been hiding in the ground come out and scurry with all of their activity and there is a smell that you can neither believe nor describe.

"The challenges of life are bigger. Because the mountains are so high, there is always the chance a snowstorm could catch you at the oddest time. Three years ago, I was trapping in the mountains in September, later in the year than I should have been, when the snows came and left me buried in a little lean-to for over a week. By the time I was able to dig myself out, I thought of my boyhood dog, not because we had so much fun when I was younger but because he always looked so meaty. Then, when I was able I headed down into the valley, slow step after slow step until I reached a low enough place where the snowdrifts did not remain. Life was just as beautiful as before but I also knew something of my ability to survive. Sometimes, life there is so hard that you learn you have strength you never believed you had. That lesson is something every man needs to learn at some point in their life.

"The people in the west are different than the ones here. People in the east are here because their grandfather and great-grandfathers lived here. They have roots but the roots are so deep that they could not move if they thought they wanted to move. Out west, people do not have the deep roots but they have the freedom to go and see things that God put on this earth to be seen and admired because they tell you so much about Him. The difficulty of the life out there drives people to extremes. In some cases, it brings out the worst in their behavior, as if their survival would be even sweeter if their neighbor did not survive. Yet, I have also seen men share their last morsel of food when there is no guarantee that the next morsel will ever appear."

When Uncle Peter spoke about his life beyond the frontier, time stood still. I tried to imagine what life must be like where there were fewer towns and more of God's amazing handiwork. Even though Uncle Peter left me spellbound, I knew somehow, in the way you know things without being able to prove them, that the reality of these sights exceeded the stories that he told me.

My mother and Bitsy had come from the store and interrupted this trance of listening. Bitsy was waving her corncob doll, Suzy, who had become her constant companion since the night Father slipped it into her bed. Mother looked for Father, glanced at Uncle Peter and then focused on the blood trickling down my cheek from my new wound.

"Jeremy, where's your father? I need my men to cart the groceries. What happened to your face?" She reached over and stroked my face, carefully, tenderly, to assess the damage.

Uncle Peter responded. "Jeddie is talking to Old Man Lucas. Jeremy put his face in front of Lucas' whip and now he has some long overdue character to his jaw line. Of course," Uncle Peter rubbed his knuckles slowly, "Mr. Lucas' jaw has a little character also. Let us get those supplies for you." With that, all conversation about my problems with the meanest man in the county ceased.

Father returned to us, squeezed my mother's hand, and climbed up into the wagon without a word. We left for home, each with our own thoughts of an adventurous afternoon in town.

Father cleared his throat after dinner that evening, an act that let us know he had words he wanted us to hear. Father spoke in the same quiet tone he used when he was in the pulpit of our church. Instead of speaking about God, however, he started to talk about our lives:

"Mary, Jeremy, Peter: I have made a decision. I have made it because I love my family and though I may not always show it, I want the life provided for you to be rich with good things. This is not easy, for I am a man who likes my life and hates changes in it." He paused and looked around at the walls of our home in which I had lived my entire life. Mother looked carefully at her man; my uncle put his guitar down and sat forward in his chair.

"Peter is the butterfly of the family. He dreams of California and goes; he wonders what it would be like to drive cattle and he does. He sees a mountain and climbs it. For me it is different. I was born ten miles away from here. I planned to live here on this good bottomland, see Jeremy and Bitsy grow here, and eventually I would die here. Peter, you have come here and told me stories of buffalo as big as elephants and mountains that reach the moon and I have decided that this is something I want to see before I die. When Peter rode onto our farm this spring he spoke to me about Oregon. Every time we have been alone since that day, he has spoken to me about Oregon. If for no other reason than to quiet his talking, I have decided to move to Oregon.

"Old Man Lucas, as mean as he is, knows nothing of people, but he does know good land. He wants ours. I asked him for an amount of money that no one should pay for our farm and he has agreed to pay it. That will be more than enough for us to make it to Oregon. He has agreed to let us stay in the house until the spring and then we will move west."

Mother spoke, when she was sure he was done. "Jeddie, I have been hoping to do this since the day Peter rode into our yard. I know I have three good men to take your women west and I will rely on you and on the Good Lord to see us through. When I heard Uncle Peter tell of those mountains, I realized that if I don't see those mountains in my life, I will not feel like I have lived a full life." She walked over to him, kissed him on the top of the head, and rubbed his shoulders. I smiled, realizing that my life of sameness was about to change in an adventure worthy of the stories of Miss Spencer.

Preparations for our trip dominated life that winter. Father worked with his tools building wooden chests to place in the wagon to contain our clothing and the necessary storage areas for the food for the journey. Mother spent her time canning fruit and vegetables for the trip. Bitsy ran around the house with her inseparable companion doll. Her job was essentially to stay out of the way, which was a task she consistently and joyfully failed to accomplish.

Before we realized it, Christmas, with its glorious traditions, was upon us. My mother cooked a feast. She began with nice light rolls and all sorts of preserves, crab apples and wild plums and dried apples. She then served us roast spare ribs with sausage and mashed potatoes and plain gravy. With this, she served chicken stewed with the best of the gravy and another chicken that was stuffed and roasted in the Dutch oven by the fire. For dessert, she had cake and pumpkin pie, so sweet and satisfying. The food took so long to prepare and yet when we ate, we devoured the treats so that the food was gone and our stomachs stretched within minutes.

Following the meal, Father read us the story of the birth of Jesus and we sang familiar carols. We passed out the little gifts that we had made for one another and enjoyed the warmth of home and family. Then, we each retreated to our world. My father nodded in his chair. My mother sat by the fire and sewed. My sister played with her new toys while holding Suzy.

The sounds of bells and the whoops of Uncle Peter from outside our cabin broke this scene of serenity. We ran outside of the home and there he was driving a team of six oxen, all with little bells attached to their yokes. He was sitting up on top of the largest wagon I had ever seen.

"Merry Christmas," he sang out. "Mary, Jeddie, and I thought this would be the perfect Christmas gift for our entire family. Here's your Oregon wagon and the friends who will be pulling you to the new home."

I yelled as loud as I could, which caused my sister to jump, but just caused the oxen to lift their heads as if a great announcement had been made that did not concern them. Father hugged his beaming wife and told her in his quiet way:

"Mary, we're really going in the spring. We're heading to Oregon."

Mother said nothing audibly but the smile on her face spoke volumes as clearly as the great books that Miss Spencer read to us. The oxen lowed while my parents kissed and winter flurries of snow danced in the wind around our family.

CHAPTER 3

PREPARATIONS AND GOOD-BYES

Our lives changed that winter. We shifted from maintaining normal life on the farm, which involved preparing for the next year of planting to making sure that the family was ready for the impending journey to Oregon. The prospect of traveling to Oregon excited me, but the actual preparation for the journey made me think more about the people left behind. I was scared.

Uncle Peter helped prepare us for the trip. He told us, frequently by the light of the fire, that we needed to be very careful in picking what we took to Oregon. He would lecture us. "Deciding what to take and what to leave is the most important part of making it to Oregon. You need to pack food and more food. Clothing for the trip is essential; it is important that you neither be too hot nor too cold since either one can make you ill. Medicine is important, since this is a long and difficult journey. You will see along the side of the road huge iron stoves and grandfather clocks." Here, he would laugh. "Can you eat a grandfather clock? Do they not have stoves in Oregon?

"Anything that helps you survive the long journey ahead of you is important. If you do not need something and if you can buy it in Oregon, then leave it behind. You are committing dreadful, and perhaps deadly, waste if you pack something not needed for life on the trail. You could become fabulously wealthy with the things left behind on the trail. That is not the plan. The goal is to arrive in Oregon safely."

Listening to this, Mother nodded her head and mentioned to Uncle Peter that we were neither "rich enough to bring a large measure of worldly effects nor foolish enough to ignore the advice of a man who had seen so much."

Mother was the busiest of all of us in preparing for the trip. Her first job, which she attacked with the gusto of a starving man attacking an offered banquet, was preparing the cover for the wagon. She sewed a double cover that Uncle Peter and I fastened to the wagon. This layer would keep any moisture out but would be sufficiently airy that it would keep the wagon from being too hot. The outer layer was made of clean white linen that would do the majority of the work in keeping the temperature reasonable and would keep our possessions dry when the spring thunderstorms hit.

Covering the wagon was just the beginning of my mother's sewing duties. She and her friends from neighboring farms gathered at our house and started work on the clothing that would take us west. My uncle assured us that clothing needed to be sturdy. Stylish garb meant nothing when leading oxen through the mud of freshly moistened roads or the endless dust of a desert trail. When the temperature was too hot or when the mountain snows hit, people did not care whether clothing met the style dictates of the cities.

With these words in mind, Mother and her friends took the good muslin and made loose-fitting shirts for the men and dresses for the ladies. Our pants were homemade jeans that the ladies worked on all day in order to make sure that they met the equally important requirements of strength and comfort. My mother took this work very seriously; she told her friends that she loved her family far too much to allow them to arrive at their new home looking like common ragamuffins.

School occupied only a portion of my time. Miss Spencer was still a wonderful teacher, but my real-life prospects for adventure pushed the lessons of mathematics and the stories of adventures on the high seas out of my mind. Miss Spencer also acted differently; she spoke to me individually more than before and always of the adventure on which we planned to embark.

One day, as the cold of January shifted to the moisture of February, and as the call of the school was waning, I joined my father and uncle in their job of cutting additional wood to ensure that we had enough to stay warm for the remainder of the winter. We hitched up the six oxen to the old wagon that we had previously used around our farm and drove them to a stand of good trees. Learning to drive this team of oxen was a job that my father took very seriously that winter since it was essential that he turn this group of oxen into a team on whom we could rely in the coming months for our long journey over the mountains.

While these animals were all of limited intelligence, they did have distinct personalities. Bob was all brown and in his docile manner would do any task that a person holding a whip would command. Bill was a little smaller than Bob and his personality was that he did not like the transition between movement and inactivity. It would take a whip to cause him to move, and a whip to cause him to stop. The most challenging of our animals was Todd, the white and brown speckled oxen. He was larger than the others and father frequently sighed that he felt Todd was probably too smart to be an ox. Todd was convinced that the grass outside of the pen was better than the grass we supplied in the pen. Unfortunately, his intelligence allowed him to use his head to open the gate, make it to the open ground, and sample fresher grass. Todd was always willing to move as long as there was a promise of green grass at the end of his journey. His personality made him the most difficult of the animals to handle; my Uncle Peter was convinced that we would be better off with five oxen and a large supply of roast beef. The other three oxen followed the lead of these animals, reliable, sturdy companions who would safely work to bring us west.

Once we reached the woods and began chopping the wood, my father started talking:

"Jeremiah," he said in his low tone, "you are no longer a little boy, and it is largely that fact that has allowed me to feel comfortable in moving my family across the country to our new home. When you were a child, we could only rely on you to act like a child. Now, however, you are closer to a man and we need to start asking things of you that we would need from a man."

I looked at him with surprise. Father called me a man and yet when I thought and saw the seriousness on his face, I said, "Certainly."

This response brought a smile to his face. "Careful, Jeremy, you don't want to promise until you hear the request. This is not going to be an easy request and it is something that I need you to do cheerfully. You know that your uncle and I are driving the team to Missouri, where we will meet up with our expedition in St. Joseph's. This journey will be difficult and I do not wish to wear out your mother and little Bitsy in arriving at the beginning of the trail. Therefore, we are going to be leaving your mother and

Bitsy with your Aunt Doris and Uncle Pierre for a month and then have them take riverboats from Nashville to St. Louis and on to St. Joseph. Since you are a man now, we need you to perform as a man and stay with your mother, taking care of her and helping her with Bitsy."

I noticed my father's face was serious and would tolerate no disagreement. I nodded my head at this request since it is frequently easier to lose a battle before it is seriously engaged, although I knew that this surely would be one of the worst months of my life. While Aunt Doris and Uncle Pierre were rich in possessions, they were not gracious. Like Old Man Lucas, they strictly measured the worth of an individual with their wealth and let all of us know that our good bottomland rendered us a source of constant disappointment to them. My cousins also constantly registered their disapproval of my family in a form of pity that angered me more than a person who would be aggressive in hatred.

Old Man Lucas had demanded possession of the farm by the beginning of March. This timing was perfect for us since it would take weeks for my father and uncle to make it to St. Joseph. This meant that we needed to pack our belongings at the end of February and leave behind the only home that I had ever known.

My mother rose very early on the last Monday in February. We backed the wagon to the front porch of our cabin to allow her to load the wagon. She packed a large box that my father had built for her. This box was large enough to fit in the wagon bed and contained bacon, other meats, and salt. On top of the box was a cover made of light board nailed on planks. This top had a hole in each corner. Father had fashioned strong legs that would slip into the holes to make it a strong table for our journey. Since it sat in the wagon bed, it would let my dad or me sit on it and steer the oxen from above while the other one walked with the oxen, urging them forward.

Following the box, we loaded a chest full of clothing that would be necessary for the journey, together with some of the little luxuries my mother managed to secrete away from the watchful eye of my father, who was determined to take only the barest of necessities to Oregon. My mother then slid into the wagon a medicine chest full of the cures that Uncle Peter told us we would need for such a long, dangerous journey. My father attached cleats to the bottom of the wagon bed that held these chests in place. Next, my mother loaded my parents' rocking chairs into the wagon. She planned on sitting in one of these chairs while playing with Bitsy with our covers rolled up on the trail.

We left the middle of the wagon vacant so that Bitsy could play with Suzy and her other toys. Mother packed the dishes and little tablecloths for the trip into the wagon. At the back of the wagon, we loaded our groceries. We packed long hand- sewn sacks of flour and cornmeal, each weighing one hundred pounds. With them came a series of smaller sacks containing the dried fruit, beans, rice, and sugar that would let us have some variety on the trip.

Finally, Mother slid the bedding on which my parents would sleep with Bitsy. Uncle Peter and I planned to sleep on the ground under the wagon, covered from the rain by the sturdy vessel that would contain everything we owned. Once we finished loading the wagon, we stepped back and stared at it. The empty wagon that was so huge on Christmas appeared so tiny when it was loaded with everything we would take to Oregon. I walked over to my thinking tree one last time, climbed it and pondered life.

I slept little that night. I lay upstairs in my loft and thought of the friends who I might never see again. While the legends of buffalo and mountains appealed to me, so did the fun times with my friends at school. With these thoughts in my head, I was startled to hear the ladder steps creak, a noise that announced the coming of someone to my room. I forced my eyes closed, but they opened when I felt the cool hand of my mother on my forehead.

"Jeremy," she whispered. "Are you asleep?"

"No, Mother, I can't sleep tonight. I am thinking about the trip."

"I know," she said. "The only place we know is this farm. Leaving it behind is so scary and it has cost me a lot of sleep. However, your father and uncle are good men who would not take chances with our lives if it were not worth it. Every crossroads taken in this life comes at the cost of the adventures and opportunities that the other choice might present. Yet, we all need to put our trust in our good Lord and move in the direction that He wants us. We all know this means that we should move to Oregon. So, we need to move on to Oregon and not look backward toward the choices that might have been."

With these words, she stroked my head lightly and kissed me gently. I knew then that everything would work out and my eyes closed easily in sleep.

We quickly ate breakfast that morning. While we understood that the journey would require energy, excitement precluded appetite. Following breakfast, Father gently lifted Mother into the wagon while Uncle Peter placed Bitsy onto the neck of his large horse. We lashed the carriers for our chickens on the side of the wagon and tied Flossie, our milk cow, to the back of the wagon. Walking alongside the oxen, I snapped the whip in front of Bob's eyes and Bob and Todd led the team forward away from our cabin for the last time. Remembering Mother's counsel, I kept my eyes focused ahead and not backward. As we moved out of the gate, we passed Old Man Lucas with three of his slaves moving toward our home. Without a word, we passed each other and with an imperceptible nod, our relationship was over. Perhaps not all good-byes were sad.

Once we left our farm, we walked past our church toward the Nashville Pike. At the church, my father called for the oxen to stop. He looked at me and told me to stay with the wagon and tend to the oxen. Then, he gently lifted my mother from the wagon and they moved, with arms linked, past the church to the tiny cemetery behind it.

While I was their oldest child, my parents had two other children born between Bitsy and myself. Charlotte was born two years after me and she died after six days. Two years after Charlotte, my brother Jedediah, Jr. was born. I remember he lived for six sickly months until, as my father said, one night he finally passed into the arms of Jesus. While my parents never spoke about these children, I know that there were times when following church Mother would walk to the cemetery and spend silent time before returning to our family with her eyes reddened. These days always meant a silent trip back from the church to our home and a quiet supper.

I watched my parents staring alone in the cemetery. Uncle Peter spoke to me, as if the silence was too loud to endure. "Jeremiah, you know there were times when I thought your parents would lose their minds with the grief caused by these babies."

"Really," I questioned.

"Absolutely. I was out west when Charlotte died but when I returned there was a different silence in the home. You could feel the unhappiness in the room much like you can feel humidity on a summer day before a storm. When little Jedediah died, there were times when I worried that your mother would not survive. Your parents are people of great faith but this was so sad that their grief almost overwhelmed their faith. I stayed with them longer than I planned simply because I worried about them.

"The death of a baby is dreadfully hard on the parents. A child dying before its parents is the cruelest trick life can play, since it is not the natural order. A parent spends so much time dreaming of the child and making plans and preparations for the child and when the birth does not lead to long-lived life it saps all spirit from the home.

"As bad as it is for a man, it is much different for a woman. Women are different. She invests her life and emotions and body in the birth of the child and to have this not be rewarded is enough to cause her to turn her sorrow inward to a place from which she may never emerge. I worried about your mother in that way."

"I never knew, Uncle Peter. Why did I not see this?"

"Because you were not supposed to, Jeremiah. Children assume a parent will always be there to care happily for the child. When you were young, you did not think of your parents as people. This is nothing that you did wrong. Instead, it is just the way that God created people. Now that you are older you can see that your parents are imperfect people with hurts, hopes, dreams, and disappointments."

We then stood silently and waited for my parents to return. When they arrived, I noticed that my mother had traces of tears on her cheeks. My father silently lifted her into the wagon. As I watched them together, I felt sad for my brother and sister, who would sleep in this lonely cemetery far removed from the loving care of our good parents.

My father twitched the whip in front of Bob and the group moved forward in silence. This did not last long as Bitsy and Uncle

Peter started a song of their own composition that made us laugh and sing. Just before we reached the Nashville Pike, we passed my school. Much to my surprise, all of my classmates and Miss Spencer were outside by the fence of the schoolyard. My classmates shouted farewells from the school while Miss Spencer silently studied our progress. For each shout of farewell, we replied with an invitation to visit us in Oregon. This continued until the unchanging pace of our oxen moved us out of view.

My Aunt Doris' manor was just outside of Nashville. My father planned that it would take us a day and a half to arrive and so we stopped along the way at a farm where a boyhood friend of my father and uncle lived. Once we arrived, we unhitched the oxen and penned them in while we dined on a scrumptious feast of fried ham and potatoes. We spent the night laughing with long loved friends and then we gratefully went to bed and fell asleep immediately.

We awoke to the smells of eggs and bacon and pancakes on the griddle that transported us, virtually floating us out of bed and into our places around the table. Following a breakfast that we devoured in full gratitude for the wonders our hostess prepared, Uncle Peter and I waddled outside to hitch up our team to the wagon. Much to our surprise when we arrived at the pen, we found an open gate and only five oxen. As we looked around, we noticed that on a distant hill, there was a solitary brown and white figure grazing in fresh green grass.

Uncle Peter saw this at the same time I did. With an exasperated sigh and a shrug of his shoulders, he mounted the bare back of his horse with a single leap and rode out toward the ox, waving his hat in the air. With skillful turns of his horse, he maneuvered Todd back toward his comrades. Finally, Todd, the well-fed and contented ox, came straggling back toward our wagon and assumed his place of responsibility.

Once Todd was back in his assigned place, we left our hosts and moved down the Nashville Pike toward my aunt and uncle's home. Finally, around noon, we pulled off the pike onto the tree-sheltered lane that led to their home. As we pulled in front of the house, a door was opened and a house slave who showed us into the front hall of the home and offered us cool lemonade to take the dust out of our throats greeted us.

My Aunt Doris was never a person who would greet anyone, even family, unless she wore her finest and her face was perfectly powdered. After a delay of ten minutes, she appeared from her upstairs bedroom. She greeted us with a tone of forced joy.

"Welcome, sister. Jedediah, I am so glad you are here. Elizabeth, you are growing like a perfect little princess. Jeremiah, do be a dear little boy and help Isaiah move those beasts to the back of the house where they will be so much more comfortable."

The invitation to leave this house even for a moment was beautiful to my ears. I even ignored the little boy comment in my hurry to escape this taffeta prison and move the beasts who showed, even in their limited mental state, more kinship with me than my aunt. I studied Isaiah, my helper in this task. He was a young man, tall, dark-skinned, with the beginning of a beard. While he might be a slave, I noticed that when we worked together, he worked as a peer and not as a man who was required to take all orders. In his eyes there was a look of pride; pride not in his status as a slave but rather his stature as a man.

Once I returned from penning up the oxen, I joined the remainder of the family at the large dining room table. While the china was lovelier than any that I had ever seen, beautiful place settings in a sterile room do nothing for a boy. Listening to this stilted conversation made me long for an escape onto the road. Finally, after the house slaves removed the last dish, my Aunt Doris spoke what was on her mind:

"So," she said turning toward my father, "what is this nonsense about moving my sister all the way across the country? Do you not know that if you could not succeed on your little farm, all you had to do was tell Pierre and he would have found you a position in his trading house that would allow you to feed your family? It is dreadful pride that drives you and causes you to take your family onto the road where they will be eaten by wild savages."

My Uncle Peter silently groaned and rolled his eyes toward both the floor and the ceiling. My father quietly answered my aunt, in a tone that spoke no anger, but contained volumes of determination:

"Doris, I appreciate your concern. We could have lived on the farm, prospered all of our life, and raised our family. However, we believe that this is not what God would have us do. We have sold our farm and are resolved to go west. I do not wish to discuss this topic. Thank you for your wonderful hospitality in providing us with this meal. Uncle Peter and I need to continue our journey."

"Surely, Jeremiah, you can wait until tomorrow. Stay with us another day."

"No, Doris. I plan to meet Mary in St. Joseph's on the twenty-second day of April so we can worship together on the twenty-third. This means that we need to leave now."

With that Uncle Peter, my father and I stood and moved toward the door. Uncle Peter and I went and hitched the wagon. I snapped the whip in front of Bob and moved them to the front while my uncle climbed on his horse. Once we reached the front of the house, we saw my father saying his goodbyes with Bitsy. He lifted her up, twirled her around, and rubbed his nose against hers.

Then, he turned to my mother and kissed her with the kiss of a man who would not see the love of his life for weeks. They lingered for a practical eternity until my uncle coughed and commented that if they did not stop it would be midnight before they actually made it off the farm. My mother giggled and playfully pushed my father away.My father stopped by me and squeezed my shoulder. "I am relying on you son," he said and then he took the whip and showed it to the oxen who started their slow steady gait toward the road.

We stood and watched them depart. I felt a sad longing as they moved over the hill and beyond our sight.

CHAPTER 4
TO THE BEGINNING OF THE TRAIL

As Uncle Peter and Father led the team into the distance, another of my Aunt Doris' house slaves offered my mother a cool ice water. My mother smiled and took the drink with just the slightest nod of the head and murmured thanks. I had never previously seen her allow other people to wait on her. Sitting on the front porch of the manor home of Uncle Pierre and Aunt Doris, she looked around her and a look of relaxation crossed her face. I was glad that she had the opportunity to rest, but I could not help but wonder what my father would think of this scene of laziness and reliance on unpaid labor.

My cousins interrupted my thoughts with their sudden arrival on their horses. Andre, the boy, was my age; Ann-Marie was two years younger than I was. Andre turned to his sister and pointed at me with his riding crop saying, "Look, sister, there is the poor country cousin."

"How very common," was her answer and they rode laughing toward the stables without a word directly passed to me. Watching the two of them move on, I realized that this could be the most trying part of my journey. My parents had always told me that relatives are a shelter in a time of storm; what I did not know was how to respond when the shelter was more dangerous than the storm. I clenched my fists and glanced at my mother, who met my gaze with a frown and a barely perceptible shake of the head.

Dinner was the longest meal of my life. Not only was the food of a refined nature that did not appeal to me, but the number of forks and plates confused me. This dinner made me feel as if I had been transported to a different world where all of my knowledge had slipped away and I was left a living monument of ignorance.

My Uncle Pierre joined us at dinner. While I especially felt a need at this time for male companionship, Uncle Pierre was a man who did not waste mere words on children. Bitsy, perhaps, held some interest for him due to her fundamental cuteness. He tolerated his own children because social convention required him to acknowledge their presence. For a ten-year-old country cousin, however, there was little attention or tolerance. I could not see him fishing with me in the Stones River or teaching me of places that I had never seen.

Conversation at dinner was stilted and largely bilingual, a fact that did nothing for me since Miss Spencer, for all of her educational talents, did not introduce us to the French language. My cousins would ask me a question in English about my prospects of surviving the wilderness savages. Then, after I gave an optimistic answer and tried to tell some of the stories that Uncle Peter had shared, they would make a comment in French and laugh as if they had been told the funniest of jokes. What the joke was I did not know, but there was no doubt as to the target of the joke.

Finally, after dinner, we went into the music room, where my cousins read their school lessons and Doris played the latest pieces on piano. My mother played with Bitsy and Suzy. I sat alone, watching the scene and thinking about my father and uncle, who were moving down the road with our earthly possessions. The oddest aspect of this entire scene was the ease with which my mother shifted into a woman I did not recognize. I expected Aunt Doris to laugh and tell shallow stories like a schoolgirl, yet, when my mother reciprocated with stories from their common childhood, I was shocked. My father wanted me to protect my mother, I did not fully understand from what I was supposed to protect her. More importantly, after having spent five hours with my cousins, I wondered who would protect me.

Bedtime came none too soon. While the comforters were warm and the feather bed was luxurious, my sleep was troubled as I dreamt of my father and uncle driving Bob, Todd and the other oxen toward Missouri. The more my cousins surrounded me, the more I envied my father and uncle their time with each other and the oxen.

Morning came and I awoke in my strange surroundings. Blinking my eyes in the bed, I tried to remember where I was. Knowledge came flooding in when the house slave greeted me with a friendly but subservient greeting. When I was on our farm, I longed for a servant to allow me to indulge my desires; however, now that there were no chores but plenty of servants, I found myself missing my daily labor.

Moving downstairs, I found my mother and Doris sitting on the back veranda sipping coffee from fine cups with beautifully painted saucers. These appeared to be the everyday stoneware of their home. Both women smiled at me, although only one of the smiles contained any particular warmth. My aunt spoke first in her affected tone:

"Jeremiah, do be a dear. Your cousins have gone to school. Please entertain dearest Elizabeth and allow your mother and me to catch up on the affairs of the day."

I looked at my mother but saw no reprieve in her eyes. Determined to be the man that my father expected of me, I nodded my assent. Anyway, a day with Bitsy and Suzy was preferable to a day sitting around the manor or enduring the pity of my cousins. Any thoughts of my unfortunate fate, however, were lost in the excitement of my sister who relished the opportunity to run on the front lawn of the home and bounce on her older brother. Reluctantly, I had to admit that her laughter and games masked the unhappiness in my heart.

This became my daily routine. I would awake, eat breakfast with my mother, play with my sister, and spend the remainder of the day with the entire extended family. Weekend days found me seeking out the company of my sister or the solace of some of the books of my uncle's library to avoid sessions with my cousins. These days seemed so lengthy and limited in pleasure that I feared we would never leave for Missouri.

The times I spent with Bitsy, Suzy and their tea parties were far more enjoyable than the time I spent with my cousins. Once they came home from school, Bitsy would lie down for her afternoon nap. My aunt and mother, oblivious to the tension between my city cousins and myself, thrust us together for our afternoon play times. My mother would caution me to behave in a manner that would make my absent father proud. This injunction left me defenseless from the cruelty I faced on a daily basis.

My cousins had a number of tactics that they used. One of their favorite tricks was to make fun of me in French while I could do nothing but create my own thoughts as to what aspect of my life was really causing their humor. They also loved spinning pictures of the failure of my father that must have occurred to lead him to take the dangerous step of leading us to the plains to die the most hideous deaths imaginable. As Andre learned that I would not fight back, he increased the description of the eight-foot-tall Indians who would scalp me while alive and eat my heart while still beating. Uncle Peter never mentioned these creatures and, therefore, while I did not really believe Andre's stories, any story, when repeated enough, can find some home in the imagination of a boy.

While my stay at Nashville was miserable, my mother clearly enjoyed the time that she spent with her sister. Before my eyes, I saw my mother appear younger as she stayed in her sister's luxurious home. Yet, while she grew in physical beauty as she rested, the beauty that she showed now was less attractive as she became more like her icy-mannered sister.

One cool spring evening as we sat outside on the veranda, my Aunt Doris was sipping a glass of sherry and my mother was drinking a glass of lemonade. I was sitting on the floor. My aunt renewed her earlier themes with my mother:

"Dearest Mary, we need not talk about this Oregon foolishness, need we? Why must you try to cross this country? Just say the word and I will send a messenger ahead to let Jedediah and that wild brother of his know that you shall not be coming. You can live on this land and resume the life that our parents raised you for and train your children to be the people they should be, not little savages."

This angered me. I looked at my mother and saw in her face a momentary look of indecision that troubled me. My mother responded in a quiet voice:

"Doris, I have loved my time here. It is true that I love this sort of life and there are certain aspects of it that I miss greatly. As much as I have loved the luxuries of this country, I long to see the land where I believe God would have us go. I would not disappoint my husband for all of the riches this world has to offer. You tell me that my children will be like little savages. I tell you that I would tenfold rather have the rough-hewn Christianity of my Jedediah than the cruelty of fine manners that our finer society sometimes offers. So, sister, I will be on the boat for St. Louis and then on to St. Joseph's when it leaves two days from now."

When I heard these words, my heart leapt. My fears that my mother would leave behind our dreams of the mountains for the luxury of this life of tedium had proven false. That night, for the first time since my father and uncle left with our oxen, I dreamt of the mountains that touched the sky and buffalo that shook the ground when they ran.

The last evening at the manor, I excused myself from dinner early, claiming a slight bout of indigestion. Slipping out of the back door of the manor, I made my way to a stagnant pond that was just behind the tree line surrounding the house. During my solitary time alone in the afternoons when I had been trying to avoid the company of my cousins, I noticed that there were a large number of toads surrounding the pond. Taking a basket that I had, with permission of my new friend Isaiah, borrowed, I found a number of these toads. Using some of the tricks that my Uncle Peter had taught me on the farm, I managed to capture four toads and place them in the basket. Then, I hid them under the back door steps of the manor.

My mother, Bitsy, and I awoke very early the next morning. We needed to make an eight-mile carriage journey to the docks, where we would catch the riverboat destined to take us to St. Louis and onward to the beginning of the trail. After a quick breakfast and our feigned emotional good-byes with Aunt Doris and Uncle Pierre together with its equally insincere invitations to visit us in Oregon, Isaiah loaded our bags into the carriage. Then, looking at my mother with a look of panic that I had practiced in the mirror the prior night, I told her I had left my prized pocketknife in my room. Before she could respond, I quickly ran to the back of the house, seized my secreted basket, and quietly made my way up the stairs to my cousins' adjoining bedrooms. Then, slipping first into Ann-Marie's room, I quietly placed one of the toads in the water jar that she had by her bed in case thirst overwhelmed her in the middle of the night. Then, I slipped another toad into the foot of the bed in which she lay snoring. Then, I moved to Andre's room and repeated the process. Finally, I snuck downstairs, returned the basket to the kitchen, and ran outside to the carriage. Once I climbed into the carriage, I produced my knife as if that was evidence that the purpose of the detour was successful.

With a quick snap of the reins, we started moving down the lane away from the manor house. As we moved, I heard a bloodcurdling scream come from first one of the bedrooms upstairs and then the other. Involuntarily, I laughed. My mother looked at me and with that all-knowing way of parents asked:

"Jeremiah, what did you do to your cousins?"

While I was tempted to tell a lie, I decided I would not compound sin upon prank and admitted: "I placed toads in the bed with each of them and in their water jars."

My mother smiled at me. She squeezed my shoulder and said, "Oh my, Jeremiah, you should not have done that." Then she gave me a huge hug and laughed aloud. Bitsy joined us in our laughter, although she did not understand why, and we left this manor laughing with more sincerity than had been heard within its walls in a number of years. As we passed the gates of the manor, I heard Isaiah's deep voice join our laughter at the prank.

We drove along the Pike into the heart of the capitol city of Nashville. I had never seen so many people as I did that morning, when we moved in the traffic of a city of 10,000 people. People moved all directions at the same time and it would be easy to be swept along in the tide of humanity if only there was a well-defined direction for the tide. Finally, we made our way through the city to the river and there, we watched as our travel bags were loaded onto the boat. As we were about to climb aboard the boat, I turned, smiled at Isaiah, and then shook his hand and slipped him my pocketknife as a gift from one friend to another. To some he was just a slave. To me, he was a friend who lived in difficult circumstances and yet never abandoned his dignity. Then, we waved at the people on the shore, as the boat left its dock and headed out into the Cumberland River.

The first thing we did once we were on board was to unpack our bags and try to arrange our goods into something that would be tolerable for the trip to St. Louis. We needed to travel down the Cumberland River to the Ohio River and then continue down the Ohio River to the Mississippi. Once on the Mississippi, we would travel north to St. Louis. In St. Louis, we would change boats and move onto the boat that would take us on the Missouri River to St. Joseph where the rest of our family and possessions would be waiting for us.

Once we had our clothing unpacked, Mother decided that she wanted to have Bitsy take a nap to refresh her from the excitement of the day. This left me to roam the boat on my own while promising my mother that I would not cause any harm. Walking along the deck of the boat, I was stricken with how wide the river was when compared to my own Stones River. To call them each a river was a disservice to the Cumberland or an exaggeration to the Stones.

When we arrived in St. Louis, the size of the city amazed me. Fortunately, we were able to move our belongings down just a few docks and step back on the new ship that would take us upstream on the Missouri River to St. Joseph.

Just as the boats were different, I also found the rivers different. The Missouri River had more sandbars than the Mississippi, which caused the crew to be vigilant. Once a boat landed on these sandbars, the entire crew would have to work a full day in order to dislodge the boat from the sandbar. The crew hated this job. Therefore, they watched constantly to avoid them and loudly cursed the helmsman if they allowed the boat to come too close to the sandbar.

Finally, the voyage was over. The boat pulled ashore in St. Joseph's and let us off. I was never so happy to feel the firm ground beneath my feet. We stood there for a brief moment attempting to adjust our eyes to the sights when we heard the loudest whoop and were nearly knocked over when my Uncle Peter and Father pulled alongside us sitting on Uncle Peter's horse. My father leapt off the back of the horse, picked my mother and Bitsy up in the air, and kissed my mother as if he had not seen her in six weeks. Uncle Peter hopped off the horse and picked me up to where we were looking eye to eye. "We are really going to Oregon, Jeremiah. We are on our way."

CHAPTER 5

ST. JOE

During my trip to St. Joseph, I had created in my mind a mental picture of a metropolis worthy of the struggles of the journey. Once we arrived, I knew that I had been mistaken. While there were a number of wagons and people bustling about, St. Joseph was a small town with a number of stores that promised to supply western travelers but it was nothing like Nashville or St. Louis.

My father and uncle had been in St. Joseph for a number of days waiting for us to finish our river trip. Once the initial embraces were concluded, Father helped Mother climb on Uncle Peter's horse. Father walked alongside the horse down the streets carrying two of our bags while Uncle Peter and I grabbed the remainder of the luggage and walked down the street. Bitsy laughed and ran around Uncle Peter's feet while telling him about the adventures on the river. I lagged behind this group, partially because I was loaded with baggage and partially because I wanted to watch the activity of all the people who were heading for unknown places west.

We walked a few miles outside of town. We reached the crest of a hill and I saw a series of wagons parked in a large, grassy meadow. In the middle of this cluster of wagons, I recognized our oxen in their constant grazing stances. Even Todd waited by the wagons as if he had decided that something could be more exciting than the hunt for fresh grass. I ran all the way to our wagon and wanted to leave that minute, but the adults cooled my spirit by reminding me that we needed to be fully supplied before we could leave and the rest of our wagon train had arrived. Having waited all winter, I could endure another week.

My thoughts were interrupted by the arrival of a tall gray-haired man clad in buckskin. "Symons," the smiling man said in a deep voice, "who are these strangers who are with your wagon? I have warned you in the past not to trust people who just show up on the trail."

My father laughed. "These are no strangers, Captain Watkins. These people are my family; my beautiful wife, Mary, my son Jeremiah, and my little daughter Elizabeth. Family, this is Captain Israel Watkins, who is going to guide us to Oregon. Peter tells me that there is no more experienced guide than Captain Watkins and that should help all of us to reach the West Coast."

"It is truly a pleasure to meet you," Captain Watkins responded with a laugh. "I think what Tenderfoot Pete was telling you is that I am really old. I remember meeting Pete about ten years ago when he was just learning how to survive on the frontier. Now, though, he knows all the ways of the mountain men and he should be able to help you arrive at your new home."

Uncle Peter laughed. "When I met Captain Watkins, I thought he was about one hundred years old. He was trying to decide what to do with his life after the beaver pelts stopped bringing him enough money. I never knew if he was a hero or a villain, and what was more important, he did not know either. The problem is I am still not sure, but since we knew this man needed to eat, we had to provide him a job. Seriously, this man taught me more about living in the mountains than any other person; I know that we will be safe. Just watch your billfold while you are in his hands." With these words, my uncle slapped Captain Watkins on the back and they went away together laughing.

Father turned to Mother and spoke softly: "Uncle Peter says he is a good guide, Mary, but not necessarily a good man. Evidently, the talk of his being an outlaw is not false, although nothing could ever be proven by courts. Still, the Lord sometimes uses sinful men to accomplish His purposes. Just let us not trust him with the silverware."

Mother laughed and said, "Jedediah, if he is a thief, then he will need to find more profitable places to practice his craft than with us. The only thing we brought enough of to attract the attention of a thief is bacon and more bacon. He need not steal from us to obtain it."

That night was precious as we were together as a family for the first time in a long time. My mother's cooking tasted wonderful, my uncle's stories were funnier than I remembered, and even the relatively silent presence of my father was comforting in a way that I did not readily recall. When I crawled to sleep in my blankets under the wagon, it felt like I was home, even if the home had none of the walls of a house.

The next morning, we rose early and hiked into town to attend church. While I had always been comfortable in the church that we had attended at our home beside the Stones River, I found it equally comforting to attend a church hundreds of miles away from that home and hearing the same prayers spoken in the same tones by different people.

As we left the church, an elderly woman dressed in a long black dress stopped my mother. This woman clearly wished to speak to my mother and she appeared agitated. "Oh, sister, are you going on the trail to the Western lands?"

My mother looked at this lady quizzically as if she could not discern the motivation of the question. "Why yes, dear lady, we are heading to Oregon."

This answer struck the older woman like a knife. "Repent of that dangerous desire. My daughter left us behind last year with her husband and their dear children. I warned them not to try this adventure but they would not listen to me. My dear grandbabies died on the trail long before they reached the mountains and my son-in-law, foolish man that he was, may God rest his soul, died at Fort Hall. My own daughter returned home alone, penniless and broken from her experience. She has not left the house since the day she arrived back home, nearly starved to death. I beg you, sister; do not put your family through the torture that awaits you."

Mother stepped back as if the woman had struck her violently with an open hand. Father stepped forward, leaned down, and spoke in a loving whisper to this woman. "Dear mother, I do not doubt that you have suffered greatly due to your experience. I pray that you may find comfort and that your daughter may be restored to health. But, as for me and my family," and with these words he placed his arm gently around my mother and smiled, "we believe that the Good Lord would have us move to this wondrous good land that He has made and we will not avoid the task that the Lord has given us. We know, Mother, that your prayers will help sustain us along the long trail ahead."

With these words, my family moved forward from the lady who was determined to perpetuate her mourning on every soul she met. My father held my mother around the waist as the two of them walked away. Uncle Peter broke the silence of the moment.

"There are people in this world who would take their sad tales and use them to make all people lie down in their place and die. There is danger on the trail; there are people who perish and never reach their promised land. Far more people survive and prosper in their new homes. People who doubt this fact should keep their doubts to themselves and not use their Christianity to discourage good people of faith who step forward in reliance on that faith."

My father shook his head and said, "Peter, there are people who have suffered beyond the measure that they will allow their faith to support them. This dear lady must have our prayers and concern. We have chosen our path and we will not look back no matter how many people tell us to do so."

The next day, my family traveled to St. Joseph's with our wagon to spend some of our money. The men stopped at the cooper shop since Uncle Peter had convinced my father that there was a need for an additional two water barrels. After that, we ordered a wagon wheel and axle for our wagon that we would carry to protect us from the damages we could suffer on the trail. Mother replaced some of the food that the men had eaten on the way from Tennessee. When we returned, we felt more comfortable that we were ready to leave for Oregon and the merchants felt more comfortable that they had obtained additional funding from us.

More wagons arrived every day in the clearing where we were gathering our wagon train. Captain Watkins promised us we would leave on Monday if we could gather at least twenty wagons. By Friday, we had grown to twenty-two wagons and we knew that no matter what we would be on the road on Monday.

Uncle Peter and I picked up the spare wheel and axle and a few trinkets for the ladies; we took advantage of the opportunity to drive the team through town looking at all the sites. After having exhausted our ability to see new things in this town, Uncle Peter and I turned and started our way home. A distinguished-looking gentleman stepped in front of us, stared up at us, and pointed a finger at Uncle Peter. "Trained mountain men do not drive oxen, young man."

With great effort, we halted the oxen. "Mr. Robidoux, trained western men do drive oxen if they wish to lead their family over the mountains." Then Uncle Peter hopped off the wagon and clasped the gentleman's hands.

"Jeremiah," my uncle said, "this is truly a great man. This is Joseph Robidoux, a trader who has done much for this me personally and the western country. For the last forty-five years, Mr. Robidoux has been trading with the Indians and sending men to the west. He has done more in opening up the West to people like us than any man I know.

"When I first came from Tennessee, he took mercy on me and let me work with him in his fur trading business. At first, I worked here at his outpost doing all of the jobs that no sane person would do. Yet, through all the labor, he taught me how to trade with the mountain men and natives, how to manage the business of a trading post, and how to keep the books fairly so that the company would prosper but not in a manner that would give the company the reputation of a cruel and untrustworthy employer. If I were a smarter person, I never would have left Mr. Robidoux, but if I had never left Mr. Robidoux, I never would have seen the sights about which I have told you. Knowing that Mr. Robidoux started this city is why I convinced your father to come here to leave for Oregon."

I shook hands with this man immediately, and remembered to greet him in the courteous way that my parents had taught me: "It's a pleasure to meet you, sir."

Mr. Robidoux smiled at my courtesy which was out of place for a meeting on a muddy street surrounded by oxen. "Master Symons. I wish your uncle had stayed with me. Your uncle learned everything that I had to teach him, but like many young men, he needs to see what is over the next hill and around each bend of the river. If he has decided to go west with you now, then you are quite fortunate because he knows how to survive in the West. I envy you that you are able to see for the first time places and sites that I saw for the first time nearly thirty years ago. Traveling west is not easy, but understand that in this life the truly enjoyable experiences are never easy."

With that, Mr. Robidoux waved us on and my uncle and I lifted our hats to him. I felt honored to have met this man at this time in my life as I was about to leave on a great adventure.

When we returned to our wagon, Captain Watkins was bellowing in his deep voice that he wanted to meet with the men of the wagons immediately. Uncle Peter unhitched the oxen and started to join my father at the meeting on the hill. While I was going to stay away from the meeting, Father waved to me and said, "Jeremiah, come with me. This is a meeting for men, you have proven yourself a man thus far, and you will need to be a man for thousands of miles to come. There is nothing that Captain Watkins can say that you should not hear, as one of the men of the wagon train."

I found myself smiling at these words from Father who was not prone to easy praise. Perhaps my experience helping my mother on our adventures without his protection had made a difference in me.

We hiked up the hill and joined a group of about twenty-five other men who formed a circle around Captain Watkins. He stared at us and waited until we were silent before he began speaking.

"Gentlemen, we are just a few days away from leaving for Oregon. I will do everything that I can to make sure we take the best routes and arrive safely at our destination. It is important to understand that you are not individuals moving to the west. For the next six months, you are part of an army. My army! It is important that we agree to what the laws are that govern this army.

"You can make your own rules and I will follow them with one exception: Do not delay us. Delay is deadly. Wake up when we tell you and move your wagon promptly into line. We have mountains to go over and if the group is delayed then we could be stuck in snow up to our axles in the mountains and you will never see your new homes. Whatever you need to do to keep up with the pace that I wish to set is essential.

"I am responsible for all of you. That does not mean that I want to discuss decisions with all of you. We need to elect someone who will be the general of this army. I do not want to discuss any decisions about routes with anyone but your elected leader."

With that speech, Captain Watkins sat down on a stump and looked at the rest of us. After a few minutes of staring at one another, one tall gentleman with long, silver hair and a thick mustache stood and addressed the group. "For those of you who do not know it, my name is Major Stephen Smith. I have led men my whole life, both in the army and outside of the army. I have led men into battle and defeated the scourge of the savages. I would be honored to lead this brigade into the wilderness and cause us to arrive safely."

As Major Smith sat down, some of the men spoke words of approval. Another gentleman stood. He was a short, heavy man who was odd looking in that he had a full beard but very little hair on the top of his head. He cleared his throat and looked around at the group. Once he felt he had all of our attention, he spoke in a low tone of voice:

"It may be true that Major Smith has a record in the military. Do we, however, know what that record entails? The wilderness is full of men who have spent a few weeks in the military chasing savages in the wilderness. This does not impress me.

"I am Thomas Richardson from Ohio. I have been a state senator in that state and have shown true leadership for years. I expect that I will lead men on the way to Oregon and once we arrive there. Do not make the mistake of confusing a title for leadership."

Once Senator Richardson was finished, some of the men who had been supportive of Major Smith started shouting at him while others who supported Senator Richardson continued their criticism of Major Smith. While this was going on my father and uncle turned to each other and just smiled. "Politicians," my father said in a tone of disapproval as he spat on the ground. This caused my uncle to laugh and poke at the ground with a stick.

After the groups had finished yelling at each other, Captain Watkins stood and told us that we would vote by marching to one end of the circle or the other. Those who wanted to vote for Major Smith were to move to the right while those who wanted Senator Richardson moved to the left. Once we counted the number of people who had moved from one side or the other, we decided to follow the command of Major Smith. Senator Richardson scowled and we watched as his baldhead turned very red and he stormed down the hill alone.

The next two days we spent dealing with working on the constitution of the wagon train. The men, under the nagging from Captain Watkins and Major Smith, needed to agree upon a written set of rules that the wagon train would use to settle disputes. Much to my uncle's amusement, we noticed that Major Smith had started wearing a sash and sword as he walked around the camp. "Look at that, Jeremiah," my Uncle Peter said as he elbowed me in the side. "He thinks if he wears a sword we all will believe that he is a military leader of great renown. People will do anything to make themselves appear important."

Finally, once all of the debating about the rules of the wagon train finished, the men all came forward and signed their names to the document, as if, as my father observed, they were signing the Declaration of Independence.

Once Sunday arrived, my parents discussed whether to attend the same church as they had the previous week. My mother told my father that while she desired to worship prior to the departure, she would rather forego any amount of glorious worship than be accosted by the professional mourner who had foretold so much suffering the prior Sunday. My father nodded his silent agreement and announced that he and some of the other men of the train would lead a small worship service that would allow us to bond together as a group. My mother smiled gratefully.

Finally, Monday came and Major Smith and Captain Watkins led us into line to move toward the ferry that would take us over the Missouri. We moved into town and joined other trains that waited for the ferryboat to take us across the river. The line for this boat moved so slowly, but finally by the end of Tuesday we guided the team onto the boat and rode it to the other side of the river. Snapping the whip in front of Bob's face caused him to step off the boat and onto the western side of the river. Once we stepped off of the ferry, we realized that we had left the organized United States behind, a fact that Uncle Peter noted by turning in the saddle of his horse, raising his hat and shouting, "Farewell, America."

We led the oxen to the top of the hill overlooking the river and waiting for the rest of our group. I looked back over the river and saw a long line of adventurers waiting for their turn to cross the river. Some of them were in wagons like ours; others were larger families in larger wagons; others, still were individuals pushing small carts. Some of the people were wealthier than we were while others only dreamt of being wealthy. Whether rich or poor alone or in large groups we joined in the dreams of a new land, a new life, and new hope and were willing to risk everything previously known to try to achieve these dreams.

CHAPTER 6

ON THE TRAIL

Since our crossing was delayed by the wait at the ferry, the wagon train stopped for the night just a few miles west of the river. In a large field with just a solitary stand of trees, we formed our wagons into a rough circle. The train placed all of the livestock into the center of the circle, protecting it from any thieves who might be interested in helping themselves to a horse or cow, while also letting us know exactly where the animals were at all times. Todd looked wistfully at the grass on the other side of the wagons, but ultimately he rested with his friends on the inside of the circle.

While Uncle Peter and Father dealt with rounding our reluctant prisoners into their wagon-barred prison, I gathered the fuel for our evening fire. Uncle Peter warned me this might be a difficult job as we moved further west and lost any semblance of trees, but for tonight, gathering limbs that had fallen from the trees was relatively simple. It was odd that while these families depended on each other for survival during the day, this companionship did not extend to the night fires. Each group naturally maintained its own individual fire as if this preserved their identity as individual families.

When I returned from the trees with my armload of wood, my mother was busy preparing supper. This evening, she promised, we would have a scrumptious feast of bacon and beans, together with freshly baked bread. Mother always made two batches of the bread. She would always first bake a loaf for dinner and then prepare a loaf of salt rise bread for a breakfast treat.

My last job of the night was to milk our cow. Mother then strained the milk into little buckets and placed them under our wagons. In the morning, we would then pour the cream into a bucket, cover it with the lid, and with minimal attention the rest of the day, allow the bouncing of the wagon to convert this cream into the richest butter ever known.

That evening, our prospective field marshal, Major Smith, announced that he had divided the train into six companies who would travel together. When he read off the names, we found that our closest companions would be the Elliott family, the O'Donnell family, and the Johnson family. These total strangers would become key parts of our life in the next months, as we adventured together on the way to our new home.

Mr. Elliott was a banker who had left Ohio in search of new areas and people needing his financial expertise. He was older than Father, with a stern expression and extremely thick spectacles. His wife was a gray-haired lady who rarely spoke to us. They had three daughters, but only two of them made the trip with us. Their oldest daughter had married a young merchant and they had decided to remain behind in Ohio. The two daughters who traveled with us, Emily and Allison, were teenaged girls, constantly looking for attractive boys and spending their time, upon awakening, trying to prepare their hair just so to induce the praise of young men, as if the dust of the roads would not turn the hair designs, within an hour, into limp strands of dusty ropes.

The O'Donnells were an Irish family who had managed to

move from the cities of the east to make this trip. I had never met any Irish men before and so I was afraid that they would prove to be the legendary drunks of whom I had always heard. Much to my surprise and delight, the O'Donnells were wonderful people, full of life, music, and fun, rising naturally from a happy heart. Mr. O'Donnells eyes sparkled with fun whenever I looked at him.

As much as I loved the parents, my favorite part of the family were their twin boys, Liam and Patrick. They were my age. I hoped the boys would become replacements for the friends I had left behind in Tennessee. They were smaller than me, but what they lacked in physical size, they made up for in their spirit and willingness to play games and run races.

The final group in our company was the Johnson family. They were a young married couple making the trip with Mrs. Johnson's older, widowed mother. While Mrs. Johnson constantly talked with her mother, Mr. Johnson at evening frequently wandered from fire to fire seeking male conversation. Father observed to Mother, after one of these fireside wanderings, "Being a newlywed is a wonderful thing, as long as there are only two in the wagon. Having a third in the wagon could make this trip extremely lonely."

It felt like I had only slept a few minutes in my blankets beneath the wagon when I heard Captain Watkins fire his gun in the air as a signal that it was time to awaken. I rolled out of the blankets, folded them, placed them in their assigned corner of the wagon, and splashed some water on my face to convince myself that it really was time to move. From all of the small fires that were being kindled in the camp, smells of cornmeal, bacon, bread and beans were arousing my sense of smell and my appetite. Once we ate, Uncle Peter and I gathered the oxen. Our four-legged friends sensed that it was time for the day to begin and, therefore, relatively passively allowed themselves to be hitched to the wagon. Then, at the appointed hour, Captain Watkins fired his gun in the air again and the first wagons in the first company of the train lurched forward. Slowly, each group started to move until finally it was our turn. My father snapped his whip and in response Bob and Todd started the oxen team moving forward and we joined the caravan.

In the morning, I walked alongside our company with the O'Donnell boys. We stayed beside the wagons, but off the trail to avoid the rocking of the wagons and the oxen, both of whom had developed a steadiness on the trail. Being there allowed us to play games and search for the tasty berries that Uncle Peter assured me would supplement our typical diet of bacon and beans. We walked alongside most of the morning, until the three of us decided to hoist ourselves on the back of our wagon and ride.

At noon, Captain Watkins fired his gun. Like obedient soldiers in a marching column, we halted our advance and unhitched the oxen, allowing them to chew their cud in peace. Mother prepared a quick meal of cheese, dried fruit, and leftover salt rise bread. Following this meal, the adults and younger children all rested while the older boys and girls took advantage of the inactivity to play games and gather some of the fuel we would need for the dinner fires. After an hour of rest, Captain Watkins fired his gun again. The men of the train hitched the animals once more to their place of responsibility and we began moving forward.

Our afternoon journey lacked the same energy as the morning. I found myself riding my perch in the back of the wagon more than I had earlier, while my new friends the O'Donnell boys were less inclined to roam and they stayed at their appointed places. The Elliott girls looked much less primped than they had at the start of the day as they also moved in the dust of the trail. Mother rocked

Bitsy to a fitful slumber and Peter rode his horse at a slower pace than he had followed in the early morning. Finally, as the reddish sun headed down on its never-ending journey to the horizon, the train passed Cold Spring and Captain Watkins fired his gun once again to signal our halt. We formed into the same circle as the day before and gathered the beasts into the circle.

Mother asked me to go to the springs to gather our evening water. Bitsy looked at me with eager eyes. I asked Mother if Bitsy could come with me to the springs. My mother smiled at me, nodded her head and told me that she could go if I kept a good watch on her.

Holding her hand in one hand and swinging the empty bucket in the other, I walked and Bitsy skipped to the fresh water. I lowered the bucket into the water and filled it with the cool water while Bitsy waded barefoot at the side of the creek. Just as I was about to start back to the wagon, I heard a soft mewing noise by the side of the springs and I heard Bitsy say, "Look at the kitty."

Sure enough, in the underbrush next to the river was a small gray kitten that was meowing in a low tone. My sister ran to it. Much to my surprise, the cat did not bolt immediately into the woods. Bitsy dropped to her knees and started to pet the cat on the nose. The cat stood up and lurched out to Bitsy. I saw immediately what the problem was with the cat, as the little creature held its front paw tenderly in the air. I pointed out the problem to Bitsy, who started to cry softly. She pleaded with me, "Jeremiah, we can help the kitty, can't we?"

Not wanting to cause my sister to cry, I told her that we could bring it back to the wagon and see if Father could help the poor creature. This pleased Bitsy, who stopped crying and snuggled the cat close to her. I held the water with one hand and started to walk back to the wagon. The cat spent its entire time resting in my sister's arms, watching her, as if it understood that my sister's love was its best hope for survival.

Once we saw our wagon, Bitsy ran ahead leaving me with the water. Lugging the water, I suddenly felt a special kinship with the oxen as a fellow beast of burden. Father came back toward me with my sister and his strong hands took the water from me. Mother stepped out from behind the wagon and asked my father what my sister had in her arms. My father looked at her and responded softly, "Mary, it's just one of God's little creatures who we can help."

Bitsy thought nothing of this spiritualizing. "It's my kitty, Mommy."

The expression on Bitsy's face would allow no argument as to whether keeping the cat was appropriate. Father took the cat's paw in his firm hands and examined it. "It's not broken, Mary. I think it is a sprain. I think we can do some good for the poor creature. A little pet for Bitsy will make the hard journey go by quicker for her."

With these words, our family grew by one. Father worked with the cat, placing cool mud on the paw and trying to make it more comfortable. Bitsy introduced the little doll, Suzy, to the cat. After some discussion, we decided that her name was Sally. As Bitsy stroked Sally, and Father worked with her injured paw, the lucky kitten's eyes became heavy and soon she followed with the quiet purring of sleep.

Our night on the trail was much like the first night. I gathered the fuel for the fire and my mother cooked a wonderful meal for us that tasted better due to the activity of the day and my minor involvement in its preparation. My blankets felt so good to me that night as I fell asleep under the wagon.

The next morning my father and uncle woke me before Captain Watkins had an opportunity to provide his gunpowder alarm clock. "Come on, Jeremiah," Peter said, "there are fish that need catching and we aim to do it."

I crawled out from my blankets. I immediately saw that Father held my fishing pole. I gratefully took it from him and we marched silently away from the sleeping wagon train and toward the springs. Without a word, we each assumed our position at a distance along the spring and prayerfully considered how good a breakfast of fresh fish fried in a cornmeal batter would taste.

Our prayers were answered mercifully and positively. Evidently, the fish were as hungry as we were and they attacked our bait. Within a short time, we had caught enough bass to provide us with a bountiful breakfast with enough left over to provide my new friends a taste of fresh fish. We returned to our wagons as silently as we had left them and cleaned the fish. Just as we were finishing the task of preparing the bass filets and starting up the fire, we heard Captain Watkins blast his gunpowder reveille in the distance.

What a feast! While I was certain that there would be other mornings on the trail where hardtack and bacon would be our means of survival, I would gladly endure them for the memory of these golden fried fish filets. We cleaned our plates, with little of the delicacy desired by Aunt Doris. We gladly shared our bounty with the O'Donnell clan. Once this meal was finished, we eagerly began another day on the trail.

With our stomachs full, we began this day much as we had the day before. The O'Donnell twins and I walked alongside the wagon train. We played a game of throwing small rocks to hit select targets. Finally, we retreated to ride on our wagons. While the energy used in sitting was less than in running races, we paid for our laziness since the wagons jolted us with every bump in the road.

Bitsy sat in her play area with Suzy and Sally. Sally slept more than she stayed awake, contentedly purring as Bitsy continually stroked her new friend. Perhaps Sally knew, somewhere in her kitten brain, that she was extremely fortunate to have been rescued from her life as a wounded cat by the side of the springs by a loving little girl.

Throughout the day, Captain Watkins and Major Smith rode up and down the column of wagons, urging us to stay together. Major Smith periodically rode the length of the train, waving his sword and shouting encouragement. When he left, Uncle Peter would ride alongside the oxen on his horse, waving his arms in a perfect imitation of the stylish acting of the major, encouraging Todd to move toward the next fresh grass with all speed. All of us laughed.

That night, we bedded down as before, but Peter looked worried. When I asked him what he saw, he told me that it was not what he saw, but what he did not see that concerned him. I looked west and noticed that the reddish sky that had accompanied us each of the prior evenings did not appear this evening. The air was unnaturally still.

As I lay down that evening, I fell asleep quickly. I also awoke quickly in the middle of the night to the sensation of the wind blowing under the wagon and surrounding me. Then, a flash of lightning illuminated the entire sky. As soon as my eyes adjusted to the lightning, the sound of thunder filled the air, clearing my mind and totally waking me up.

The rain then started, coming not in individual drops but in sheets of water. I sat under the wagon, bundled in my blankets, in wonderment at the power of the first prairie thunderstorm I had ever experienced. The pattern of wind followed by lightning, thunder, and torrents of rain sustained itself in a divine show of power throughout the entire evening. Uncle Peter and I sat up during the evening watching the spectacle and dozing from time to time when our tiredness outweighed the spectacle of the storm.

Morning came and breakfast fires were impossible in the continuing rain. The men hitched the oxen in the rain. We ate hardtack and cheese for our breakfast without any of my mother's special cooking touches. Captain Watkins rode through the train urging us to move onto the trail as soon as possible.

The leading wagons moved out into the trail, but we waited longer than usual for our turn to move. Suddenly, Major Smith rode through the camp, waving his sword and shouting at the top of his lungs for all of the men in the army to move to the front wagon. The urgency in his commands caused Uncle Peter, my father, and me to leave our place with the wagon immediately and run to the front of the wagon train. There we saw a sight that depressed me far more than the rainy, sleepless night I had just endured. The first wagon, pulled by a team of mules, had sunk into a muddy mess of the road that the day before had been a dry trail that allowed us to move quickly. Captain Watkins was standing at the side of the road shaking his head, while Major Smith rode around shouting orders to the men that confused more than helped.

Finally, Captain Watkins stopped the confusion. He called Uncle Peter over to him and whispered a few words to him. Uncle Peter nodded and walked over to Major Smith. Uncle Peter held Major Smith's horse and whispered some words to him. Then, Major Smith flushed, tensed as if he wanted to say something, but he thought better of it. Major Smith then pointed at the second wagon in line and instructed them to unhitch their oxen from the wagon and double the animals attached to the first team. Uncle

Peter connected ropes and hooks to each of the front wheels of the wagon. Major Smith ordered the men of the first company to handle the ropes and pull the wagon out of the mire. Once the wagon struggled to the higher ground, the men disconnected the ropes and extra animals.

When it was my turn to pull on the ropes, I thought that my arms would fall out of their shoulder sockets before the wagons would move free of the mud. I thought my wars with the weeds at our home on the Stones River had been difficult, but I realized as I pulled on the ropes that I had no idea of how hard work truly could be.

In this way, we managed to keep the train moving at a very slow pace in the morning. We all collapsed at our midday break, exhausted from the labor of pulling wagons through the mud. In our first two days we had traveled about twenty miles each day; this morning we had moved the wagon train forward about a half mile and we all felt more tired as we sat down to another cold meal of hardtack and pemmican.

At our midday meal, Father asked the question that I had pondered all morning. "Peter, what did Captain Watkins whisper to you and what did you tell Major Smith?"

Uncle Peter laughed. "Jedediah, he had me tell our good major that if he did not stop waving the sword, Captain Watkins was gong to break it over his head. Then he had me tell the good major that he needed to calm down and help attach ropes to the wagons and help the train make it through the mud."

We all laughed at the thought of our grizzled captain breaking the sword of position over the head of the military one.

Captain Watkins understood our exhaustion, so the midday break was a little longer than usual. Uncle Peter and I crawled into the wagon and actually slept soundly for the time of our break. It was a truly bitter noise when I heard Captain Watkins announce the time to begin again with his rifle shot in the air.

Fortunately, the rain stopped. The afternoon was less laborious than the morning but the travel was still slow as the animals worked their way through the deep mud. More than once, we needed to stop our wagons and help our companions escape the deep muck.

I barely found enough fuel for the fire, but my evening meal went largely uneaten as I fell asleep sitting with my family. The next thing I was aware of was rolling over in the wagon where Father had placed me before he assumed my usual position of sleeping on the ground.

Fortunately, the rain that plagued us stayed away from us for the next two days. We returned to the pace of the first few days and continued to move westward over the land. I had always heard of the prairie grasses of the west; while the grasses were not as tall as my head, as I had heard they could be in the heat of the summer, these spring grasses grew taller than I had ever seen. Walking through these grasses, I learned to love the sensation of the wind slapping the grass against my thighs.

Finally, at the end of the first week on the trail, we found our train camped just next to the Vermillion Creek. There, we found the most complete stand of wood. When we camped at the edge of the creek, my mother sent my sister and me to gather dandelions in the fields. She wished to feed us something different that evening and the fields of dandelions had given her ideas of a new meal.

I gathered the plants in a pot. Bitsy and Sally joined me in this job, although their contribution was mostly running through the field of dandelions. Sally had showed much improvement since she had arrived with our traveling band; somehow, constant love

WEST TO THE SUN

and fresh cream had turned her from an ailing animal to a frisky companion.

While working, I noticed slight movement on the edge of the fields. I looked carefully at the tree line, convinced myself that there was nothing there, and returned to my assigned task. Then, I saw more movement and again glanced at the tree line. This time, though, I clearly saw that there was something there and moved toward the trees. Then, suddenly, a figure stepped out from the tree line. I looked carefully and realized I was looking at my first Indian.

I turned and ran to Bitsy, telling her to pick up Sally. I then picked them both up in my arms together with my bucket of dandelions and half walked and half ran out of the field toward the wagons. I glanced over my shoulder to see if the native warrior was following me. Once convinced that we were alone, I moved Sally and Bitsy quickly to my wagon.

"Where's Uncle Peter," I called to my mother.

"Here I am," Uncle Peter replied.

"Uncle Peter, come quickly," I said. "There are Indians here."

"I know," said Uncle Peter. "They've been following us for the last two days."

I have often been scared in my life, but never more than at that moment.

CHAPTER 7
TO THE PLATTE

Uncle Peter startled me with his calmness in the face of the knowledge that Indians were following us. I had never seen an Indian before and my fear increased due to the commentary of my cousins, who had painted a picture of certain death and dissection at the hands of these eight-foot-tall savages. How could he be so calm? All I could ask was, "How did you know, Uncle Peter?"

"First of all, Jeremiah, you need to understand that this entire western land is their home. We are just passing through on the way to our new home. Always assume that we are being watched and followed. In addition, when you live in the wild for a long time you learn there are times when you sense in the small of your back that you are not alone. Sometimes a plant moves when the wind is not stirring. A fire burns where one should not; perhaps a fire is not burning where it should be burning. In due time, the Indians will make their approach to us, but for now, we need to just continue on our way. The Indians in this area are not usually hostile."

With these words, my uncle sat by the bonfire, picked up his guitar and started to play. I listened and watched the sparks from the fire extending into heaven and mixing with the million stars that looked down on us until my eyes became heavy and I gladly crawled into my blanket bed beneath our wagons. My dreams that night were haunted with the sights that I had seen and had not seen, but truly supposed, visions of a tribe of hostile Indians circling our wagons.

The next morning, we woke as usual and crossed the Vermillion River. I liked crossing rivers early in the morning because these crossings were very hard work. I believed it was better to complete the tasks when fresh than when tired from a long journey. If a river rose due to recent rainfall or had powerful rapids, we would send one of the stronger swimming men to the other side of the river with a rope that would be tied to a tree. Then, the animals would lead their wagons into the water and we would use the ropes to guide them to the other side. If any animal lost its footing, or nerve, it would not be swept away because of the rope barriers.

Crossing the Vermillion took the wagon train a good part of the morning. The road leading to the river was muddy; in preparation for the crossing, we frequently had to stop and pull the wagons from the muck. Major Smith rode back and forth across the river, yelling and swearing at us to move faster and move our oxen to the other side. The animals timidly felt their way along the slippery bottom of the river and made their way cautiously to the other side of the river. Then we needed to climb the slippery, muddy bank to reach level ground. Once we were on dry ground, we started again down the road, pushing our teams to make up for the delays caused by crossing the river.

Upon stopping for the evening, we built our fires in the middle of the circle with the animals and cooked our meals. The routine of the camp had developed in just a week. The children gathered fuel, milked the cows, and released the chickens from the coops attached to the wagons while the adults prepared the food. Once these tasks were complete, we ate our evening meal. My uncle played his guitar and poor Mr. Johnson would wander from fire to fire seeking male companionship outside of his wagon of women. The Elliott girls wandered around the fires, seeking the attention of the young men while I played some games with the O'Donnell twins or listened to my uncle's guitar. This evening, the routine would change dramatically.

As the families were completing their meals, into the middle of the wagon fires came a group of six Indian men. The men were tall and their hair was cut with a forelock that pasted into a high point. Once they were in the middle of the circle, the normal activity ceased and the women and children retreated from the fires toward the perceived safety of the wagons. Captain Watkins stepped forward and met them.

My uncle whispered in my ear. "Pawnees. You can tell because they grease their hair with buffalo grease into a point. They are great hunters of the plains and this is their normal territory."

Captain Watkins met the Indians. The men spoke quietly. The Indian leader gestured with his hands pointing to the wagons and the people around the wagons. Captain Watkins nodded, turned, and moved away from the visitors to address the men of the wagon train.

"These men want gifts. They say that we are disturbing their hunting grounds. Since they are allowing us to travel in their territory peacefully, they are demanding that we provide them with presents to pay them for the inconvenience. They want food, clothes, blankets, and any pretty things that will make their young women happy. We can either give them the gifts or send them away. If we send them away, they will come to steal whatever they want and we will fight a needless battle."

Major Smith chose this moment to exert his leadership. He stood and raised his voice to the group. "Men, we need to resist the entreaties of these godless heathen. If they want food and clothing, then let them labor for it as we have done. Send them on their way with nothing. They are nothing but savages. They will run from us as soon as we open fire with our rifles."

Some men murmured agreement. I heard a voice reply. It startled me when I realized who was speaking. My father, in his low voice of authority that he only used when the corn went unworked by lazy boys, said: "That is foolishness. We have supplies to share. Have each family give something, whether a shirt, an extra blanket or five pounds of bacon. Do not create an unnecessary enemy so close to the beginning of our journey. Anyway, Major, since you appear to be citing these men as being godless foes, you might want to remember that true religion is to look after widows and orphans in their distress. Who knows how many widowed and orphaned Pawnees we may be feeding?"

More men, including Captain Watkins, expressed support for this view. We all gathered some of our excess and handed it to the Pawnee leader, although I noticed that Major Smith handed over this bounty with less than a charitable heart. I looked at my father differently following this debate. Perhaps the Bible that he preached on a Sunday did have value in persuading people on the other six days of the week.

Captain Watkins joined our family by our fire. "Can you believe what a fool Major Smith can be at times? He would have started a battle over fifty dollars worth of excess food and clothing. Better to be rid of them and not endanger our livestock. We gave nothing that will harm us, and our hearts and wagons will be that much lighter for the charity provided."

Uncle Peter replied. "Captain, you are absolutely right. However, you also know that we had better watch our horses very carefully tonight. Jedediah, Jeremiah, and I will stay awake. You know that this was a group that came to gather supplies and to examine our horses."

Captain Watkins nodded, took a drink from the hip flask that he always kept in his pocket, and walked away from us. My father spoke: "You are a wise man, Peter. I noticed that while the leader was discussing matters with Major Smith, his braves were looking at our horses."

That was a restless evening. Uncle Peter played his guitar a little longer than usual and told Father that the three of us needed to crawl beneath our wagon as if all was well and we were pretending to fall asleep.

When I was back in my school by the banks of the Stones River, I had heard stories of soldiers in long-ago wars executed for falling asleep on guard duty. This fear of falling asleep when coupled with the excitement of the evening did fierce battle with my tired bones and the youthful desire to sleep for just a few minutes. Then, as the dark of midnight turned into the gray, predawn light, I started to feel my head nodding into my chest. Suddenly, I felt a strong shake at my shoulders. Uncle Peter looked at me, put his finger over his mouth in a sign telling me to be very quiet, and crawled out from under the wagon.

Father, Uncle Peter, and I stepped out into the open. We all cocked our rifles. Then, Uncle Peter whistled low in the direction of the horses. A solitary figure, with a greased forelock, stopped, turned, and looked our direction. Without saying a word, my uncle stared at the figure, shook his head, and raised his rifle over his head. The Pawnee looked our direction, scowled, and, without turning his back on us, moved quickly out of our wagon corral without taking any of the animals he had coveted.

Once our uninvited guest left, my uncle stirred up the fire from the evening before and made my father a pot of coffee to help with the day ahead. While making coffee, Uncle Peter turned to me and said, "The Pawnees, like most Plains Indians, are noble in their bravery and way of life, but they do not believe in owning things the way we do. Horses belong to everyone, as a gift from their gods. It is not a sign of dishonor to steal one."

Father nodded his agreement and added, "Never confuse, Jeremiah, a different way of living life with being evil. A man in our culture who is a horse thief is a horrible man; but, if there is no ownership of horses, then there can be no theft of horses. What we need to do is to learn what we can from people like the Pawnees while keeping a strong grip on our beliefs."

I silently listened to this advice. Sometimes, wisdom came from educated strangers, but more often than not, it came from the men who had helped raise me and cared to teach me of the ways of men.

That morning we sleepily continued our path west. At midday, we reached the Big Blue River, which, was far more difficult than the other rivers that we had crossed. While Captain Watkins and Major Smith explored the crossings, Mother had me gather some of the black mustard that grew along the river. Any time my mother could, she had Bitsy and me gather some of the plants along the rivers. While I believed there was no one better at cooking than my mother, there was a limit to the variety that she could provide given our diet. Our daily food consisted of bacon, beans, bread, and more bacon, beans and bread. It was enough to make a boy want to eat the green plants that ordinarily he would reject without second thought.

It was at this crossing that my father did something very unusual. He pulled on the plants from the side of the road and called the families in our little company together. "Do you see this? This may look like a wild pea plant, but you need to be very careful about this. This milk vetch is very poisonous to our oxen. Boys," he said to the O'Donnells and me. "It is your job to keep the oxen away from this. If we are not careful, our animals will die and we will be stranded on the side of the road."

Uncle Peter looked at the plant. He nodded his head. "The Mexicans have a name for this plant. It is locoweed. Loco is a Spanish word for crazy. Any cow that eats too much of this plant will act crazy in its last days and then die."

My comrades and I promised to take this job seriously and for the next day, we saw nothing but locoweed along the side of the road. Whether or not it was locoweed, I do not truly know. However, when told that our friends, the docile oxen, could die from eating too much of this plant, I could not be too careful and tended to see the danger in every grass.

Moving past the Big Blue River, we camped alongside the junction of the road where the people who had begun in Independence joined with the folk who had started at St. Joseph. From this point forward, the road would be more crowded and dustier as all the people heading west joined a single trail. As we moved further along the trail, the trees that reminded me of my home in Tennessee became scarce. In place of the trees, the grass grew thicker and taller. When the strong wind blew through the grass, a song played as the tops of the bluestem grasses thrashed against each other. This tune continually played for us as we continued, always forward, toward the land beyond the sun. Day extended into day, the constant marching moved us closer to our new homes.

Finally, Captain Watkins took mercy on our caravan. At a beautiful place called Alcove Spring, Captain Watkins announced that not only would we take our noonday rest, but also that we would allow the train to rest in this park for the remainder of the day. Mother was especially grateful for this news; the tasks that she wanted to accomplish in tending to her family and their appearance were impossible while we continued on our never-ending march of twenty miles a day. Clothes needed mending. Children needed cleaning. The carefully packed wagon needed reorganizing.

In contrast to the labor that Mother anticipated, I knew that Uncle Peter and Father looked forward to an extended rest in the afternoon. The gear needed checking, but I also knew that they wanted to rest in the heat of the afternoon sun and that there would be little activity beyond the gentle breathing of napping men, once the inspections were made.

The O'Donnell twins and I escaped quickly from our chores. Near the springs was a field of flowers that was as colorful as the intermixed colors found on a painter's palette. Beyond the flowers of the field, a waterfall fell from a twelve-foot ledge and splashed onto the smooth rocks below. The O'Donnells and I jumped under the waterfall, feeling the cool water bouncing on our heads and necks. The cool water refreshed our tired bodies. We ran faster that afternoon due to the waterfalls.

After we left the falls, we wandered along the paths in the woods. Along the side of the path, I noticed a lonely grave dug under an oak tree on the side of a hill. While we would become immune to the sight of graves the further we went along the journey, this one remained in my memory the entire journey. I knelt down by the gravesite and read carefully the crudely carved gravestone: "Sarah Keyes, Died May 29, 1846, aged 70."

I was eleven years old. The trip from home, leaving the friends and memories of my youth, seemed like a huge gamble to me worthy of the riverboat gamblers I had met on the riverboats. Why would someone leave behind a full lifetime worth of memories? What sort of spirit must reside in a woman who would travel in this way, knowing the likely outcome, when she was seventy years old? Could the quest for new sights compel someone to abandon a full life of friends and knowledge? Perhaps home and certain knowledge paled when the family moved. Regardless, there was a spirit in Ms. Keyes that propelled her on a journey that she had to know she was unlikely to finish. I wondered what her thoughts were as she realized she was dying on the prairie and would never arrive at her new home. Now, she lay forever in this beautiful park, a warning to future travelers and a memorial to the spirit of a woman willing to leave an entire life behind to stay with family on a journey to the sun.

That night, Peter pulled out his guitar while Mr. O'Donnell pulled out his fiddle. They struck up lively tunes while the families danced around the fire, laughing and enjoying their moments of rest and relaxation. The joy of that evening washed away the drudgery built up in our souls caused by the constant marching, just as surely as the afternoon splashing in the waterfall cleansed us of the dust of the trail. My parents did not dance; however, Father presented Mother with a bouquet of wild flowers that caused her to blush like a schoolgirl who has received a prized gift from her young beau. They then stood by the fire listening to the music and tapping their feet in time to the fast beat of the music. Even the usually dour Captain Watkins stood at the side of the group, smiling and taking slow pulls from his hip flask.

We danced, sang, and laughed deep into the night. Bitsy and

Sally crawled into bed early; I stayed awake as long as I could until the urge to sleep overcame my desire to hear another song and I crawled into my blankets under the wagon.

When Captain Watkins fired his gun the next morning, the adults groaned as they felt the impact of the long hours of the dancing and longed for the mercy of additional moments of slumber. Realizing that there was no mercy, however, we crawled out from our blankets, put them in their appointed locations, and stumbled out to stoke the breakfast fires. We ate silently. Then, we moved slowly to hitch up the oxen, and pushed forward onto the trail.

Compared to the beautiful variety of Alcove Springs, the road drained us with monotony. The sea of grass continued as it had before. Dust increased and started to choke us as we moved down the trail. At my uncle's suggestion, we all took handkerchiefs, wetted them, and wrapped them around our nose and mouth. While this made us all look like highwaymen of the stories that Miss Stewart read us back in our schoolhouse, the relief that we received from the dust was immense and worth any of our comical appearances.

We moved as quickly down the trail as the flow of wagons would allow us. Our speed soon slowed. We did not know why, but the wagons in front of us stalled to the pace of a sloth. This frustrated us greatly because we remembered Captain Watkins constant reminders that speed was essential if we were to avoid the early snows in the western mountains.

Uncle Peter waited one day in this new pace. Then, he could take no more. He pulled Bitsy up onto the neck of his horse, whispered in her ear, patted his horse, and urged him forward with speed. Bitsy giggled as the animal responded with a quick canter. These two youngsters at heart, if not in body, left singing their little kids songs as Uncle Peter's horse moved beyond our wagon train. An hour later, they returned. Uncle Peter shook his head and reported his findings: "We need to be patient. The road squeezes between the Little Blue River and the bluffs ahead. There is just enough room for every wagon to move in single file. The milk cows and cattle need to walk with the wagons and cannot wander off on their own, because there is simply no room."

Slowly we moved forward, delayed by the crowd and the landscape. Finally, we entered into the land that Captain Watkins called the Narrows. Entering the Narrows, Uncle Peter rode around the train with Captain Watkins. "Be careful men," the experienced travelers told us. "These grasses are the perfect hiding place for rattlesnakes."

Rattlesnakes, I thought. Just what we needed. "Uncle Peter," I asked when he returned. "Are rattlesnakes really ten feet long? Do they really eat cattle? My cousins told me this when I was staying with them."

Uncle Peter laughed at my questions. "No, Jeremiah, rattlesnakes are only three or four feet long and they eat small animals like mice and rabbits, not useful oxen or useless Todd. They are more afraid of you than you are of them, but they are stupid creatures and often feel threatened where no threat exists. So, be careful, especially when you wander from the trail. You may accidentally step near one and be bit before you see it and then the war for your life will be engaged. So, stay near the wagons and we will push through the Narrows as quickly as possible."

Hearing this advice, I climbed onto the back of the wagon and rode through this little slit in the land between the river and the butte. I looked for the snakes and found none. I felt disappointment at this omission. Having heard so much about them, I felt that the snakes owed me at least a momentary glimpse of their presence.

Once we left the Narrows, I noticed that there were fewer and fewer trees to provide us with the necessary fuel for our fires. I began gathering grasses to provide the flame we needed to light and sustain the blazes that gave us the warmth for the evening and the heat to cook our food. Uncle Peter laughed when I complained about the lack of trees. "Do not be surprised, Jeremiah, if you do not see another tree like those at home until we arrive in Oregon. The world is different here in the middle of this continent."

With this story, I ceased looking for the tall stands of trees I loved so much. Instead, as my mother told me when we left our home in Tennessee, I simply kept my eyes looking forward. We kept moving through the ever-growing grass fields. Then, at the end of one day, we climbed a slight hill and saw a sight that startled me. Beyond the hill was the long, wide Platte River that flowed unimpeded in both directions as far as I could see. In every direction, I saw nothing but waves of grasses, dotted only by an occasional tree, apparently rolling and sinking like waves of a green sea that crashed together as the gusts of wind moved them wherever the wind desired.

Looking at this endless sea of high grass, I felt as if this landscape could surely swallow me, much as the blue-green oceans could swallow ships that dared too much and drifted too far. Yet, much as sailors ignore the dangers of Davy Jones' locker, I felt compelled to move forward to find the joy that the continued adventure promised.

CHAPTER 8

BUFFALO HUNT

Once we reached the Platte River, we were a day's journey from Fort Kearney. Mr. Johnson's mother-in-law, Old Mrs. Parker, wandered over to our fire after supper. She warmed her hands and spoke: "I can tell when those young kids want me to leave for a while. That husband of my 'Liza acts very strange and before I know it, she is a blushing schoolgirl again. So, it is better that I find someplace to be than continue to stay where I am not wanted."

My mother answered: "Well, it is a difficult circumstance when there are two women in one kitchen. It probably is harder when they are in one wagon. So, any time you feel the need to remove yourself from the young couple, feel free to join us."

I silently groaned. During our short time together, Mrs. Parker had proven a unique capability of wringing a single drop of rain out of any sunny day. Some company made time pass faster; Mrs. Parker made every moment feel like an hour long with her constant grumbling. I knew that Mother was placing her personal Christianity into practical action. Somewhere, I knew that Mrs. Parker would, before this journey was complete, force me to exercise a little of my own.

"This has been a hard journey," Mrs. Parker started, "but at least tomorrow we reach Fort Kearney. It will be a heavenly oasis of civilization. It bothered me when my 'Liza told me that we must move. It bothered me even more when I was required to dispose of some of the beautiful things that I accumulated over the course of my long life. Now, that awful Mr. Johnson tells me that we need to lighten the load and we must leave some of my beautiful furniture along the road. That will never happen. But, at least tomorrow, we will have a breath of civilization instead of this constant savage traveling."

Onward her complaints continued. Like a stone rolling downhill, her complaints gathered speed and threatened to crush anyone standing in their way. I have no idea how long she spoke with Mother, for I wandered away and joined the lively company of the O'Donnells. Uncle Peter and Bitsy joined me by the fire where Mr. O'Donnell played his fiddle, and my uncle strummed along with the lively Irish songs with his guitar. Sally crawled up into Bitsy's lap and we swayed back and forth and sang along when we knew the words of the tunes of freedom denied and love lost. Soon, we noticed that Mrs. Parker had returned to her wagon and Mother waved that it was safe for our spirits to return to our own wagon and climb into our blankets.

From that point on, there was an entirely new set of remarkable sights. The Platte River looked to be a mile wide and an inch deep. The river was so brown and slow moving that it was unclear to me whether it should be drunk or chewed. I walked along the banks of the river with my friends, the O'Donnell twins, searching for tadpoles and small creatures we could trap, as if we were the mountain men of old. Bitsy either rode in the wagon with Sally, or when Sally slept, she rode on the neck of my uncle's horse.

At midday, our column ceased and my uncle and I seized our

fishing poles in desperate search for a hungry catfish or two. The sensation of the cool river water and mud on our bare feet felt good enough to make up for the failure to catch the fish. "I fear Mrs. Parker will be disappointed in Fort Kearney," my uncle said in a sad voice. "She expects elegant St. Louis and she is not going to be happy with what she sees."

I did not grasp what he was saying, but that knowledge came quickly. In the middle of the afternoon, as we passed a small hill, I saw a few sod buildings so poorly constructed that they were barely able to stand on their own. Uncle Peter rode over as I looked at them and said, "Look, Jeremiah, there is Fort Kearney. The buildings are so weak that sometimes snakes crawl through the holes in their walls." I could only imagine what Mrs. Parker would be feeling when she saw this collection of huts.

Our wagon train passed through Fort Kearney. The ladies stopped at the fort's store while we set up camp just west of the town. Captain Watkins wandered over to my uncle and asked, "Do you feel like hunting buffalo?"

Uncle Peter smiled and told our guide that there was nothing he wanted to do more.

Captain Watkins nodded. "I think these greenhorns could use a taste of buffalo meat. I guess I could let you go hunt some buffalo if you would agree to meet us at O'Fallon's Bluffs. I believe there are some buffalo herds south of us and I know you can go hunt us some fresh buffalo meat."

Uncle Peter replied, "If you round up for me an extra horse and a couple of mules, I will go hunt some buffalo meat with Jeremiah."

Captain Watkins spit on the ground. "That is a good idea. I wish I could go with you, Tenderfoot Pete. I do get terribly tired of being around that Major Smith and his military foolishness and all of the whining women. If you promise that you'll meet us at O'Fallon's Bluffs in one week's time, you can go and we will carry on without you, but only if you bring me back some fresh meat."

Uncle Peter nodded. "I know O'Fallon's Bluff. We will kill our buffalo, bring the meat, and be waiting for you there. We'll be dangling our feet in the river while you are trying to keep Major Smith from making people loco."

I could not believe my ears. Not only was I going to see my first buffalo, but also we were actually going to hunt them. Uncle Peter and I gathered our supplies quickly. We packed hardtack and bacon for food; salt to cure any meat we obtained, and large knives to butcher the enormous animals. We took some spare sacks in which we would wrap the meat. We carefully packed our rifles and ample ammunition for our hunt.

My sense of being a grown-up slowed when Mother, who had returned from the commissary, hugged me and warned me to mind my uncle. I could feel the concern in her embrace and for a moment, I doubted the wisdom of the adventure. Father, though, smiled at me and assured her that this was a task well within my capabilities. Then, Captain Watkins rode up with a spare horse and two mules. All of my concerns vanished. I put on the confident face of an eleven-year-old buffalo hunter, climbed into the saddle, and waved to my parents and Captain Watkins. Then, without a further look backward, I turned my horse to the south and followed Uncle Peter out of camp.

Once we were out of sight of the wagon train, I urged my horse to move forward and join Uncle Peter. Once I was alongside him, I asked, "Uncle Peter, how are we going to find buffalo?"

Uncle Peter laughed. "Jeremiah, in this country and at this time of year, it is not hard to find the buffalo. The herds stay close together since the young have just been born. When we are within a few miles of the herds, we will see dust in the distance. The real danger is in hunting the buffalo."

"Uncle Peter, how dangerous can it be to hunt buffalo? I have been deer hunting before and I have never felt that hunting was very dangerous, as long as you are careful with the rifle. Father taught me how to handle a rifle almost as soon as I was large enough to hold one, just like your father taught you."

Uncle Peter stopped his horse, turned, and faced me. "Hunting buffalo is one of the most dangerous, and exciting, things you will ever do. They usually travel in large herds. There are two ways of hunting buffalo. First, you can tie up your horses and try to sneak up on one of the animals at the edge of the herd. If the wind shifts, or if the herd is spooked by anything, they will turn and run at you and you will be in the middle of an angry herd on foot. This happened to some friends of mine who wound up losing their horses and mules which were swept along in the sea of running animals."

"The second way to hunt buffalo is more effective, but even more dangerous. What we could do is to tie up the mule and chase the buffalo on our horses. When we come alongside one, we shoot it in its hump and then veer away from it quickly. The animal will always leap at you and while you need to reload while on horseback, you need to steer away. Usually, the second shot will kill the animal.

"I know a man who was hunting buffalo this way and his horse stepped into a prairie dog hole and the horse stumbled and he went flying fifteen feet ahead of his horse and barely managed to avoid being trampled by the running herd. So, Jeremiah, while I know that you know a lot about deer hunting, this is not the same thing."

Uncle Peter gave his horse a little kick and we started moving more quickly. This week we needed to find the buffalo, hunt them, butcher them, and return to our wagon train at O'Fallon's Bluff. This was not going to be a relaxed vacation. I rode behind Uncle Peter. I was proud that he trusted me to be his hunting partner, but it was scary to hear his stories. Part of me wanted to protest that I was only an eleven-year-old boy and that I should be home with my parents, but the rest of my heart steeled me to prove myself worthy of the trust that was being shown in me.

We rode the rest of the evening, stopping only when it became too dark to follow the trail. Uncle Peter knew where he was heading with only a few glances at the trail. I asked him about his ability to make these decisions and he told me it was easy since buffalo tended to travel on certain trails that had enough grass and water to support them. Therefore, we simply followed these trails and knew that we would find the buffalo.

That evening, Uncle Peter showed me a new way to start a fire. I had started to gather some grass, as we had been doing for the last week on the trail. Uncle Peter stopped me and told me he had a much easier way to provide fuel for the fire. I watched as he gathered big brown mounds; he called them buffalo chips and said that the animals we were hunting had provided this fuel for us. I laughed at the thought of using their droppings to cook our food. Uncle Peter assured me that I would soon become used to using them for fires since this was the primary fuel as long as we were on the plains.

I was scared to cook my food on these droppings, but they left no taste and they burned very cleanly. The bacon tasted just as good as it did around the fires of wood that we had made earlier in the trip. The fire kept me warm that night as I lay under the stars and dreamt of riding in the midst of a large herd of racing buffalo.

My uncle shook me awake before the sun rose. The smell of

coffee cooking on the ashes of the prior evening's fire welcomed my nose to a new day. Peter gave me bacon from the night before and hardtack for breakfast. We ate quickly, saddled our horses, and were on the trail before the gray of the night had been fully replaced by the red of the dawn.

We rode silently most of that day and the morning of the next. Around noon, my uncle stopped his horse and pointed in the distance. I saw, much to my excitement, a large puff of dust on the horizon. "Buffalo," my uncle said. I nodded and felt my heart leap with excitement inside of me. We slowed our pace and carefully determined the direction from that the wind was blowing. As we crossed the grassy plains, I said a silent prayer that I would keep my nerve and not embarrass my experienced uncle, who had trusted an eleven-year-old boy to be his companion on a buffalo hunt.

For an hour, we followed the dust clouds. Then, as my excitement grew to a level that I could barely contain, I saw a herd of the largest animals I had ever seen. Their brown fur was thick, giving them the most amazing beards and a fierce look that made me glad I had a rifle to protect myself.

Uncle Peter leaned over and pointed at a bush that was growing alongside of us. "Let's tie the mules up here and keep them safely out of the way. Load your rifle, Jeremiah. Put a few extra cartridges in your shirt pocket and extra powder in your gun. Once we are in the herd, take the shot and put it in your mouth because you will not have enough time to reach in your pocket for it. Remember, once we get them running, they are faster and bigger than our horses. Be careful. Let's each shoot one buffalo and find our way out of the herd to safety."

I leapt off my horse and tied up the mules. Part of me wanted to stay with them, but I had come this far and I wanted to see if I was man enough to do this job. Following his instructions, I loaded two extra charges of powder into my rifle. Then, mounting my horse, I swung away from the mules that gladly stayed eating the greenery of the bush and grass around them.

Uncle Peter moved ahead. He motioned for me to steer my mount to my right. I carefully guided my horse until Uncle Peter and I were the length of our old cabin apart from each other. He nodded at me and gestured when I was where I needed to be. We slowly cantered toward the herd, waiting as long as we could before we added speed to our horses. Suddenly, one of the larger animals turned, looked at us, and instinctively started moving away. As if this beast had communicated in its own language, the entire herd began moving the other direction. Peter nodded at me and we both began adding speed to our approach. Finally, the herd realized that danger was at hand and began to run as fast as they could.

What amazing creatures! They were so big and graceful. As they ran, the earth shook beneath my mount as we moved into the herd. I dug my heels into the horse and felt him start to gallop along with the buffalo. I could not stay silent if I had wanted to; a yell rose from deep within me and came out as a scream that was as powerful as if I had waited my whole life to utter it. I glanced at my uncle and saw that he, too, was waving his arms and screaming at the beasts. Suddenly, he lifted his rifle and fired his gun between the shoulders of a large animal that had the misfortune of straying too closely to him. This reminded me that I was not here solely for running with these powerful, magnificent creatures but that I also had a task to perform.

Steering my horse with my legs, I turned it closer to a large running buffalo. Ceasing my screams, I shifted my spare cartridges into my mouth. Taking my rifle in my hands, feeling the perspiration building and my heart racing, I trembled slightly as I took aim while my horse raced like the wind under me. Finally, I thought of my family waiting for the meat and pulled the trigger. I felt the gun shudder, although the sound of the herd drowned out the report of my rifle.

The animal lurched, staggered and as my uncle had predicted, jumped at my horse. Fortunately, I remembered his caution and while I was reloading my rifle, I pushed with my legs, guiding the horse away from the onslaught. I fired again and then this time the beast stopped in its tracks, turned its head looking at me in pain, and collapsed to its knees as its eyes finally closed.

I slowed my horse. This herd of animals held nothing more for me. I wanted the hunt to stop, as exhilarating as it had been. Part of me mourned for this one of God's magnificent creation.

The herd of bison, minus their two dead comrades, ran beyond us and continued galloping into the distance. Uncle Peter turned his horse and rode to me. "What did you think of that," he asked me in a breathless voice that could not hide his excitement.

I realized that I was not only laughing but that tears were involuntarily flowing from my eyes. I replied, "That was the most incredible excitement I have ever had. These animals are magnificent. They are so big and fast. It scared me to death, but I would not stop my horse for anything. Then, when I fired the gun and saw how the animal responded, I felt horrible. It looked at me with such pained eyes that I could not bear to look at it. I knew what I had to do though to provide the meat that our wagon train needs and so I just pulled the trigger again."

Uncle Peter nodded his head. "It is sad that the way to have meat from these creatures is to kill them. They are so wonderful. I think you learned a lot about courage today. A braggart can put himself in a dangerous situation. You though, put yourself in a dangerous situation and did something that you really did not want to do, so you could help feed your family. That is true bravery. I am proud of you. You did a man's work today."

He put his arms around me and I felt better.

Then we needed to do a slow, tedious job. Cutting through the fur was incredibly hard work. The hair was thickly matted and much denser than the hair of the oxen and horses. My uncle sawed through to the meat quickly. He had warned me we needed to complete this task quickly since we did not want to waste this huge amount of meat. Skillfully, Uncle Peter cut the muscle from the bones of our buffalo and then turned this muscle into buffalo steaks. I placed the steaks in the salt we had packed in order to preserve them from spoiling.

Once we had taken the choice steaks from these animals, we worked on the other pieces of meat. Uncle Peter found some wood and made a long framework, under which I built a low fire with the buffalo chips. Uncle Peter cut the meat into thin strips and I placed them on the framework. In this way, we dried the least tasty pieces into jerky that would provide sustenance while taking little of our wagon's storage room. We spent the rest of the day tending this fire and cutting strips from our buffalo for jerking.

That evening I had my first feast from the buffalo. Uncle Peter told me that the roast from the hump of the buffalo was better than any meat I would ever taste. We carved the meat from this area of the buffalo and roasted it over the fire we built to the side of our jerky fire. Nothing that I have eaten before this dinner compared with the meal I shared on the open prairie.

Following dinner, we continued with our jerking of the meat. Allowing any of this meat to go to waste would be a tragedy that I could not imagine. Finally, my uncle nodded to me that it was time to go to sleep. We lay our weary bodies near the jerky racks and fell asleep. While we heard coyotes talking in the distance, we knew they would content themselves with the parts of the buffalo that we did not turn into meat and would not approach us.

That morning we loaded the jerky into sacks that we closed as tightly as possible in order to keep them dry. Then, after we loaded up the mules with all of the meat they could carry, my uncle placed the coats from the buffalo on top of the mules and we left the scene of battle.

It was a slow journey back toward O'Fallon's Bluffs. One of the skills that Uncle Peter demonstrated is that he always knew the direction he needed to follow. Many people carried guidebooks and crude maps, which might not be accurate; Uncle Peter carried his guidebook between his ears. For the next three days, we slowly moved along the trail. While we always stayed vigilant, we knew that we did not have the ability to save and move any additional buffalo meat to the wagon train, so we did not hunt any more. We made ourselves content with buffalo steaks and bacon on the way back to the wagon train. While I enjoyed my uncle's company, part of me wanted to return immediately to the family to tell them the stories of how I rode into the herd of buffalo and emerged with hundreds of pounds of meat. I knew that my attitude probably included too much pride, but pride came on easily with accomplishment.

After three days of travel, I rode over a slight hill and saw the Platte River on its brown journey. My uncle smiled, pointed at a slight incline perhaps a mile in the distance and said "O'Fallon's Bluff. I told Captain Watkins that we would be cooling our feet in the Platte River before he arrived. You should never doubt my ability to find my way." I laughed and realized that pride was a shared human characteristic.

We rode our horses over to the river and allowed them to drink their fill. I started gathering the sticks, grass, and buffalo chips for the fire and we watched as wagon after wagon drove past us. We swam in the river and tried unsuccessfully to catch more of the reluctant Platte River catfish for our meals. Mostly we waited and dozed.

Around noon of the next day, I saw Captain Watkins riding his horse with Major Smith riding alongside, gesturing with his sword over his head. Uncle Peter and I emerged from our hiding spot by the river and greeted them: "Does anyone want some buffalo meat?"

Captain Watkins grinned. He shouted for the wagons to form a single column to pass by the bluffs and told Major Smith: "We pass by these bluffs and then we make camp. Tonight, we feast on buffalo meat and celebrate. Tomorrow, we will work to make up the time lost."

Major Smith started to protest, but the look on our guide's face told him that this would be pointless. I ran on from these men looking for my family. Finally, in the third group of our wagon train, I saw the familiar faces of Bob, Todd, and Bill. My father saw me at the same time I saw him. He pulled the reins to halt the animals and both he and my mother hopped off the wagon. I hugged my mother and started to speak, but thought differently. Words are sometimes the worst way to speak. Therefore, I just hugged and received a hug in return. Home was not a building, but a place and a people to which we always enjoyed returning.

CHAPTER 9
ALONG THE RIVER

After I told my parents the stories of my conquest on the buffalo hunt, I immediately found my friends the O'Donnell twins and shared my victory with them. In certain stories, it might be necessary to embellish the details; in this situation, no fictional account could be better than reality. The speed of the buffalo, the power of the racing herd, and the fear that they caused deep inside me needed no exaggeration.

Unlike our usual evening meals, the community ate this meal together. We gathered the buffalo chips that abounded in the area and together with dry grass we created a huge cooking fire in the center of the circle of wagons to roast the good rib meat of the animals. Each family brought forth some of their hidden store of luxuries to make this feast something truly worthy of a festival. Fruits, long hidden fresh vegetables and freshly baked sweets all appeared on the tables. Each family sat under the warming sun and joined to feast as a new community.

The musicians brought out their guitars, fiddles, and other instruments following the conclusion of the meal. Around the former cook fire, the musicians sat and played while the married couples danced and the teenagers sought out new partners. The

Elliott girls glanced my way, since the whole community knew of my exploits. Instead of pursuing me, as I was far too young for their interest, they instead pressed Uncle Peter for details of the hunt. He responded with the amusement of someone who saw through the courtship desires of people whose immaturity made them more likely daughters than girlfriends. He quickly wearied of their attention, seized his guitar, and joined the merrymaking.

The O'Donnell boys and I drifted away from the party and spent our evening in pursuit of fish. We chatted briefly about the events of the last week, but mostly we sat on the side of the Platte River and let our lines dangle listlessly while listening to the music in the distance. When the music stopped, I gladly crawled into my spot beneath the wagon and fell quickly into a deep and contented sleep.

The morning came and the routine to which I had grown accustomed fell back onto my shoulders like an old, comfortable set of clothing. My mother, humming some tunes from the night before, set the bread and bacon out for our breakfast. Once we ate, we cleaned the dishes, placed the food back in their appropriate storage locations. We hitched the animals into their accustomed place. Bitsy climbed into her wagon play area with Sally and Suzy; my mother sat in her rocker working on some of the mending, Father sat up top and drove the oxen, while I walked alongside the oxen, urging them on and showing them the end of the whip when they wanted to stop. Westward we moved, tracing the path of the Platte River, one step after another, one roll of the wagon wheel following the prior roll.

Mercifully, this day was without unusual activity. After the excitement of the buffalo hunt, I felt I needed the opportunity to stop thinking and simply walk. The height of the grass obscured me from any long view. Instead, I marched forward, step after step, seeing only the wagon in front of me and the grass on the side of the trail. Hours passed and we soon consumed our midday meal. We rested. Then, the journey continued through the afternoon. The routine lacked the excitement of the buffalo hunt, but in an odd way, the lack of adventure allowed my mind to rest and process the excitement of the prior week.

The next morning came early. While we had grown accustomed to the early dawn serving as a clock alerting us of the time to move, the dawn this day was dark and foreboding. We ate breakfast with many glances at the western sky. Even the animals responded to the conditions. The chickens made more than their accustomed clucking. The oxen assumed their position in the front of the wagon more reluctantly than usual. Even Sally refused to take her morning romp through the bushes for mice, preferring to stay with Bitsy in the safety of the wagon. Usually, I loved being in the front of the wagon train; today was our day in front but somehow I would have preferred the relative ignorance of being at the end of the train, hiding, ineffectively, behind my fellow adventurers.

We continued tracing the river. As if the river was bored with its single channel, it split into two different streams. We followed the southern branch of the river, continuing westward. Soon, the sky answered the questions that we all held about the day. Lightning lit the sky; first one bolt followed by a sheet of lightning that lit the entire sky without a clear definition of a single bolt. The thunder followed the lightning that shook the ground. Uncle Peter's horse danced a jig of nervousness, requiring all of Peter's skills to keep the horse moving in a straight line. Following this announcement of the pending storm, the wind which had been calm the entire day started to blow, quietly at first and then with a force and power that alerted us that this would not be a day like any other.

The rain started. First, a discernable drop and then a second, followed by a steady stream of water from the skies and finally a sheet of water that slapped into our faces and destroyed both our will and ability to move forward. We were all soaked; even Mother and Bitsy found that the double covering was no match for the sheets of water descending from the skies.

I glanced backward at my friends the O'Donnell twins and envied their ability to avoid the oxen-steering duty and hide in the wagon. Mrs. Parker started to complain loudly to poor Mr. Johnson about this rugged world to which he had thoughtlessly brought her to die.

Captain Watkins rode over to Uncle Peter. "Probably need to stop and protect the animals."

Uncle Peter glanced at Captain Watkins and then turned his eyes to the horizon. "This could be bad. The only good thing about the rain is it reduces the chance of a prairie fire."

Just then, our good major rode over to them. "Move forward, men. We can not let a little water stop us from our goal for the day."

"Major," my uncle, replied loudly, "this looks like a cyclone. We need to protect our animals and families."

"Coward," the major snapped. "You are afraid of a little water. I am tired of your insubordinate tone. I will not trade words with you. It is time to move. I order it."

Uncle Peter clenched his fist. I knew that he wanted to punch the major in his insulting mouth, but instinctively he knew that this was not the time and that the major's empty words were not worth the bruised knuckles that would inevitably follow. The major realized how close he had come to starting a fight that he would surely lose, so he turned the head of his horse and rode off yelling at the rest of the train to speed up and continue moving. We continued forward, out of a doomed sense of obedience to the Major rather than due to any strong belief in his leadership.

The sky turned black, then a green that I had only previously seen in glass bottles, and finally, a red of the dirt around us. The rain continued in sheets falling from the sky, turning the sandy ground into a quagmire. The oxen struggled forward slowly. Suddenly, Uncle Peter shouted, "Look, twister."

I watched in fascination and terror as a cloud appeared, starting to spin, reaching toward the ground with its bottom tip emerging from the cloudbank. The cloud started moving toward us faster and appeared certain to land in the middle of our wagon train. Father pulled the oxen to a halt, hopped off his perch on the wagon, and led the oxen by their halters into a slight valley next to the road. "Get under the wagon", he yelled at us. We all jumped into the valley and hid under the wagon while the wind howled above us. Uncle Peter jumped off the horse and slapped it in its haunches to let it find shelter in its own way.

We lay flat on our stomachs under our wagon as time stopped, with Bitsy crying and Father holding her close, whispering comfort into her ears. We heard the sound of the wind passing over our heads, which made a howl that scared me more than the wind itself. Looking out from under the wagon, I saw branches and limbs fly past our wagon. I buried my head in the dirt and prayed that the storm passed quickly.

As quickly as it came, the wind ended. The rain continued to fall heavily, but the wind died. We emerged from our hiding place and looked at the rest of the train. Uncle Peter's horse came nervously back to the train. The storm had tipped several of the wagons, and portions of the belongings were scattered in the midst of them. In the distance, I could hear a little girl screaming. I heard some of the adults talking and they said that her leg had been shattered. I knew that the rest of the day would be spent in cleaning the mess caused by the storm. While this was hard work, I was grateful for witnessing the splendor of the storm and the safety that God had provided us underneath the wagon.

As we lit the fires that evening, Captain Watkins rode up to our group. "There is a meeting after supper tonight," he explained. "Some people want to talk about what happened today. I think it probably is a good thing to do. All of the men need to attend."

My father nodded. "Yes," he said, in his low voice. "Can't say I am real happy with what I saw today."

Mother hurried us along. She clearly wanted us attending the meeting and offered to do some of the chores with the animals that I usually did at night. It made me feel good that my family still thought of me as a man, although I knew the rest of the wagon train saw a boy when they looked at me. I noticed that whenever my parents said something encouraging to me, it welled deep inside of me and made me believe it was true, even if my internal voice denied the reality of the compliment.

After we washed up from dinner, my father, uncle, and I walked to the designated area. We saw all of the men of the group coming into the clearing. The faces of the men were largely tired, with occasional angry looks When the group had gathered, a younger man stood up. I had never heard him speak before, but I knew that he was a farmer from Pennsylvania. He cleared his throat and began talking in a voice that shook with anger:

"Some of you may not know me. My name is Josiah Braun. My little girl Amy is the girl whose leg was shattered today. I believe the reason her leg was broken is that our leader, who loves pretending that he is the general of a mighty army, failed to lead us safely. Rather than using common sense, he pushed this group out of safety just to prove that he was in charge. Now, my little girl lies in the wagon with her leg shattered because of him. I hope we can save her leg and her life. But, regardless of whether the leg is saved, this so called major is a man who is unfit to lead." He tried to say more, but all he could do, thinking of his daughter was weep and wave his hand in disgust at the major.

Senator Richardson stood next. He looked around at us and scowled. "I tried to warn you that this so-called major was not the man to lead us to the west. He has waved his sword at us for the last three hundred miles and has contributed nothing to the journey except a comical figure. This would be acceptable, if it were not so tragic. Now, he has mangled poor little Amy Braun with his criminal negligence. I tell you, good people; it is time for a change. Raising a sword is showmanship; it is not leadership! We cannot rely on the man with the raised sword any longer. We need a leader. In the papers we signed at the beginning of this journey, we wrote that we could replace the leader at any time. The time has come."

Major Smith looked at the crowd united against him and spoke: "Responsibility is never easy. I have labored hard to bring us this far in the wilderness. Leadership is difficult and lonely and I have spent many hours worrying about our moves. We need to move this wagon train to the west and have it arrive on time. Do any of you want to be stranded in the western mountains in the snow? I think not.

"As for today, I am truly sorry about little Amy. Who would not feel sorrow at the injury of that precious young sprite? Am I God? Can I start and stop storms? Do not make a rash change to new leadership at a time when the road is about to become more dangerous."

Once the Major sat down, the decorum of the meeting vanished. Every man needed to make his voice heard above the fray and, therefore, in the mixture of voices no single man could be heard. Father, Uncle Peter, and I watched the spectacle with concern mixed with amusement. Suddenly, Mr. Braun punched Major Smith in the jaw, sending him falling backwards from the stump on which he had been sitting. Then, Major Smith's friends attacked Mr. Braun and his friends and before I knew what was happening a general battle erupted. My father pushed me hard into the relative safety of a space beneath one of the wagons. Finally, Captain Watkins fired his rifle into the air.

Fistfights were one thing; gun battles something entirely different. The sound of the rifle stilled the aggressive spirit and stopped the fight immediately. The captain waved his rifle and shouted: "Enough! Let's just have a vote before someone is killed."

Just like the first election, we all voted by walking to one side of the clearing or the other. When we counted the votes, the men had voted to have Senator Richardson lead the group. Major Smith stormed off away from the group, swearing aloud and hitting the tall grass with his now functionless sword. The good senator smiled and shook hands with each of us as if we were long-lost comrades. The three of us smiled and rolled our eyes at one another as our posturing friend, the senator, left us. Father just muttered, "He is a politician to the core."

We awoke early the next morning and started our daily travels just as the sun rose over the horizon. We yoked the oxen and moved them through the moist sand in an effort to make up time that had been lost in the previous day's events.

At noon, we turned the oxen loose to find the grass that would sustain them through an equally long afternoon. The grass was good along the Platte and the fear of the oxen wandering into a patch of locoweed dissipated. As they moved to find the best grass, we sat down for our noonday meal of cheese, fruit, leftover bacon and bread. While we were sitting and resting following the meal, I heard a bellow from an ox that would have been comical if not for the desperation it held. The noise started low and built in pitch, desperation and volume until it was a high-pitched scream. Then, when the noise stopped, it repeated itself and the lowing demanded our attention.

Curiosity made me run to find the cause of the despair. When I saw what had happened I did not know whether I should laugh or cry. Our own Todd had seen a sand spit near the edge of the river on which there was a large clump of sweet, green grass. Since it was impossible for Todd to ignore fresh grass, he had moved toward the island and had become stuck in the quicksand that lined the riverbed. I turned and ran back to our wagon: "Father, Uncle Peter, come quickly. Todd is stuck in the quicksand and can't free himself."

My father and Uncle Peter ran to the river. Sure enough, Todd was struggling with the quicksand and with every movement he was making himself stuck firmer into the muck. I turned to my uncle and asked if he should try to slip a rope over his neck and pull him out. My uncle laughed and said, "I would love to do that, but there is too much danger of injuring him by trying to pull him out."

Father climbed onto the bank of the river, shook his head, and laughed. "I would hope that this experience cures Todd of his love for fresh grass, but I doubt it. Jeremiah, gather an armful of fresh grass. Peter, get me some large slats of wood, as long as you can find. We need to meet in the river as quickly as possible. As irritating as our good friend Todd is, he is a good, hardworking ox."

We all ran to our appointed task. With the help of the O'Donnell twins, we picked an armful of the tall grass that grew alongside the river. Father then directed me to a place on the river that he felt would support our weight. Uncle Peter joined us with slats of wood about six feet long. My father stood a few feet more into the river from Todd and had me stand directly in his line of sight. Taking the slats from Uncle Peter, Father slid the wood into the muck, at an angle that would put them under Todd's feet. Then, Father had me call Todd and wave the armful of grass in front of his nose.

Todd lifted his head and stared at the grass. He lowed as he always did when he saw fresh grass. Slowly, he started to move forward. Uncle Peter laughed. "I can feel his hooves on the slats." My father nodded and told me to hold the grass closer to Todd's face but not to let him eat any of the grass. As Todd moved forward toward the fresh grass, he walked on the slats and managed to free himself, inch by inch, from the quicksand. Finally, Todd managed to walk away from the slats. I looked at my Father who told me to give the grass to Todd. I gave it to the muddy animal and led him back safely to the other oxen. Uncle Peter laughed, looked at Father and told him, "I know that you don't agree with me, but we would be so much better off with five animals and a huge side of beef." Father smiled and told us that Uncle Peter was probably right, but if Todd were a steak, he would find a way to run off the plate.

Once the adventures of this noon rest time had ended, we hitched the animals to the wagon and continued on our road west. Finally, we reached the place where we would cross the South Platte River, climb the hills on the other bank, and head back to the north fork of the Platte River. The river was wide. Crossing a river of this size promised to be a strenuous exercise. Our typical method of using ropes to mark off the borders of the ford that we wanted to use was not practical; the river was simply too wide and there was not enough rope. Captain Watkins stopped our train at the banks of the river. He took all of the boys of the train aside and gave us our instructions:

"Your parents are going to be in charge of wagons. Your task is to drive the livestock across the river. We need some of you to drive the livestock. The older boys, we want to stand downstream from the crossing. If any of the cattle or horses veers too far from the crossing, you need to drive them back towards the wagons. You need to watch carefully also should any of the cattle appeared stuck. Give a holler if you see one of the animals struggle as if they cannot move forward. Sometimes, there are holes in the riverbed where one of their hooves can become stuck. This is the most dangerous thing that can happen on a river. Your job, boys, is more important than the driving of the wagons. We need you to be men this day and do a man's job."

We divided ourselves into two teams. The first group, to which I belonged, gathered the train's cattle and horses driving them into the river. The second group stood across the width of the river, prepared to block any animal from drifting downstream with the current. When we were finally prepared, Captain Watkins fired his gun into the air and pushed our train forward into the water. Uncle Peter, being the boy at heart, rode behind the cattle, waving his hat and whooping loud yells.

As so often happened, we prepared for events that did not occur. The cattle willingly crossed the river. A few cattle wanted to find their own way across. Uncle Peter on his horse, and the boys forming the picket line with their staffs would not allow them to become explorer cows. Slowly, carefully, the wagons crossed the south Platte until they reached the other side.

Any sense of victory quickly disappeared. When we had the river in front of us, all we saw was the water. Having crossed the river, we saw what next faced us. In front of us, we needed to climb a mountain. I looked at Uncle Peter and the despair of my heart must have been etched on my face. Uncle Peter, upon seeing the look, smiled at me and said, "This is California Hill. You will see mountains that dwarf this little hill before we reach our new home. However, no matter what the size of the hill, there is only one way to reach the other side. Climb it."

With these words, I assumed my place by the oxen, showed them the whip, and urged them on. The leg muscles of the animals strained, rippling through their skin. Their power was never more evident than as they climbed this hill, straining to gain traction through the sandy soil. I noticed that the more they struggled, the more my father spoke to them in encouraging words. There were people in our train who beat their animals to move them forward; Father simply spoke gently and had me show them the whip and their power took us where we wanted to go. When I told my father about this, he simply smiled and observed, "There are people who treat their plows better than they treat their livestock. Where would plows go without the oxen to pull them?"

At the top of California Hill, I turned around and looked below us to the river and beyond. Then, I looked to the land ahead of us and while we had come so far, we had so very far to go. Then, I knew that the only way to reach my goal was to put one foot in front of the other, driving the cattle and causing the wheels to turn one turn at a time.

CHAPTER 10

PAST CHIMNEY ROCK

While the adventure of going uphill was new and exciting, this was nothing compared to the labor of descending hills. A day after our California Hill crossing, we reached Windlass Hill. This was a large hill overlooking the northern fork of the Platte River. It rose several hundred feet above the North Platte River and while the grade was not straight downhill, it felt that way when we first approached the edge of the hill and looked down to the river below. Captain Watkins and Senator Richardson stopped the wagons before we reached the edge of the hill and conferred with each other. After their meeting, Senator Richardson addressed the rest of us:

"This is a difficult hill for us to descend. It will not be the last one, but it is important that we learn how to perform these tasks correctly. We are not going to drive the wagons down the hills. This hill has a series of declines similar to stone steps that are about two feet apart. To drive the animals down the hill would crash the wagons and injure our animals. Hard work will let us descend this hill safely. Captain Watkins will tell us how we are going to make it down the hill to Ash Hollow."

Captain Watkins nodded to Senator Richardson and then started speaking in his rough voice. "We are going to take each wagon, one by one, down the hill as far as it can go safely. We will unhitch the animals and have the boys move them to the bottom of the hill. Then, we will lock the rear wheels and attach ropes to the wagon. A team of men will ease the wagon down the hill, while other men steer it and yet another group will lift the wheels so they make it down the steps. Once a wagon makes it to the bottom, the young boys will hitch the animals to his wagon and move it out of the way. We will camp in Ash Hollow and rest up from today's labor. The women and little children will need to march ahead of us down the hill. Someone will need to carry little Amy Braun on a stretcher to the bottom."

Captain Watkins did not exaggerate the amount of work involved in moving these wagons. While we waited our turn to move down the hill, Father, Uncle Peter, and I took our turns guiding other wagons down the hill. This strained every muscle in my body; yet, I considered myself lucky that I was not on the team that needed to lift the wagons over the rocks. These men needed to hoist heavy, loaded wagons over the steps and make it to the next level. Somewhere, in my mind, I imagined our oxen laughing at the thought of men doing their work.

Moving the wagons down the face of this hill took all day. We arrived in Ash Hollow tired, sweaty, and sore. This was a beautiful location, with groves of ash trees and cedars. The trees lent a sweet smell to our campground. Ash Creek ran through the campsite and refreshed us. Our spirits lifted as we washed the sweat and grime from our bodies. While we appreciated the cool shade and beautiful surroundings, all of the men who spent the day guiding wagons down the steep hills appreciated the rest more than the beauty of God's creation.

Had I known what awaited us beyond Ash Hollow, I would have appreciated the shade, sweet smell, and cool springs more. When we left this oasis, we traveled into open sandy country. The grass turned more from the green sweetness into dried brown vegetation. Ugly sagebrush littered the ground. Dust became more of a problem as we moved onto this arid plain. The wind swirled the dirt, and the lack of green vegetation helped the dust come into our noses, mouths and throats. Uncle Peter suggested, and we all readily agreed, to take bandanas and dip them into cool water and keep them over our nose and mouth.

The lack of vegetation allowed me to see clearly that on the other side of the river, walking along the north bank of the river, was a large group of people moving the same direction as we were. I found it interesting how we moved on without any particular notice of them at the same time that we remained anonymous to them.

I looked at Father sitting in the wagon and pointed this group out to him. He nodded and said, "Mormons," as if that word answered all of the questions that were swirling in my mind.

Hearing his answer did nothing for me. I let a series of questions flow from my brain to mouth. "Who are Mormons? Are they going to Oregon? Why are they traveling on the other side of the river? Is that a better route than our route?"

My dad chuckled. He stopped the wagon and let me climb up onto the seat next to him. "I forgot how many questions you can ask. Mormons are a group of people with significantly different religious beliefs than ours. Because of some of those different beliefs, their neighbors have violently chased them out of a number of states. Now, they are heading west to find a land from which they cannot be moved. A great salt lake is to the southwest. They travel on the north side of the river not because it is any better but rather because they want no contact with us."

I thought about these answers. "That doesn't feel right, Father, that they would be chased out of home just because they don't believe what we believe."

My father did not answer immediately. He whisked the reins on the back of the oxen and appeared deep in thought. Finally, he spoke: "Jeremiah, it isn't right. I believe that the Mormons are terribly wrong in their beliefs and that we are correct in our faith. I wish that all people could come to the knowledge and beliefs that we have developed. However, chasing them out of town will not help me to reach them with the truth. People need to be careful before they run folks out of town because they may be the next ones to be forced out of their homes. How is burning down a house showing the love of Jesus? What we need to do for these people is pray for them, not attack them. All that the attacks succeed in doing is creating their own martyrs and giving excuses to evil people on both sides to act violently."

I hopped off the wagon seat and resumed my position beside the oxen. I thought a lot about this conversation the remainder of the day. I had never thought there were people who disagreed with me so much that they thought contact with me would be corrupting. I had never thought there were people who agreed with me so much that they would set fires to houses of those who did not share our beliefs. Both thoughts scared me; both thoughts left me quietly thinking about what I believed and what I would be willing to do to convince others of the rightness of my faith.

When we stopped for the evening, we continued our usual routine. Our peaceful chores were suddenly disrupted by loud cries coming from one of the wagons. I looked and saw Mr. Braun holding the limp body of his little girl, Amy. Tears were flowing down his cheeks in a constant stream while his sobbing wife leaned against him, as if her troubled soul would not allow her body to stand on its own. Words were unnecessary; we all knew what had happened. Little Amy had died from the injuries that she had suffered in the tornado.

No one knew what to do. We had traveled so far and while we knew that danger was all around us, the cool touch of death had stayed away from our band. After a pause that lasted a few moments, my mother and father walked over to them. My mother wrapped her arms around the grieving woman while my father spoke lowly in the tone he used whenever trouble was near. His words were too quiet for us to hear. They were not intended for us.

Father returned from this brief conversation. "Peter, would you direct the preparation of the grave. Jeremiah, please ask Mr. Johnson to help us dig the grave for little Amy."

Mr. Johnson agreed. Uncle Peter, Mr. Johnson, and Father selected a site overlooking the river. These men dug the grave, a labor slowed by the heavy hearts created by the sad task that needed completion. While they worked in the soil, the O'Donnell twins and I gathered large rocks and brought them over to the gravesite. These rocks would cover the grave and protect the body from coyotes. While the men worked in the dirt, the women of the camp visited with the grieving parents. Men showed concern by labor; women comforted the parents with soft, loving words.

When the grave was dug, Mr. Braun wrapped the little body of his daughter in a quilt that had been lovingly prepared by Mrs. Braun. We carefully lowered the body into the grave by the river. My father took his wide-brimmed hat off, bowed his head and slowly recited the 23rd Psalm in the voice that he used at the church on Stone's River. He then prayed.

Before Father spoke the final amen, I left this scene of sorrow. I wandered away from the graveside service and walked along the riverbanks, alone in my thoughts. I was aware of the moisture that had built, unbidden and unwanted, in my eyes. I simply wanted to think, feel and understand, yet, I knew these were things I would never fully think through, feel, and understand.

I felt a hand on my shoulder and I looked into the tear-tracked face of Father. We simply walked, each in our own thoughts for a while. Finally, he broke the silence:

"I will never understand sad things like this. I am not sure we can ever fully understand them. Faith grows in times of sorrow, and in times of great sorrow, it grows greatly. I know this from the death of our own little Charlotte and Jedediah, Jr. It never feels fair. I always wondered why my precious infants were taken while that mean old Mr. Lucas lives forever.

"Sometimes, God's ways are truly wondrous and deeply mysterious. If he had taken Mr. Lucas when our babies died, no one would have been around to buy our farm and let us move to wonderful new ground with Uncle Peter as a family. Think of things all you want, Jeremiah. Question all you want because the answers to these questions will always lead us to God and not away from Him. At the end, come to realize that our God is great, powerful, and mysterious and His ways are not our ways, but also that He is great beyond measure."

With these words, my father turned back. I continued my walk alone with my thoughts and prayers. I returned to our camp as the sun sank in the western sky. My thoughts were quieter but the answers I thought would come easily did not flow easily through my soul.

Early the next morning, the wagon train moved on into the west. We passed by Amy's rock covered grave, but none of us paused for long. It was as if we were afraid that the sorrow of that place would consume us, much as if a fire consumes a piece of meat left too long in the flame. Finally, we passed a hill and the grave was gone from our sight.

At the end of the day's journey, I saw an astonishing sight. In the distance, there were large oddly shaped pillars stretching into the sky. They surely reached all the way to heaven; yet, somehow I knew they were miles away from us. It looked to me that God had taken time out from His work of creation to amuse Himself by carving some pillar to His glory in the middle of this flat, dry land. Uncle Peter saw my look and pointed to these pillars:

"Courthouse Rock and Jailhouse Rock. We will be there tomorrow. They are amazing structures to see. No one built them, but you will love their sculpted shapes. Tomorrow we will take a detour and march over to them. You will see more wonderful things in the west, but you should not miss an opportunity to see them up close."

I was excited when I crawled into my blankets under the wagon that night. I had been walking through this country for a long time and yet, while the land was different than I had ever seen growing up on the banks of the Stones River, I could not say that I had ever felt like an explorer seeing land for the first time until I saw the pillars in the distance. Seeing this sight let me imagine myself as an old-time conquistador exploring the west. I desperately wanted to examine them closely.

The morning of our side trip took forever. Finally, we stopped for our noonday break. Uncle Peter approached Captain Watkins and with some mixed form of bribery and threats convinced him to lend me one of the spare horses. With that, we were off on our exploration.

We rode towards these towers. When we arrived, the site was so much more than I dreamt possible. While these towers conceivably could have been carved by an ancient civilization, I knew that the sculptor was divine and not human. I agreed with the names of this site, since it reminded me of our hometown courthouse and jail stuck into the skies on top of a pillar reaching towards heaven.

Uncle Peter and I tied our horses to a scraggly tree at the base of the structure. We started climbing the side of the cliff that held the towers. The people who had hiked this way before had worn a trail we could follow. Upward we worked, slowly, yet with a sense that what awaited us was well worth the end of the climb. When we reached the base of Courthouse Rock fastened to the tower, I could not believe my eyes. The land stretched infinitely into the distance. While being this high made me feel huge, the breadth of the land also made me feel very insignificant. Neither one of us spoke as we stared out into the distance.

Once we had looked at the sights and rested from the exertion of our climb, we moved down the side of the mountain. Uncle Peter told me the old time mountain men who navigated in the western world used this monument. "Robert Stuart had recorded this monument on his desperate journey back from Astoria to the east in 1812. Robert Stuart had left Astoria when he was trying to reach his employer, John Jacob Astor, during the War of 1812. Without a map, he made it all the way from the Pacific Ocean to his headquarters in New York, avoiding hostile Indians; living without enough supplies and without reliable men on the journey. Ever since, Courthouse Rock has been an important place that all manners of people use."

The fact that I had been there made me feel like I too, in spite of my size and age, was a mountain man. I wonder what it would have been like to be a teenager like Jim Bridger, making my way on my own in the western terrain. I would be looking for beavers and muskrats, finding anew the old Indian paths that followed the streams into the mountains, surviving when the countryside was both the supplier of needs and the taker of life. It was with a trace of sadness that I realized the world had changed enough that I would never experience the ways of the past. That sadness was replaced, however, with the realization that my life would have different adventures; adventures that would provide me with sights, sounds and experiences the mountain men of prior generations would never dream.

We mounted our horses and returned to our wagon train. Excitement filled me as I realized that if I were the master of all I could see, then for a brief moment I had been the king of an empire that stretched from nearly endless horizon to endless horizon.

At the end of the day, we camped in full view of another spire reaching the sky. It also reminded me of the ruins of an ancient civilization balanced on a pillar stretching into the sky. My uncle told me this was Chimney Rock. Listening to this, Mother commented, "I hope that the day comes when I have a chimney that large. Not even Doris' house could hold that chimney."

As we left Chimney Rock, we started feeling that the plain prairie was tilting upward, ever higher to the west. When we mentioned this to Peter, he nodded his head and told us that we were coming to the end of the plains. Once we passed Scotts Bluffs, we would be heading towards the mountains that would be our next adventure.

Moving onward, we continued to pass the little animals that Bitsy regarded as the cutest attractions of the west. These little creatures were prairie dogs. The animals would stand and watch for intruders and when a person approached, they would screech a warning and scurry into one of the hundreds of burrows the animals had dug into the ground. Bitsy begged Mother to take us out into the field nearer to the prairie dogs, so they could watch the creatures in their activity. Seeing no reason to say no, Mother agreed to take Bitsy and me into the field after we cleaned the dishes. Mother carried a large walking stick for no apparent reason other than it looked good and she wanted something to lean against while she watched Bitsy play.

Bitsy and Sally ran in the field. My mother cautioned her not to go too close to the prairie dogs or too far from her. I spent my time watching the animals and chatting with my mother, when all of a sudden, my mother moved quickly away from me and towards Bitsy. Bitsy did not see Mother; she continued playing with Sally and chasing after the skittish prairie dogs.

Suddenly, Mother raised her hand and struck the ground hard with her staff. Once, twice, three times, Mother raised and violently slammed the stick down onto the ground. Then, as quickly as the violence began, it ended. "Bitsy," my mother said in a breathless tone, "it is time to return to the wagon. Jeremiah, go fetch your father and uncle. I have just killed a rattlesnake."

My feet caused me to fly back to the wagon. "Dad, Uncle Peter, come quickly. Mother has killed a rattlesnake."

Father grabbed a rifle and sprinted into the field where Mother and Bitsy remained. Uncle Peter and some of the other men of the group followed behind with me. "Mary," my father shouted, "step away from that creature. That snake did not bite you, did it?" His voice rasped as he tried to make himself heard at the same time he ran as fast as he had ever run.

My mother held up her hands. "No, Jeddie, I am not bit. But that snake wishes it had never been near Bitsy."

My father smiled a look of absolute relief when he heard this news. He took his rifle and shot the snake, just to make sure it was dead and not merely stunned. Perhaps it was my father's caution; perhaps the audacity of this creature that dared approach his beloved family caused this unnecessary shot. Once he was convinced that it could no longer bite his family, he lifted the snake with his rifle and flipped it into the bushes along the trail. We all marveled to see the three-foot rattler that Mother had killed with nothing more than a stick. My father shook his head "Pray for me, men. I am married to a woman who kills deadly creatures with sticks. Can you imagine what she could do to a husband?"

We all laughed and walked back to our wagon in time for us to make our afternoon journey. We were amazed at my mother; thankful to God for protecting my little sister and mother, and reminded once again how close danger was and how we needed to be cautious to reach our new home in Oregon.

CHAPTER 11

FORT LARAMIE

We camped that night next to Scotts Bluff. The trail went south around the bluff, but since the oxen were showing signs of being tired, Captain Watkins and Senator Richardson decided that our group could use a day off with a picnic on top of Scotts Bluff. Early in the morning, we gathered our food and started to climb up towards the top. Uncle Peter carried our food on his horse while Bitsy rode on my father's neck. At the beginning of the climb, I ran ahead with the O'Donnells seeing who could reach the top of the bluff first. The steepness of the climb soon tired our legs and forced us back to the group with a more measured pace.

The day was bright and sunny. Unlike our eastern skies, where even on the sunniest day there were always cotton-puff clouds, there was not a cloud in the sky, which made it bluer and bigger than any I had seen on our farm. Upwards we climbed, picking our way along the rocky trail, until we finally reached the top. Once there, we were awestruck at the sight. Turning east, we saw our constant companion, the broad Platte River valley with its wide, shallow river stretching as far as we could see. Along the river was a steady stream of wagons, each moving west with us, seeking the new beginning that we also wanted.

Turning west, we saw on the far horizon, mountains reaching into the sky. The tops of the mountains were covered with white snow that was barely separable from the line of the horizon. As a community, we looked at this sight, stunned at both the enormity of the mountains that could be seen at such a distance and the size of the task that crossing this mountain range presented us as a group.

At the top of the bluff, we set up our picnic lunch. After we ate, we ran a sequence of games designed to prove which of us was the best athlete. Once the sun became too hot for us to stay atop the bluff, we loaded our remaining food and walked down the mountain to the waiting wagons. Our family rested the remainder of the afternoon, although we told one another that the reason for the laziness was that we needed to allow our oxen the rest to which their hard work entitled them. The only task of the day was to gather water, since we knew that there was little water on the next twenty miles of the trail.

Every day not spent marching blessed our spirits. Even the good Lord took a day off from creation, so it made sense that we, too, occasionally rested on the journey. While happy days at home needed activity to fill time, the constant physical exertion of life on the trail made me happy to have a single day where we could simply rest our tired feet. By the end of the day, though, we all felt anxious to continue our journey to the mountains.

This sense of excitement led to our waking earlier than usual and quickly finishing the morning routine. We hitched up our oxen and began our ascent south of the bluff. In the middle of the morning, we passed a trading post on the side of the road. Captain Watkins stopped the train and announced that those of us who needed some supplies could visit the trading post. Peter shook his head: "I know the people who run this trading post. They are very sharp business people. Unless we really need something desperately, we need to wait until we show up at Fort Laramie. Everything will be very expensive at this stop. I don't even think my family connections will let you have a good deal at this location."

"Family connections?" my mother asked.

"Yes", my uncle responded, "this is the Robidoux trading post. Two members of the Robidoux family run this store. Joseph Robidoux is the son of my friend Joseph Robidoux, who Jeremiah and I met in the St. Joseph. The other owner is his uncle, Antoine Robidoux. I have never met Antoine, but he was very famous in the time of the mountain men. He never really trapped animals, but he was very good at trading. He never paid any more for furs than he needed to and he never gave anyone a lower price on supplies than he could avoid. Still, I always liked these men, in spite of the money I left behind. It is always best to talk to men on the trail, since they may know something that would be of value to us, but let us try to avoid doing business with them."

Uncle Peter and I wandered over to the trading post. In addition to the store, there was a building housing a blacksmith who manufactured spare parts for the wagons that were waiting at the trading post and those who would arrive later. The blacksmith knew there would always be a customer for whatever he prepared since the trail was extremely difficult on the wagons.

Uncle Peter walked over to the cabin that served as the trading post and opened the door. The room was dark. Goods for sale were everywhere: blankets, bottles containing liquor and medicine, bags of dried food, and salted meats hanging up front. Through the dark, dusty surroundings, I could see a man and a woman standing behind the counter, talking to some of the members of the wagon train, trying to sell some of their goods.

"I come all this way and cannot leave the Robidoux family behind," my uncle called out to the man.

The man turned to the voice and squinted through the dark. Then, a moment of recognition passed over his face and he briskly walked over and slapped my Uncle Peter on the back. "Howdy, Tenderfoot Pete. You never know who you will find in the wilderness. The last time I saw you, we were trading buffalo hides together by the Arkansas River. Those were very fun times and we made a lot of money for the company. That must have been about seven or eight years ago."

My uncle smiled at Mr. Robidoux and turned to me. "You always did have a great memory. Jeremiah, I would like you to meet Joseph Robidoux. He is the son of Mr. Robidoux, who we met in St. Joseph."

I shook hands with him and smiled. "It is a pleasure to meet you."

"So, Peter, are you heading to California? Everyone is heading there, particularly now that I hear there may have been gold found out there."

"No, digging for gold is not for a family. I am going to Oregon with my brother and his family. I am going to set down roots and become one of the farmers about whom we used to laugh. I do not want to wake up one day on the road with white hair, no family, and nothing built in my life."

I left my uncle to share experiences and tall tales with his former colleague. I walked outside, joining my family in adjusting our wagon so we could be ready when the shoppers finished. Finally, we left the trading post and continued our route around Scotts Bluff. We rejoined the Platte River at the end of the day. This day we learned how precious a cool drink of water could be. Fortunately, our family prepared well for the lack of water, but other families did not and were especially overjoyed to see the river on such a warm day.

We continued along the Platte River through the rough country. Grass gave way to more and more sagebrush. For a boy who was used to growing up along the lush banks of the Stones River, I knew as much about this type of landscape as I did about the dark side of the moon. Some people could find beauty in the land we were passing through; for me, the landscape simply existed and was an area we needed to move beyond to arrive in our Oregon promised land.

Our daily goal was to make it to Fort Laramie, or as the owners of the fort called it, Fort John. Captain Watkins promised the train that we could have two days rest to restock provisions and rest the oxen. He warned us that the next place for rest would be Fort Bridger, which was four hundred miles away, so if we needed something desperately, we needed to buy it at Fort John. This was welcome news to Mother, who wanted days away from traveling to let her restock and reorganize the wagon thoroughly and spend some time mending the clothes that had become worn with the exertions of the trail.

While we were sitting around the campfire, Uncle Peter told us, "Fort Laramie was founded by William Sublette, as Fort William. Old Mr. Sublette was one of the mountain men who founded the Rocky Mountain Fur Company. He was one of a group of brothers who loved to trade and make money instead of being out in the mountains. Every year, Mr. Sublette hosted a rendezvous in the mountains to trade furs for the goods that everyone needed for the next year, but mostly for the whiskey that some mountain men could not resist. One year, after the rendezvous, a big battle broke out between some of the mountain men and some of the native tribes. In the middle of this fight, one of the tribesmen shot Mr. Sublette.

"After this fight, Mr. Sublette lost interest in being out west, since he, like most people, preferred to make his money without lead injections. Mr. Sublette sold the fort to American Fur Company, which officially renamed it Fort John, but everyone called it Fort Laramie because it was located where the Laramie River met the Platte River."

"Laramie is an unusual name. Where does it come from," I asked.

"Usually, out here, unusual names are old Indian words. Not so in this case. Jacques LaRamie was a French Canadian fur trapper. One year, he went to catch his furs and he was never again seen. No one really knows what happened to him. He may have been killed by Indians, he may have gone home to Canada, or he may be living in a tree laughing at us for all we know. Someone decided to name the river after him and everything else just naturally followed.

"You will like Fort Laramie. Everyone heading west stops there. In addition, they always have some Lakota Sioux, or Northern Cheyenne Indians around the fort trading with the townspeople or working to cure buffalo hides. The young men will be gone now because they are out hunting buffalo now so they can have enough food and supplies for the winter."

Finally, we arrived along the banks of the Laramie River. The river promised to be a difficult crossing and the reality fulfilled the promise. The riverbank had green trees, but beyond the river, past the initial green, was a flat, treeless plain. On the other side of the river, an adobe fort was looming. While the buildings were not resplendent mansions of St. Louis, they also were not the grass huts of Fort Kearney. Mrs. Parker would not be happy, but to us, this looked like civilization after weeks on the trail. Along the river, there were a series of tipis, around which I could see a series of women, children, and older men. We drove our wagons to the river, crossed over to the other side on a ferry, and moved our wagon train past Fort John about a mile before we set up our camp alongside the river.

Once our camp was set up and the oxen taken care of, the O'Donnell twins and I ran to the fort. The activity of the fort excited me. Not only were there people who were from other wagon trains, but there were different types of people. Traders who lived in the fort; single men traveling west in search of their fortune; Mormon families from the other side of the river; buffalo hunters with their large rifles; Lakota Sioux women and children. All of these mixed into a picture of different sights and sounds that shocked my senses, which had become used to the same people and routine day after day.

Everywhere we turned, we saw something new. The Sioux women worked on the buffalo hides, spreading them over wooden frames and scraping the hair. Then, I saw them curing these with the buffalo brains, which would help turn the hide into usable clothing. Every part, even the brains, of the buffalo were used somehow by the tribes. Once finished, the Indian women would trade these hides for supplies from the fort. Then, the fort would send the hides east for trade and everyone would be happy. Except, of course, the buffalo.

Wandering through the fort, we stopped at the general store. Our mothers had given each of us a small, silver half-dime to spend. Looking at the storehouse full of practical goods, we managed to look beyond them and find the honey sticks that would sweeten our entire day. In our view, we had plenty of bacon, cornmeal, and rice at the wagon, but where on the trail had we found any candy? It took very little thought for us to decide to spend all of our money on the available sweets.

Pushing our way to the front of the store like three dangerous men on a deadly mission, we explained to the storekeeper our plan. He smiled at us as if he had seen this drama played in the store every hour of every day during the season when people came west. Wordlessly, he took our money; he handed us a king's supply of honey sticks and peppermint candies. Then, he reached underneath the counter and gave each of us a small bottle of sarsaparilla. "On the house, boys", he said. "Enjoy your treat."

We all thanked him as if he had provided us the keys to a golden city on a hill. Running outside of the store, we found our way to a large stone beside the store and we opened our precious sarsaparilla bottles as if they contained the elixir of life; drinking them, we carefully poured the sweet liquid down our throats. For once, I felt like a boy again instead of the sometimes man responsible for helping his family transplant from one home to an unknown location. I know that my friends felt the same way, since the jokes we told were funnier; the games more intense, and the conversation more like the ones I used to have back home with Billy Hollis. For this one day, I was back in the skin of the eleven-year-old boy who had grown on the banks of the Stones River. I missed those days and the friends left behind.

When our candy was gone, we left our rock and wandered through the bustling community. We enjoyed watching the people and listening to the snippets of conversations as people spoke about their life and journey. Suddenly, I heard a familiar voice call my name. I turned around and could not believe my eyes. There in front of me was my teacher from Stones River, Miss Spencer. I blinked, rubbed my eyes, and looked again, as if my brain would not believe what my eyes were communicating to it.

"I guess you didn't expect to see me," Miss Spencer said.

"No," I replied in a stammering, stunned tone. "What are you doing out here? How did you travel here? Who is teaching school?"

"Those are a lot of questions that require a detailed answer. When you were talking about moving west, it excited me, but I was afraid to do anything about it. That day when you left Stones River and walked down the road with your family, I stood and stared down the road until you had disappeared. Then, sadly, I knew that I had to return to teach the rest of the children. While I worked with them on their lessons, my heart was not with them that day. I went home and assumed that the next day would be more productive. It was not.

"Day after day, I would teach the children sitting in the room but my heart was never inside the schoolhouse. Each night when I walked home, I thought about heading west and I wished that I could be on the way west. I remembered that I was just a single woman and I would have to live where I was and not be concerned with dreams of life out west. These unfulfilled western dreams just made me sad.

"Then, one day, I thought about your uncle. He once told me that when he was a fifteen-year-old boy, he left his home and just followed his dreams. Before he left home, his mother cried and his father threatened him with a whipping to end his life. Peter knew though, that for him to be happy, he needed to be on his own. One night, he snuck out the loft window of his parents' cabin, climbed on his horse, and followed his dreams. Surely, his parents were upset, but when he returned he had done what he needed to do to be happy and they respected him all the more for his following of his heart.

"I thought about Peter and I prayed about the decision I needed to make. Finally, I thought about what life would be like if I never went west. I would probably be married, become an old lady, and have children and grandchildren running around in front of me who loved me greatly. That would bring me great joy. Somewhere, though, deep in the recesses of my heart, there would be a sad voice telling me that I missed something very important by not following my dreams.

"Once I thought about that, I realized I had no decision to make. I spoke to the school board and told them that at the end of March, I would leave the school. They were unhappy, but when they listened to me, they knew there was no way they could keep me in that school. I left the school and I packaged up the few things I owned and walked to Nashville. Then, I boarded a paddlewheel boat and took it as far as I could. Then, I unloaded my limited belongings into a pushcart and was going to head west.

"Fortunately, before I made it too far, a family took mercy on me. They had eight children and the parents wanted help controlling them on the trail. We marched along the Platte River and finally arrived here. I fear this is where I am going to stay, however. The father has died and the mother now wants to return to her family back East. Having come this far, and spent about all of my money to take the steamboat, I have no other choice but to find a job here at Fort Laramie and earn enough money to continue next year to the west. The funny thing about dreams is that as long as you are making progress towards fulfilling them, the sorrow of having the dreams unfulfilled drifts away, due to the magical healing of activity."

Talking to Miss Spencer made me momentarily forget my friends, the O'Donnell twins, who had disappeared from my consciousness. Finally, I remembered them and did the introductions. I realized, upon meeting Miss Spencer, how much I had missed my friends in Tennessee. For once, I remembered my manners and stammered out an invitation to dinner. Miss Spencer smiled warmly at my newfound formality and graciously agreed to come with me to our wagon.

Walking back to the wagon, I dominated the conversation. My pranks at my cousins' house, our nighttime vigil to protect our horses from the Pawnees, the excitement of the buffalo hunt, all of these occupied our conversation and left me breathless with excitement again. Children loved Miss Spencer because she always listened to our stories, not just heard our voices. This was as true on the trail as it was in the school, which made me feel important.

When my parents saw Miss Spencer coming toward our moving home, thoughts of work ceased. Mother put down her mending; Father dropped the work he was doing on the harnesses, and Uncle Peter stopped cleaning his gun. All thoughts shifted to hospitality for the long-lost friend. That evening, we pulled out the dishes that had been packed away, sliced some of the good ham, and made a meal that would have made gracious society, even my Aunt Doris, proud.

Following the evening meal, we cleaned the dishes and spent the remainder of the evening around the fire telling stories of the places and people we knew so well. Finally, as the sky was shifting from its evening pink into nighttime black, Miss Spencer stood to leave. Uncle Peter volunteered to escort her to her possessions. When he left, Bitsy and Sally were put into the wagon for the evening and I crawled under the wagon for my sleep. When I was dozing into my slumber, I was aware that Mother kissed me on the forehead and covered me with a large, unfamiliar blanket into which I gladly stirred to protect myself from the cool breeze of the early summer night. That was the end of this wonderful day.

I awoke the next morning to the strong smell of coffee brewing on the coals of the stirred fire. Throughout our camp, mothers started breakfast. I lay on the ground so cozy under my blanket that the will to rise left me. Finally, Father gave me a gentle kick and told me to climb out from under the blanket. As my eyes focused, I noticed that the blanket that covered me was a buffalo robe that had magically appeared. When I crawled out of my resting place, I pulled the robe out and looked at Mother. She must have understood my question immediately from my expression, because without me saying a word, she explained that the women of the wagon train had been working on curing the skin of the buffalo I had killed in thanks for the meat my hunt had provided. I immediately hugged the robe closer to me for it was more than just a source of warmth but it was a very personal treasure, a reminder of one of the most exciting moments of my life.

"Jeremiah," Father said, "we need to talk to you. Uncle Peter, your mother, and I have an idea about which we want to know your opinion. Uncle Peter and Miss Spencer discussed the possibility last night of her joining us on our trip west. Oregon will need teachers far more than this outpost along the trail. Yet, while we believe this is the hospitable thing to do, we would not put you in an uncomfortable position if you do not want to continue with your teacher."

My whoops of joy provided the answer. What could be better than being on both an adventure to remember with beloved family members and now with a close friend?

CHAPTER 12
EMIGRANT GAP

Mother made room for Miss Spencer's belongings in our neatly organized wagon. While Mother loved her system of organization, she gladly made changes in the wagon to accommodate a friend. Miss Spencer's possessions showed that while her young life may have made many friends, it did not lead to great riches.

Going to bed that evening was different. The family debated the sleeping arrangements. Father offered to sleep outside with Uncle Peter and myself while leaving the wagon to the ladies. After much good-natured debate, the adults decided that Miss Spencer would sleep outside when there was good weather and Father would sleep outside with the men during the rain and snow. I crawled into my buffalo robe and slept happily under the wagon.

Waking up the next morning, we prepared to continue our move west. This did not happen without excitement. While I gathered the oxen and coaxed Todd back to work, I heard loud cries and yelling coming from the wagon next to us. When I returned to our wagon, I found the source of the ruckus. Sitting in front of their wagon was Mrs. Parker, blocking the path of the oxen, with her legs and arms folded, screaming at Mr. Johnson.

"I would rather die here than move one step forward. You have brought me out here against my will. I have silently endured the loss of all my worldly possessions, the loss of the friendships of a lifetime, and now I am being forced to ride in a wagon that jolts every nerve in my body with every turn of the wheel. You have brought me to this Godforsaken place against my will; now, you are free of me. I wish you happiness in your new home. I am going to die in this spot, alone, unmourned with no one to bury my body and protect me from the coyotes who will feast on my bones. Do not think of me."

Young Mrs. Johnson ran to her mother. She threw her arms around the shouting woman, trying to calm her and reassure her with her hugs. Mr. Johnson was more direct; he tried unsuccessfully to lift the woman to her feet. This angered his young wife, who turned on him with rage coloring all of the features of her face.

"Do not put your hands on her. She is my mother. We have treated her most cruelly. Either she comes with us or we do not go any further. If you go on, you will move forward without us."

Mr. Johnson stepped back from this scene with mother and daughter wrapped in an embrace punctuated by the wailing of these women. Looking at Mr. Johnson, the frustration on his face was painful to see. Father walked over to Mr. Johnson and they spoke quietly so that we could not hear either one of them. Of course, hearing any conversation would be extremely difficult with the wordless screams of these women. Father returned to our wagon and spoke to Mother. Mother walked over to the women, knelt down in front of them, and tried to talk to Widow Parker. The crying women rebuffed these efforts and pushed Mother away.

Captain Watkins came riding over to this conflict. "We need to begin moving," he told the increasingly frustrated Mr. Johnson.

"I know, but my mother-in-law has decided that she would

rather die than take one more step towards Oregon. Given my preferences, I would leave the mean old woman to sit here until she was hungry enough to behave like an adult, but now my wife has decided she cares more about indulging the immature rants of this horrible whiner than to follow her husband to our new life. I am sorely tempted to leave them both behind and let them journey the thousand miles home, but while I may not know everything there is to know about being a good husband, I do know that this would fall far short of the protection I have promised my bride."

Captain Watkins shook his head. "Unbelievable," he said. "We can allow one more hour for this scene. Then, we will need to move west. We are already behind schedule and we cannot allow this woman to keep the entire train from reaching the western mountains before the snow flies. If you think climbing mountains in dry weather is difficult, you have no idea how hard it will be to try to move through mountains with wagons in the snow."

Captain Watkins rode away. He cursed his fate to be the guide to a group of tenderfoots who acted like the trip to the western coast was a stroll to a picnic lunch. Mr. Johnson and my parents tried to convince Mrs. Parker and her daughter to stop their demonstration and join the line of wagons. Minutes passed and nothing could convince mother and daughter to move from that spot. Reluctantly, we said our farewells to the Johnson wagon. We knew how painful this was for Mr. Johnson, who desperately wanted to start a new life in the west with his beautiful bride. Yet, we knew that Captain Watkins was right and that our journey needed to continue with all people who wanted to continue.

We marched west. My parents commented that it was their fear that poor Mr. Johnson would be in for a miserable existence with the women. Mother commented that she knew what life was like for a wife whose mother disapproved of the match. In her case, however, she had decided that when she said she would marry her man she needed to leave behind her parents. Until young Mrs. Johnson made the same decision, there would be nothing but sorrow in that home.

While rest was always welcome, moving forward on our expedition made us happy. Bitsy rode with Uncle Peter and their conversation was more animated than usual. The oxen had more energy in their steps than they had before Fort Laramie. Mother sang her songs with more joy; her joy in turn brought an unusual smile to Father's face as he urged the oxen to move. I had the largest change in the group since I was no longer alone walking beside the wagon as Miss Spencer decided to join me and carry on a conversation about what we were seeing and the places we had been. Change in this instance was joyful; Miss Spencer's presence lifted emotional burdens immediately.

In the middle of the morning, we came alongside a large series of cliffs. My uncle pointed them out to us and pulled his horse off the trail. "This is Register Cliffs," he said. "Everyone who comes through here has to carve their name and the date in the rock. This is one way you can make your mark in this world"

This sounded like fun to me. The O'Donnell's, Miss Spencer, Uncle Peter and I left the train as it continued west and climbed the hill. We looked at all the names, wondered about the stories behind the names, and then found a cliff face where there were few names. I took my knife and carved into the side of the rock:

"Jeremiah Symons
June 1848
On to Oregon."

Once we had carved our names into the rock, we needed to hurry to rejoin our wagon train. Our noonday meal was shortened, but the poor meal was well worth the time spent passing on to subsequent travelers the knowledge that I had been at that spot.

We learned an immediate benefit of having Miss Spencer join our group. Miss Spencer knew more about the plants on the side of the trail than all of us combined. That evening, she led the O'Donnell twins, Bitsy, and me into the open meadows where we found lush raspberry plants. Filling both our stomachs and pots with this tasty fruit occupied our time for the rest of the evening.

The sight of ripe raspberries excited Mother, who immediately began work on sugaring the berries and turning them into sweet pies. Before we went to bed that evening, we devoured the pie, letting the warm juices of the berries bathe our throats and slide around the edges of our mouths. I looked at my sister and laughed; all of Bitsy's mouth and a good portion of her face was covered with the red juice. My laughter was tempered by the knowledge that my face was just as juice covered. Climbing under the wagon that evening, I smiled under my robe as my stomach felt the content feeling brought on by the pies.

Driving on the next day, the Platte River ceased being the mile-wide, inch-deep companion that had been with us for so long. The river became faster, narrower, and more treacherous to cross. The trail matched the river, changing from a gentle sandy road to a rockier climb that challenged all of us.

We knew deep inside that as hard as our initial leg of the journey had been, the portion we had traveled was really the easy part of the trail. We had learned some of the lessons that we needed to survive.

Captain Watkins gathered the boys of the wagon train that

evening. "Boys, we have been a little lazy for the past few weeks. Every day, we gather just enough buffalo chips for the fire of that day. We have been fortunate that we have not had enough rain to soak the buffalo chips. There is nothing worse than a wet buffalo chip. We are coming into places where there will not be enough fuel for all of the fires needed. Therefore, boys, I need you to work harder in gathering the buffalo chips. We need to store them and keep them dry until we need them. No one else can do this job except the boys of the wagon train. We are relying on you to give us enough fuel for the fires for the next several days."

With these instructions, the O'Donnells' and I took some empty containers and wandered outside of the camp and started gathering the buffalo chips. While we did not feel that we had been lazy, we could understand the importance of the task, and even though there was certain disgust in our work, we knew our families depended on all of us working hard.

We worked on this chore for two hours after our evening meal. Only when the sun started its descent into the western horizon did we return to the wagon train, each of us with loaded with full containers. As we neared the wagon train, we recognized the two older Torrance boys watching us.

The Torrance boys were a few years older than I. In addition to the age, they were substantially bigger, which was obvious to both them and me. When I was the momentary hero for the buffalo hunt, they had spent their time, between eating bites of the good rib meat, making comments questioning whether a little child like me could actually have killed an animal. More likely, they thought, I had found it dead or Uncle Peter had killed him. They spent their time around the wagon train alternatively avoiding chores and trying to impress the Elliott girls with their masculine strength. I tried to avoid them whenever possible since a friendship with them was not worthwhile.

While they had been at the same meeting with Captain Watkins and heard the same warning as we had, evidently they had a different plan. The bags of chips were heavy. When we saw them approaching us, I was hopeful that even their conscience had been pricked and that they wanted to help us carry the bags the remainder of the way. This was, unfortunately, not to be.

"Howdy little guys," Josiah, the older Torrance brother, called. "We really appreciate all of the work you have done for us. It truly was charitable of you little boys to gather buffalo chips for our family. I only hope that you left some of them for yourselves." Adam, the younger of the brothers approaching us, laughed aloud at Josiah's comments.

I became very angry at the realization of what was happening. I thought only grown-up outlaws robbed adults, yet, here the Torrance boys were robbing us as surely as if they pulled a gun and demanded a strongbox that I had been guarding. These boys had been sitting by the fire, romancing the girls, and shirking the work while my friends and I had done the hard labor necessary for our families. It just was not right.

I looked over at my friends. Liam looked flushed and angry. I knew that this look mirrored the look on my face. Patrick, though, had an oddly peaceful look on his face. He whispered to us, "Do what I do and it will be all right."

Patrick nodded at the Torrance brothers. "I know you boys are too busy and important to do this work. None of us expected you to help in gathering these chips. So, we have set aside some of the chips just for you."

Josiah Torrance smiled. "Now, you are being sensible. Almost. I do not understand what you mean by some of the chips. We expect to take all of the chips and you will help us carry them to our wagons. Then, we will let you go without the thrashing you need."

Patrick nodded his head. "I know that is how it is going to end. But, we saved some very special chips just for you." He put his full bags down and opened them. "Would you like to see these special ones Josiah?"

Josiah moved forward towards the open bag. He bent over, peering into the bag as if he were looking for lost pirate gold. Instead, in one quick motion, Patrick brought his hand up out of the bag, slapping a large buffalo chip into Josiah's face. Josiah stood for a moment, stunned at the insult to his dignity, and then he howled with rage. As soon as he opened his mouth, I took one of my top buffalo chip, which was still moist, and threw it into Adam's face, smearing some of the moisture over his anger-contorted features.

With this attack, the war began. Each of us took our top buffalo chips and threw them as hard as we could in the faces of our attackers. Having no desire to come close to us and face more direct hits, and stung by the pain of the direct hits in the face, Josiah and Adam ran back to the wagon train with dirty faces and empty hands. The O'Donnells and I laughed; unexpected and memorable victory easily replacing the initial anger of the robbery and making this evening's distasteful job a night that we would always remember, especially when the Torrance brothers appeared to try and impress the Elliott girls. In the distance, that evening, I heard the shouts of the Torrances, parents and sons, as they dealt alternatively with their thieving ways and their unfortunately discolored features.

We put the adventures of that evening behind us and continued heading westward. After an uneventful march of a couple of days, we left the main trail and stopped at one of the most amazing sights

I had seen on the trail. An arch formed in the rock that extended high over the most beautiful mountain stream. While Chimney Rock had taught me that rocks could form into any number of odd shapes, this was the first time I had seen rocks form a natural umbrella over water. Uncle Peter assured me that not only had I not seen this formation before but also that he had never seen this type anywhere else in his travels. We spent the evening fishing for trout underneath the shade of the stony arch. That evening, fishing may not have been successful but it certainly was unique.

Traveling westward, we noticed that the dust was thicker as we followed the trails. There were more adventurers on our trail since some of the Mormons who had spent their time on the other banks of the North Platte River had crossed over and were sharing the road with us. This made the progress slower and more difficult.

We saw a multitude of pronghorn antelope standing at a distance, playing their games and bouncing over the prairie. These animals never came too close to the train, but both man and antelope showed their curiosity in the staring contests in which we engaged.

While riding along, Uncle Peter described his experience hunting these creatures. The antelope was too fast and too timid to track on horseback or on foot. Antelope, however, possessed one fatal character trait. An antelope could not bury its native curiosity and had to learn about anything that was unusual in its environment. Hunters could take advantage of this curiosity by waving white handkerchiefs in the breeze. The poor animals would wander over to the raised handkerchiefs and be rewarded for their curiosity with a rifle shot. It was unfair, Miss Spencer observed, for an animal's lust for learning to be fatal.

Having had this experience described to me, I felt that maybe Uncle Peter was telling me one of the improbable stories that old-time mountain men were famous for sharing. That evening, right before dusk, I snuck out of the camp with my rifle and a white cloth that Mother had brought with us. Moving toward a herd of antelope, I circled around the herd so that the wind would not carry my scent to them. Then, I took a long stick I had found on the ground and carefully tied the cloth to the top of the stick. Then, between my teeth, I made a low whistling noise that caused some of the antelope to raise their head. Much to my surprise, one of the creatures actually wandered over towards my hiding place on the ground. He moved so close to the handkerchief that I could almost imagine he could hear my breathing. Deep down, I felt a little sorry for this poor creature, but the thought of another day of no meat but bacon took charge of my emotions and let me fell him with a single shot. Meat is meat. Fortunately, Father had been spying on my adventure, and we were able together to move the animal back to our train.

Our brisk progress along the trail came to a sudden stop. In front of us, we could see a substantial line of wagons waiting for a ferry to take them across the river. Brigham Young, the leader of the Mormons, had built this ferry in 1847. Our situation demanded patience; yet, frustration grew in our hearts, since we knew that we lacked either the patience to wait or the means to avoid the delay. Senator Richardson called a meeting of the men and told us that the coming country had many ferryboats that would take us over the many streams we would cross in the coming days. To speed the process, he told us that it would be necessary for each member of the wagon train to pay to the good senator fifty dollars that he would use to pay the men in charge of each of the coming ferryboats for the entire train. This, in the senator's view, would speed the process of the train crossing the rivers.

This announcement caused some mumbling in the wagon train. As the always-bitter Major Smith noted, "It is just like a politician to resort to taxation whenever possible." His concerns, however, were dismissed due to the bitterness that we all knew he held in his heart towards the good senator.

Precious time was lost at this crossing of the river. All of the people felt frustration because the time of our departure to the other side was impossible to gauge; if we knew we had days we would perform productive, needed repairs; if we had only hours to stay at the ferry it would be easy to pass the time in idle enjoyment. Additionally, we heeded the warnings of Captain Watkins that our progress to the west was not as swift as to guarantee that we would not see mountain snow before we made it to Oregon.

We waited, watching the good June travel days pass on without traveling. During this time, we traded news with other wagon trains and told the tall stories that arose from life on the trail. Men repeatedly told of rumors of gold being found in California. Some men scoffed at this story, since people always heard of new places where a man could become rich without significant labor. Other men, though, insisted that the stories were true and that all a man needed to do to prosper in California was to labor for a few short days in the California streams. Once a man made his fortune, he could live anywhere and in anyway he desired.

Finally, after a two-day wait, it was our turn to load the wagons and cross over the river. Saying farewell to the Platte River, we moved further onto the trail. The colors of the trail changed from green into a brown color where the plants matched the color of the soil; in the distance, we could see red buttes rising high above the floor of the plains. The sameness of the nearby terrain made the work of surviving on the trail more like drudgery. Then, as if the trip needed more difficulty, it started to rain.

At first, the rain was gentle. Then it picked up in ferocity. The rain hit us in the face and made the progress even slower. Then, lightning started to flash in the distant skies and both people and animals remembered the horrors of the tornado along the Platte River. This time though, no tornado developed. It was just rain, more rain and still more rain that slowed our movements to a crawl. Finally, that night, we reached a gap in the rocks called Emigrant Gap, where a stream called the Poison Spider Creek flowed. Uncle Peter, Father and I crawled into a slice in the rock where we could stay warm for the evening. While the dryness was appreciated, knowing the name of the creek caused me some anxiety and made me want to sleep with a single eye open to watch for any creatures. Finally, sleep overcame the fear of spiders and the dreams of the mountains forced out thoughts of the crawling creatures.

CHAPTER 13

SOUTH PASS

Following a night of restless sleep, I stirred to find my father pulling his pants on before daylight had fully reached us in our sleeping crevice. He whispered to me, "If I have another breakfast of bacon, I may start to root in the mud like a pig. There are fish out there and I plan to have some of them in our frying pan before I take another step."

While there was no invitation in his statement, there also was no prohibition. I crawled out of my buffalo robe, slipped on my pants, and grabbed my fishing pole. Sneaking down to the stream, we let our lines dangle in the water. Blissfully, the fish were as hungry for our bait as we were for their filets. By the time the rest of our group had arisen, we had rolled our trout in cornmeal and were frying them to a crisp, golden brown. Never in the recorded history of man, fish, or pig was there a piece of bacon that approached these fish in flavor.

I struggled with determining the day and date during our time on the trail. When we were home, we had school days, non-school days and church days. Each week fell behind the next week in our lives and the seasons told us the month. We knew the time for planting season, growing season, harvest season, and repair season.

For a farmer these were as much part of the calendar as any month named for an old Roman or Norse god. On the trail, though, each day was identical to the preceding day. The scenery might change and there might be more or less climbing of hills or crossing of rivers, but the natural ability to tell time of year disappeared.

This changed one night when Captain Watkins rode up to our encampment. "Everyone rest up tonight. We have many miles to travel tomorrow if we are going to camp by Independence Rock for Declaration Day. Hard to believe that it is already July second. Everyone knows that the reason we call it Independence Rock is that if we do not reach this place by July Fourth, we will be snow bound in the western mountains. So sleep well everyone and wear your walking shoes tomorrow."

With this warning, Mother finished preparing the salt rising bread that we would eat in the morning and the rest of us crawled into our sleeping places. I wrapped myself into my buffalo robe and resolved to sleep quickly because I knew the next day would be tiring.

Captain Watkins had promised we would march a long distance the next day. He truly was a man of his word. We started our journey early and continued all day long until we reached our destination. The only rests allowed were a midday break and any rest needed by the animals. As if we needed more reminders, the strength of the oxen mattered much more than the comfort of eleven-year-old boys. The increased heat made the long walk more laborious. Water was a precious commodity, but every cool drop we drank we treasured as if it were a portion of the riches of the lost City of Gold.

Finally, Captain Watkins fired his rifle in the air as a signal to stop for the evening. The sun had already started its quick descent into the western horizon. My legs felt like two loose hanging strands

WEST TO THE SUN

of ropes dangling toward the ground unattached to anything firm. Wobbly, tired, weak; all of these were words that could describe the way my legs functioned at that moment.

When I saw Independence Rock, my heart sank. Far from being a magnificent mountain worthy of the importance we placed on it, I saw a mere granite boulder sticking one hundred feet up from the floor of the ground; this rise was no more or less impressive than any of the other rocks that rose from the floor of the desert. Disappointment must have flooded my exhausted face for Uncle Peter quietly said to me, "Not much of a bump from the floor is it? Mountain men leading these wagon trains are superstitious about being here by the fourth of July and that is the only reason this pebble has its name. But, we should be grateful to have a day to rest our feet."

Thinking about resting my feet raised my spirits. I did my evening chores quickly and with a joyous heart. Uncle Peter pulled out his guitar and started to play lively tunes with the O'Donnell clan, but before too long, I found my chin resting on my chest as my eyes closed tight and finished my day.

When I awoke the next morning, I found myself safely under the wagon. I crawled out and smelled the familiar smell of the smoky fires and the distant smell of coffee brewing. Mother was already awake finishing the breakfast of bread, bacon and coffee. Early this morning I heard her coughing. When Father asked her about the coughs, I heard her mention the dry air in a tone that dismissed further questioning.

Uncle Peter told me that Independence Rock, like Register Cliff, was a place where travelers needed to carve their names. We planned to climb Independence Rock as soon as we had cleaned our breakfast dishes. Once the dishes were clean and put away, we all walked up the rock toward the top, singing some patriotic songs and running short and losing, races with Bitsy. Uncle Peter sang loudly and intentionally off key, which made the women laugh and the men cringe and cover their ears. Father observed that it was a good thing the milk cow could not hear him because it would surely sour milk for days to come.

Once we reached the top of the rock, we turned and looked east to see the distance we had covered. We noticed that right next to our encampment, there was another wagon train that had followed us to the rock. Beyond them, we saw puffs of dust indicating that other trains were still moving on July fourth. Turning to the west, we could see in the distance the mountains stretching to heaven. Then, we knelt down on the rock, pulled out our knives and carved our names into the rock. My father smiled and told me that hundreds of years from now people would be able to trace my route from Register Cliff to Independence Rock. These future travelers would wonder whatever happened to Jeremiah Symons and whether he and his family had made it to Oregon.

We hurried down the rock after we carved our names. Next to Christmas, July fourth was always my favorite day of the year and I saw no reason why today should be any different from the days that had been spent at the side of the Stones River.

Upon returning to the wagon, one of the chickens sacrificed its life for our dinner. We cleaned and plucked the chicken and soon the smell of my mother's fried chicken dominated all of the other smells of the camp. Our noonday meal was a wonderful chicken that reminded me so much of our other dinners at home. The chicken tasted so good we never wanted the meal to end.

Following our noonday meal, all of the kids ran races for the amusement of the adults. Then, the men tested their strength to impress, or amuse, their women. Finally, we challenged our neighboring wagon train to a massive tug-of-war competition. Each group stood on opposite shores of the Sweetwater River and wrapped their hands around the rope that had been lashed together to span the river and provide enough room for the men to grab. Captain Watkins fired his rifle into the air, signaling both groups of men to pull with all of our strength. We grunted, groaned, and moaned as we bent with all of our strength and tried to move our enemy to our side of the river. My muscles strained as I pulled. The sun beat down on us as we moved first one direction and then the other direction.

The O'Donnell twins stood behind me. I heard them groaning with effort. Standing at the side of the river, Senator Richardson called desperate encouragement to us to pull harder. Hearing his voice, we bent our bodies into the rope and tried to put more of our strength into the line. Slowly, sadly, I felt the ground moving under my feet as I moved towards the riverbed.

The front man in our team stumbled. The next man fell and before I knew what was happening my legs gave way and I fell into the river. I landed hard on my face, which in spite of the defeat felt good since it cooled my sweat-soaked hair. The next thing I knew the O'Donnell twins had landed partially beside me and partially on top of me. I tried to push them off me and stand up. I spluttered as the water of the Sweetwater filled my mouth. I shook my wet hair like one of the dogs I had seen in my hometown that dried off by making everyone around them wet with their shaken fur. Then, despite the sad defeat, I simply started to laugh out of the pure fun of the contest. My friends, my father and my uncle, all of whom also showed signs of the soaking we received in defeat, joined this laughter. The men from the other train joined us in the river and we enjoyed the momentary comradeship born of good competition.

We left the river and joined the others for the rest of the day's activities. The groups sang together and our musicians played patriotic songs. Then, Senator Richardson stood in front of the group and gave a patriotic speech. He stood with his hand inside his shirt, pressed against his substantial stomach and started talking in his deep, self-important tone:

"Good people. Today we celebrate the founding of our great country. Our country we love that stands as a shining example of freedom in a world filled with monarchs and despots, a world where common people are incapable of undertaking journeys to improve their lot in life like we are currently engaged in. Yet, it is important to realize that the journey we are undertaking has much more than an individual significance. Collectively, we are engaged in a journey that fulfills the destiny of our country, the God-given manifest destiny of the good people of this country to be freed from the constraints of the eastern geography and European ways and fill the entire landscape of our land from sea to sea. As John Winthrop once dreamt, America could become a city on a hill that is a shining example for the rest of the world. We are fulfilling that dream today.

"One of my favorite speeches about the fourth of July is from a man named Jonathan Mason, who early in the life of our republic said: 'But while patriotism is the leading principle, and our laws are contrived with wisdom and executed with vigor; while industry, frugality, and temperance are held in estimation, and we depend upon public spirit and the love of virtue for our social happiness, peace and affluence will throw their smiles upon the brow of individuals, our commonwealth will flourish, our land will become a land of liberty, and America an asylum for the oppressed.'

"Our journey to the western shores of our land is beneficial to the dream of America as an asylum for the oppressed. Therefore, good people, take cheer, for the labors that we are undertaking are not merely for personal profit but are also for the fulfillment of providentially given tasks."

The good senator continued like this for quite some time. My attention to his high speaking drifted away as I thought more about our journey. I did not know, nor care, about providential destiny. All I knew was that we had a dream of a better life and we had sacrificed what we had known in a gamble to meet that goal.

Finally, the senator ended his polished oration. Some of the men brought out their store of liquor, a drink my father and uncle studiously avoided. Then, musicians from both camps gathered, tuned their instruments, and started to play lively tunes with great gusto. The younger married couples and the unmarried teenagers began dancing while the older people stood around the dirt dance floor, clapped their hands and enjoyed the music. This continued far into the night until Mother insisted that Bitsy and I go to sleep. Reluctantly, I crawled under the wagon, wrapped myself in the buffalo robe, and drifted into a sound sleep after a wonderful day.

Morning came far too early. Groans filled the air as we tried to will ourselves to move through our tasks. My personal awakening came when Mother was coughing, again, in a manner that worried us. I heard Father ask if he should fetch our doctor; Mother dismissed his concern with an observation that no one could keep from coughing in this dry air.

Finally, later than usual, we moved forward with our journey. That day, we reached the most amazing canyon. The Sweetwater River carved a narrow passage in the rocks that was probably only thirty feet wide at its base but that expanded as the walls reached higher until it was a massive gulf at the top. The cliffs stood higher than Independence Rock and were a far more impressive sight. Uncle Peter called the place the Devil's Gate and while I did not know where it led to it certainly looked like the devil had a hand in its appearance.

Captain Watkins, in particular, felt the strains of the previous night and announced that for this day, we would camp here. Since there were several hours of daylight left, this was an uncharacteristic stopping point, but I did not complain. Instead, my father and I grabbed our rifles and started to seek fresh meat and explore the canyon.

Walking along the Sweetwater River I was in total awe of the walls of the canyon stretching upward to the sky. Part of the way through the canyon, we resolved to climb higher to see more of the sights. We slowly climbed a trail towards the top of the cliff face. Suddenly, Father stopped me on the trail and put his finger to his mouth and with his other hand pointed ahead of us. There on a rocky ledge were two large animals with huge curling horns. "Bighorn sheep", Father whispered. "You need to watch this."

The two large bighorn sheep confronted each other on the trail. Their huge horns turned in the most spectacular fashion and glistened in the reflected light of the sun. Without warning, the two animals charged each other and collided fiercely. The sound echoed through the canyon. Repeatedly, they charged, with each collision shattering the air with the sharp, almost musical sounds of their violent combat. At last, one of the sheep realized he was the lesser creature and slunk away from the battle. The victor stood on the edge of a cliff extending over the river for the entire world to see the dominant ram.

Dreaming of fresh meat, I raised my rifle and took aim on the posing animal. My father's strong hand grasped the barrel of my gun and brought it down. "Jeremiah", he said, "today we will eat fish or bacon. It would be rude to kill this victor in a God-given piece of entertainment."

I agreed. I just watched as the sheep nimbly jumped along the trail and disappeared into the distance. Some creatures just did not belong in our frying pan.

The next day we drove our wagons around the Devil's Gate. My father made a comment that it was probably best to give the Devil a wide berth. I just shook my head and kept walking.

That day we learned both the good and the bad of the Sweetwater River. The river name was perfect. The water coming from the river was the sweetest water I had tasted since our farm in Tennessee. The bad thing about the Sweetwater River was that it never could make up its watery mind as to what direction it wanted to flow. Side to side it turned, either as if it did not know how it should move or as if it did not care if it ever reached its destination. For the next days, we crossed the Sweetwater River repeatedly.

After we crossed the river five times, Captain Watkins explained that the wagon train had a choice to make. Either we could cross the fast-running river three more times in the canyon within a couple of miles, or alternatively, we could avoid the crossings by leaving the river, heading south of the canyon. This would require us to drag the wagons through a sandy road. Since we felt that pulling wagons through bottomless sand would be harder than even three difficult river crossings, we opted to camp by the beginning of the first of the three crossings so we could finish our river crossings in a single day.

The next day we crossed the river. Fortunately, the sun rose hot that day, since we would spend much of the day with our legs in the cold water of the river. We tied ropes on the other side of the river to mark the areas where we needed to cross. When the boys finished lining the width of the river to block the animals from passing too far away from the ford, we allowed the animals from the first wagon into the river. The river ran quickly at this point, but we managed to maneuver the animals through the water and lead them up the opposite bank. Usually, a single river crossing was enough work for the day, but the train rolled up its ropes and repeated the process a second and third time before finally we were through the canyon.

As if this were not enough hard work for the day, the riverside trail turned swampy. This meant that we needed to help the oxen out with ropes during the worst heat of the day. Captain Watkins rode through the train shouting encouragement. If we worked hard, he promised we would see amazing things at the end of the day that we would remember for the rest of our lives. Hearing these words, we pushed forward, turn of the wagon wheel after difficult turn.

We moved forward until Captain Watkins shot his rifle in the air signaling the end of the day. Once we watered our animals in the river and put them in our nightly corral, Captain Watkins rode through the camp and had us all follow him with shovels. He led us into a small marshy creek that ran into the Sweetwater River. Then, he dug away some of the grass and there was a pool of river. Captain Watkins pointed at this water and announced, "This water is wonderful, but what is below is even better."

With this announcement, he dug beneath the water and to our surprise pulled out a huge chunk of ice. "Under this spring," he told us, "are pure blocks of the coolest ice. Come here and chip some out for your families." Once the captain stepped aside, we all attacked the ground with vigor. The sun was so hot that day that the thought of pure ice was a thought of heaven. Once we carted our quota of ice back to the wagon, we chipped off a portion of the ice for our evening drinks and used the rest of the ice to cool our sweaty heads after a day of marching.

For another two days, we marched along the side of the Sweetwater River. The more we traveled along the river, the more I learned to appreciate it. Trout eagerly ate our bait to be our breakfast meal as if God Himself had sent them magically to our fishing lines. The water was so fresh and sweet that it was almost tempting to sit by this river for the rest of my life. Yet, onward we moved. At the end of this march, however, we left the sweetness of this river. Before we left, though, we carefully filled every available container for water, since Captain Watkins warned us that ahead, water would be scarce.

The road tilted higher as we headed west. At our campsite following the last crossing, Uncle Peter told us that we were less than a day's march away from South Pass. Uncle Peter explained, "South Pass is one of the most important places on the whole westward trails. First, South Pass is a major break in the Rocky Mountains. Mr. Stuart found this pass with his desperate Astorians back in 1813. If he had not found South Pass when he did his men would have starved to death or been killed by hostile Indians. The location of South Pass disappeared from our knowledge, until, a dozen years later, Jedediah Smith, the greatest of the mountain men, found it again. Fortunately, he described it carefully enough in his journal that future travelers could find it.

"Once we reach South Pass," Uncle Peter continued, "we will cross the continental divide. All rivers flow to the west from this place forward. I do not know if it is exactly the halfway point between St. Joseph and Oregon but it feels like it. The government maps call everything west of here the Oregon Territory. This is not where we want to end. Home awaits a thousand miles to the west."

We continued to South Pass. To the north and south, mountains stretched touching the heavens. When I was a young boy and had drawn mountains on my school slate, they were always individual straight lines without interruption. Now that I stood near them, I realized the inaccuracy of that imagination. The mountains I saw were a group of snow-covered rocks extending irregularly into the skies, with ledges and uneven spikes beginning in firm foundations and pointing upward. All of their irregularity made the peaks both more impressive and terrifying.

Once we reached the top of the pass, I ran to the front of our wagon train. I looked forward to the west, eyes straining into the horizon as if my eyes could summon our new home into vision. Instead, all I could see was dusty mile after dusty mile. Home was no longer just behind me but instead stretched in front of me, far beyond the vision of my eyes, but safely within the vision of my heart.

CHAPTER 14

GREEN RIVER AND BLUE DAYS

After pausing to enjoy the view from South Pass, we moved several miles beyond South Pass and camped beside Pacific Springs. Pacific Springs was a lush meadow with plenty of good grass that Todd and his four-legged companions thoroughly enjoyed. The spring water was cool, clear, and refreshing. Uncle Peter warned us that we should enjoy an oasis like this because the quest for water would dominate our lives from this point forward. It was odd that we had taken water for granted in Tennessee; here, in the dry west, we needed to hunt for water, savor water, and preserve every drop of water.

Once we completed our evening chores, I climbed into my bed on the ground under the wagon. Rolling to find a comfortable place, I heard a family argument in the Elliott wagon. I tried to ignore it, since I did not truly care about the emotions of flighty girls, but the noise of the argument kept me awake.

Emily Elliott was sobbing. As difficult as it was to understand the inarticulate words through her violent cries, I could understand that crossing South Pass was distressing her. She wailed: "You said that we were in the Oregon Territory. We should be close to our home, and the dances of the community, and the fun of our new life with the new friends we will make. Now, that I am happy and dreaming of this, you tell me we still have a thousand miles to go before we reach Oregon City. Maybe, dear, sweet Mrs. Parker had it right. I want to be done with this trail. To realize that we have come so far, suffered so much, and yet have so much time to go just is too terrible to imagine." This explosion of words ended as quickly as it began as her voice trailed into a series of incoherent sobs.

I could not hear much more as the Elliott adults tried to comfort their emotional daughter. Uncle Peter rolled over from his sleeping place and told me, "Distances drive people crazy. Everyone knows that traveling to Oregon is a two-thousand-mile trip, but no one really understands what two thousand miles means until you are walking it or riding in a wagon that shakes your bones. I have always viewed South Pass as a victorious milestone; there are, however, people who become very sad when they finally reach the Pass look beyond it, and see nothing but mile after mile of ongoing dry lands. Poor, silly Miss Elliott is feeling that reality most harshly right now."

We awoke the next morning, left the beauty of Pacific Springs, and continued heading west. By noon, the cool water became a distant memory as the dry sagebrush took control of our lives. Instead of having the freshness of the Sweetwater, Uncle Peter explained that we needed to cross three related rivers. First, we needed to traverse the Dry Sandy River, then, the Little Sandy River, and finally, the Big Sandy River. Uncle Peter laughed and reminded us that any river named Sandy promised more dirt than refreshment.

Uncle Peter's words proved prophetic. We reached the Dry Sandy River and we found mud in the riverbed but no flowing water. This made our crossing easy, but for the families that did not store water in every available container from Pacific Springs, the sudden realization that not every river contained ample water was terrifying.

At the end of the day, we camped at a lonely field of sagebrush called the Parting of the Ways. That night, Captain Watkins convened a meeting of the men of the wagon train. This lonely outpost had its name because now, every wagon train needed to make a decision relating to its chosen route. We could follow the usual route to Fort Bridger or we could take the Greenwood Cutoff. The cutoff would be a difficult trip over desert and mountains but that would be about five days faster than the easier trip.

The men debated the merits of each route, but never reached full agreement. Finally, sadly, we agreed that six wagons, mostly those with ample supplies and no children, would move along the cutoff while the remainder of the wagons would continue as we had initially planned to Fort Bridger. Father shook his head at losing some of our traveling companions. "Shortcuts," he observed, "might lead to the same place but there is always a payment demanded in difficulty, danger, or death that may be more than the amount saved. Better, Jeremy, when responsible for the safety of a complete family, to take the easier route even if it causes a little delay."

That morning, we said our good-byes to the group moving on the cutoff. While we promised that we would see one another once we reached Oregon, we knew, somewhere deep in our souls, that we could probably never see one another again. We waved farewell and watched them move beyond our sight and into our hearts' memories.

Shortly after parting, I noticed that the wind began to blow stronger. It began as a gentle morning breeze; then, it moved to a brisk wind; finally a gale against which I struggled to walk. Unlike some of the winds that blew when we were marching by the Platte River, there was no promise of moisture coming with the wind. Instead of rain falling from above, dust began to rise from the ground. First, a wisp of dirt that irritated the nose quickly led to an atmosphere choked with the sand particles that stung my face as they hit me. It felt like I was being cut with pieces of glass as I took each step forward in the blinding sand storm.

Our pace slowed as we tried to continue our move westward. Each step was a painful struggle. Abrasive dust covered everything that we owned. Even from inside our wagon, I heard Mother coughing violently as she struggled for breath. At Uncle Peter's urging, we wrapped our faces in rags and tried to protect our eyes from the swirling sand. Finally, we stopped the hopeless walking and hid in our wagons until that night, when mercifully the sandstorm stopped. That night, the wagon train did not light its typical campfires; instead, in relative darkness we cared for our animals and dug the sand away from the wheels. We slept that night with empty stomachs and dirt everywhere embedded in the very pores of our skin.

Breakfast the next day was more of the same bacon that had become a second nature to us. Yet, the lack of the meal the evening before made it taste like the most precious meal of our trip, filling the empty crevices that were our stomachs. We continued our march through the heat, pushing through the drifts of sand.

Our meal that evening was troubled. Mother cooked a fine feast for us. Yet, while the family enjoyed the meal, Mother sat, coughing, sweating and barely tasting the food that she had prepared. Then, she excused herself, whispered in Father's ear, and climbed into bed. Evidently, the illness that had bothered her earlier had not totally disappeared. That was the last we saw of her that evening.

Recognizing our need to contribute during her illness, we all worked to clean the dishes, put away our foodstuffs in the manner Mother would, cared for Bitsy and Sally and finally put the animals and family to bed for the evening.

The next morning we awoke expecting to see Mother stirring the fire and making the wonderful breads that she made for her loved ones. When I awoke, I saw Father stirring the fire, putting his coffeepot over the coals for the strong coffee he always made. He looked at me, smiled a tense, tired smile and said "Mother is still very sick. We need to do her chores today until she is better."

Hearing this, I climbed out from my bed beneath the wagon. While I had never known her to be ill, I also knew that our tasks on the western prairie did not cease simply due to illness. I unloaded our breakfast food and dishes and handed them to Father, who made a breakfast of Johnnycakes for us. While the cornbread cakes were one of my favorite meals, the joy of the eating was diminished because of the concern for the absent, never sick, mother.

We walked alongside the wagon that day with quiet, prayerful hearts. It was a somber group. Even Bitsy and Uncle Peter spent little time that day singing their songs and laughing. Miss Spencer rode in the wagon, trying to make Mother comfortable, swabbing her head with wet cloths and continually trying to keep her drinking liquids. When Mother drifted into sleep, Miss Spencer would climb out of the wagon and walk with us. She answered our questions relating to Mother with quiet, one-word answers that let us know the illness was serious.

The rest of us just marched, silently concerned with the health of our loved one. Father said little all day, grasping the reins and focusing his entire attention on the road in front of us. Our concern made the day feel endless; the weight of our concerns made the labor of the walking far more ponderous than normal. Finally, at the end of the day, we reached the edge of the Green River, which ended our reliance on the aptly named Sandy Rivers. Ordinarily, this would have been a cause for great joy, splashing and fishing; today, however we simply ceased walking and worked through our many chores.

Once we unhitched the oxen, my father instructed me to bring Doctor Woods to our wagon. He was a quiet man making the trip west with his wife and baby. He was one of the kindliest men in the wagon train; a man always willing to answer any scientific question that a man or boy might have on the natural wonders of the world or the stars circling above us. His inherent thoughtfulness made us love him more, even though our good health meant that we spent little time with him.

I ran as fast as I could to his wagon and tried to describe what had been happening since the prior evening. While my words may not have been coherent, the concern on my face told him the entire story. Grabbing his medical bag, he followed me through the train until we reached our wagon.

My father greeted Doctor Woods and helped him into the wagon. The rest of us mechanically went through our evening chores as Father, Mother and the Doctor spent a veritable eternity alone together in the dark of that wagon.

After this lengthy examination, Doctor Woods and Father emerged from the wagon. Their faces were serious and did not invite interruption as they spoke softly. Doc Woods placed his arm on Father's shoulder, lowered his head as if in prayer, then broke off, and walked slowly away.

Father stood alone for a moment, came to us, and gathered us all around. I looked into his face, not sure what I expected to see, but clearly not expecting to see the red-rimmed eyes of a man who had been crying. I looked at him with all of the power in my body, as if by intense, focused concentration I could see into his soul. His eyes did not meet my gaze, but his voice, drawn and tired, caught my full attention:

"Doctor Woods, good man that he is, has examined my dear Mary." Father wiped a tear from his eyes before he continued. "The news is bad. Somewhere along the trail, she has contracted a lung infection that has turned into pneumonia. The sandstorm we passed through was too much for her weak lungs and she has become mortally ill. The doctor tells me that the illness is in the last stages and there is nothing that can be done for her." With this, my poor father choked a sob and continued: "We can make her comfortable like dear Sarah Spencer has done today, but I fear there is nothing that can be done to save her life. Jesus wants her more than He wants us to have her."

I did not hear the rest of the words. I felt like a strong man had punched me in the stomach and removed all of the air from my body. I dropped onto my knees in a prayerful stance, but it was not a desire to pray to the Lord who was ripping my mother from my arms but rather the failure to have enough strength in my bones and muscles to support the frame of my body. My head dropped to my chest and while I felt the strong hands of Uncle Peter on my back, they meant little to me.

In my mind, this was news that I did not expect to hear until I was an old man sitting in a rocking chair on the porch, surrounded by my grandchildren. Someday, when my hair was gray, some kind voice would tell me that my dear ninety-year-old mother had passed away. Then, we would all sadly dab at our eyes and make easy comments about a life lived fully and well. I did not expect, could not understand, that the young woman who understood me better than anyone and loved me more than anyone could be loved would be taken from me so soon.

Uncle Peter pulled me to my feet. I leaned against him and tried to recover the emotional composure I felt all grown men had to have. Maybe, if calmness in the face of this news was needed to prove manhood, I was not able to claim the title of man, regardless of the rivers I crossed or the animals that I had slain. I looked at the devastated face of my father, and the tear-streaked cheeks of my uncle. I realized that there were times in this life when the emotions of men needed to spill out from the meager containers of our bodies.

"Can we see her, Father?" I asked. My voice sounded like the high voice of a pleading boy not the strong, resonant voice of a confident, grown man.

"Absolutely, Jeremiah," Father replied. "She wants to see us all."

We carefully rolled up the sides of the wagon covers to allow the cooler breeze into the wagon. I remembered how she carefully, lovingly stitched these covers for Uncle Peter and me to place over the framework of the wagon. Those days felt both like yesterday and as if they had happened a million years in the past to different people.

Once this task was complete, I left the wagon. Better to let the others talk to her first. My emotions were exploding in my soul, much like fireworks from a Declaration Day celebration that I had attended so many times with her at home, but these emotions did not provide any comfort. I sat on a bluff overlooking Green River and tried to compose myself. Mostly, though, I wept. Finally, my father joined me, saying nothing at first, simply joining me in our shared sorrow. He then put his arm around me, a display of affection that came very rarely, and whispered to me that Mother wanted to see me.

I climbed into the wagon. Mother lay in her bed, propped up by her pillows. Her hot face had lines where the sweat and tears had flowed down her cheeks and mingled together. She gestured for me to sit on her bed and I did so, first at a far corner, then moving closer and closer to her, as I struggled to hear her gasping voice.

She smiled, a smile mingling love, sorrow, and exhaustion. She coughed and then spoke. "Jeremiah, you need not be so sad. I have lived such a blessed life. I have married a wonderful man. I have had four children, two of whom I am about to hold in my arms for the first time in a long, long time. I have seen the most amazing things this world possesses: mountains that truly touch the sky, buffalo that shake the earth, land that goes on forever and promises something new each day. But, do you know what makes me happiest?"

I shook my head. I wanted to speak but the desired words failed to make the long journey from heart to mouth.

I felt her hand stroke my hair as she had done so many times when the boyhood injuries were too much for me to bear on my own. So many times in my loft, the burdens of the day, the battles with hometown bullies, the frustrations with my father, the concerns over the trip west were wiped away by her hand. This time, though, the hand would not eliminate the pain.

"You make me happiest, Jeremiah. I have watched you grow from a little boy into the image of a fine man. I do not mean that you are a man because of the buffalo or antelope meat that you brought to our table. You are becoming such a fine man because of the way you treat people, the way you respond to difficulty, the way you are willing to overcome challenges. This is one of those challenges Jeremy. You need to help my Jedediah. I worry about him. I worry about little Bitsy. You need to be a good son and a good big brother. I know you will because you are not a boy anymore but you are a fine Christian man. Continue to grow, Jeremiah and know that I am always proud of you."

I cried. My head fell into her lap. I wept as if the flood of tears were water that had been released by an exploded dam. My body shook as her hands slowly, weakly stroked my face.

"It's not so bad, Jeremy. I do not hurt badly and I am going to see Jesus. How can that be horrible?" She stroked my hair some more and then asked me to send in Bitsy.

I left her embrace and brought Bitsy to her. Bitsy climbed onto the bed, held Suzy to her for Mother to adjust the little doll and then lay down next to her. Mother and daughter lay in an embrace, with my mother softly talking to her until Bitsy finally fell sound asleep.

Father gently lifted Bitsy and placed her sleeping form into her own bed. Then, he carefully climbed next to my mother. They hugged each other, whispering to each other in a tearful conversation that was meant for no ears other than theirs. Finally, the conversation ceased. My father stroked her hair and climbed out of the wagon. "She's gone, Jeremiah," my father said. Then, we fell into a strong, lasting embrace. Uncle Peter joined us and the three of us held tight to one another, with tears falling and blending in the dust.

Mourning consumed the remainder of the night. Mother had shown every person in the wagon train a strong Christian love whether in the form of lent foodstuffs, words of encouragement or needed hugs. Grief followed the sad recognition that this lady would travel no more. As the people ceased coming and the moon hid behind clouds, my father silently and tearfully prepared the body for burial.

When gray dawn broke, Father led some of the men to a place on the banks of the Green River for Mother's grave. They dug deep into the sandy soil, carefully constructing this final bed. Much as I had gathered rocks to cover the grave of little Amy, who died before by the Platte River, now other boys of the train gathered rocks to protect Mother from the coyotes that lurked in this area.

Once the grave was completed, Uncle Peter and Mr. O'Donnell reverentially lifted the lifeless body out of the wagon and carried it to the grave. There, tenderly, they lowered her body until she rested deep in the ground. Father stood, silently at the grave, strong hands wringing the brim of his hat. I stood by his side and Miss Spencer held the sobbing Bitsy in her arms. Father's mouth moved as if he wanted to speak, saying the words he had previously said at so many other gravesides, but this time, the comforting words that he had summoned before failed to appear. His mouth moved again but once again, sound did not come forth.

Sensing the difficulty, Uncle Peter stepped forward and began to speak.

"In the last chapter of Proverbs, King Lemeul writes: Who can find a virtuous woman? For her price is far above rubies. Mary Symons was a virtuous woman. She lived her life loving her God, her husband, and her children. Her children will long for her, her husband will love her eternally, and her God welcomed her to her long sought home. We do not always understand His ways; however, I truly can say that I would rather have known her and loved her for this short span of years than to have never known such a precious woman."

Uncle Peter prayed. Mr. O'Donnell slowly played Amazing Grace on his violin, the sweet, sad music flowing around our assembled group and echoing back and forth across the river. We wept through his playing until the final notes of the hymn ceased their echoing. Then, Father picked up a clump of dirt, dropped it in open grave, turned and walked away, tears streaming down his face.

I watched this action. My face must have silently questioned this behavior, for Mr. O'Donnell answered my unspoken question. "Lad, it is an old tradition. When a husband drops the dirt on his wife in this way, he knows surely that she cannot return to him, but that he will go to her." Nodding my head, I dropped my own clump of dirt into the sad grave and followed my father down the hill.

The men of the train quickly shoveled the dirt into the hole. Boys placed large rocks on top of the grave to protect her body from hungry coyotes. Then, the funeral was over. Reluctantly, I turned and gathered our oxen into position and with the tears still pouring from my overflowing eyes, much as water when poured into a full glass falls over the sides and flows onto a table and then the floor below, I silently hitched them into their designated place. Then Father gathered some of the honeysuckle flowers that we found around the trail, tied them together into a bouquet, and silently walked to the grave of his beloved bride and placed them there. He stood, alone, silently standing by the grave until I walked over to him and whispered, "Father, it is our turn to cross the river."

He nodded and wiped his red eyes. Arm in arm, we climbed

away from the grave and walked back to our wagon. Mother had once told me that the way to leave something precious was to walk forward and never look back. I tried to follow her advice, not only because it had worked for me before, but also because I knew that there by the banks of the Green River, I was leaving behind a portion of my soul that would never be fully reclaimed.

CHAPTER 15
FORT BRIDGER

Green River was high and rushing quickly. We crossed the river silently. When we reached the other side of the river, I hopped off the back of the wagon and snapped the whip in front of Bob and Todd with more force than usual. They surged forward out of the water, startled that their friend was challenging their easygoing ways. Uncle Peter leaned over, whispered something to Father, and drove his feet hard into the haunches of his horse. The animal leapt forward and galloped more speedily than I had previously seen him. Dust rose as horse and rider moved briskly past our group, beyond our wagon train, over the hill and out of sight.

I looked at Father. He shrugged his shoulders and said, "When Peter is unhappy, he wants to be alone with his thoughts. When he sorts things out mentally, he will return, acting like the Peter who we all love. He told me he would be back at the end of the day. I hope that is true." In his eyes, I could see a wistful glance that told me he, too, wished to ride off but that he knew the responsibility of this day would not grant him the freedom to mourn in this way.

I understood. I regretted that I could not ride with Uncle Peter in his silent, lonely quest for clarity. I wished I had a horse that I could gallop away from my life, riding into the distance until I felt the numbness that follows sorrow. Instead, I was left with six oxen, a little sister, a silent father and my own thoughts. I kicked at the ground, sending a rock into the air. I marched along, scowling, kicking the rocks that lay by my feet and keeping my thoughts inside of me.

After a long days march, we reached our evening resting place. Uncle Peter rode up to us. His face was stern. Yet, there was a relief in my heart when I saw him. While I understood his desire to ride away, deep inside of me there was a fear that he might disappear forever. Knowing this was not the truth made me feel better about life.

We sat down and silently ate. After we cleaned up from the meal, Father cuddled Bitsy tenderly until she fell asleep in his arms. He then tucked her gently into her bed and rejoined us at the campfire. We sat around and looked at one another in silence before he spoke.

"I know how upset everyone is. Last night, we all lost a great friend and we have not had the luxury of a proper mourning time. The trail is cruel in the way it demands that we leave behind our loved ones without a proper farewell. Yet, we all know that while we left her body behind us, the part of Mary we all loved is living in heaven today and in each of our hearts. As painful as our loss is and as many tears as we may all shed in the days ahead, we need to make a decision. Either we decide to continue forward toward the home of Mary's dreams as a family or we decide that we splinter apart like a dry log chopped by a sharp axe. There is no doubt what she would have wanted us to do, but ultimately, it is a decision we all need to make inside of us. If we want to make this a journey that would please her and our Lord, then, we will need to work together.

"The easiest thing for me to do would be to give all of your mother's jobs to Sarah and I know that she would do her best and would do it cheerfully. I could say it is women's work and try to make it sound natural. It just is not true, though. Sarah can never replace your mother and it is unfair to both her and us to pretend that she would. We are all going to work on all of the tasks. One day, I will cook; Jeremiah will take care of the animals, Sarah will take care of the clothes; and Peter will clean the dishes and put the supplies away. Then, we will rotate these tasks so no one needs to become too tired of a single chore. The Bible teaches us that many hands make light work and we are going to live this Scripture for the rest of the journey."

We all nodded at this thought. I did have one urgent question: "Are you sure you want me to cook? Why don't I take care of the animals on the day Miss Spencer would do that and she can cook."

Uncle Peter laughed aloud and said, "That is the best idea I have heard all day. I am a brave man; I am fierce in battle with man or beast. I have faced a bear and caused him to retreat in terror. Yet, the thought of eating an eleven-year-old boys' cooking makes me want to faint with fear."

We all laughed aloud and agreed. With this, our serious meeting was over. The moon began to illuminate the sagebrush-cluttered landscape; in the distance, I heard the solitary cries of the coyotes as they sought their next meal. Uncle Peter pulled out his guitar and strummed it lightly, playing tunes gently and softly until we all decided it was time to move to our beds and fall into a restless, sad slumber. I felt angry. Angry at life and angry at God for taking my mother. I knew, though, that I could not simply lie down and die. I needed to keep moving forward towards the goal.

For the next few days, we traveled across the arid land with the sagebrush and the dust. The July sun beat down on us and caused the sweat to pour off our bodies, soaking our shirts and weakening our legs and our spirits. When I looked into the southern and southwestern skies, I saw rugged mountains extending their rough, uneven peaks into the heavens. At their top, I saw snow covering them even in the heat of July. It lifted my spirits to know that even though I was struggling on the hot plains, there was a place nearby where the cool of winter moisture survived. If only we could be magically transported to the refreshing mountain peaks, play in the snowfields and refresh ourselves, cooling our bodies and our spirits. Deep inside, though, I knew the mountains were far off and even if we could detour to them, the mountaintops stood far above our ability to climb.

Finally, we reached the banks of the Black's Fork of the Green River. We set up camp along its banks and when I released the oxen to drink from the cool waters, I jumped into the river with them, splashing the cool water on my sweaty body, feeling the instant relief that came from the refreshing water. I splashed the oxen. They looked at me with questioning, but appreciative eyes. I knew somehow that if they had a way of maneuvering their hooves they would splash back but for now they would simply low at me and enjoy the cool spray of water from the running stream.

The next day we traveled to Fort Bridger. Captain Watkins had told us that we would rest for one day at the fort. This would be a welcome rest for all of us since the heat of the open desert was slowly sucking the life out of all of us, man and beast alike.

Arriving at the fort, we were surprised. Unlike the wasteland of our recent travels, the fort stood in the middle of a cool oasis of green trees and high grass. For a minute, I could have closed my eyes and imagined myself back on the banks of my beloved Stones River, feeling the cool, rushing water on my legs and enjoying the shade of the trees protecting my head from the hot summer sun. The fort, though, brought me back to the reality of the present.

Fort Bridger was actually two wooden stockades surrounding a tradesman's village of services for the western traveler. There was a commissary and blacksmith shop. The buildings were crude, wooden structures covered with roofs of sod and dirt. Surrounding the fort were dozens of tipis of the natives who wished to trade at the fort and with the travelers who reached the fort. It was not the architecture or the potential trading partners that brought us to this place. Rather, it was the prospect of resupply that made this such an important outpost. Uncle Peter told me Jim Bridger and his partner, Louis Vasquez, set up this trading post because they knew at this place on the journey, the travelers would have money but need refurbishing. This exchange would make the partners wealthy, while allowing the western travelers to meet their goal of continuing, well supplied, to their new homes.

Once we cared for the oxen, Uncle Peter and I left the wagon and headed into the fort. There, sitting on the porch of the wooden store, a tall man with hard, sun-soaked skin and a grizzled beard sat speaking to a number of listening travelers.

"One time when I was out alone in the desert, I was approached by a full tribe of Cheyenne. There had to be at least one hundred of them as I was just trying to find a new trail. I knew, at that time, that the Cheyenne were the fiercest fighters around and at that time, they hated all white men. I tried to move away from them, walking at first. While I tried to appear to be harmless, I noticed that all of the braves were following me. Therefore, I decided I needed to move more quickly. As I moved quicker, though, they also moved faster. Finally, I ran as fast as I could and the entire tribe chased me.

"I ran for miles faster than I knew I could. All these braves, though, chased after me and I was unable to lose them in the open land. So, I ran toward a canyon, hoping that I could hide and make them lose interest in me. I turned one way and another in the canyon until I found myself at the end of a box canyon. The walls were thirty feet high and there was no way to climb out of there. I wanted to retrace my steps but the Cheyenne were too close for me to escape them. So, I backed up all the way to the end of the wall and looked around at all the one hundred angry Cheyenne braves covered by war paint who surrounded me."

Then the speaker stopped talking. We waited for him to continue for the longest time. Finally, one voice called out from the crowd: "What happened then, Mr. Bridger?"

Jim Bridger smiled, looked around at us, and simply said, "Why they killed me of course." Then, he laughed, a hard, hearty laugh that involved his whole body, complete with a slapping of his knee. We laughed out loud realizing that a master storyteller had tricked us greenhorns. Finally, he looked at us and said, "Come on in and shop, folks. We have everything you need for the rest of your journey." He moved away from his audience and we all dispersed, heading in different directions depending on what we needed.

Uncle Peter and I followed him. Uncle Peter spoke: "Old Gabe, are you still telling that story to scared audiences?"

Jim Bridger turned around and stared at him. Then, in a moment, recognition replaced his confusion and he broke into a huge smile. "Tenderfoot Pete? How long has it been, six or seven years? We have not seen each other since Fort Hall. What brings you here?"

Uncle Peter smiled at the older man. "I am moving my brother and his family out west and I am finally going to settle down and live like a gentleman farmer. I figure all the great places have already been discovered by you, so I might as well find a wife and raise some children. Gabe, I would like you to meet my nephew, Jeremiah. He is turning into quite a man. We went buffalo hunting awhile back and he rode his horse into a herd and killed a buffalo just like Kit Carson used to do."

Jim Bridger laughed and slapped me on my back. "Jeremiah, you are practically a mountain man. You are much younger than I was when I killed my first buffalo. If you do what your uncle tells you to do, you will be just fine out here. Your uncle was green when I first met him, but he worked hard and learned how to survive in the wilderness. I have to admit, though, of all the young explorers I met he is the one who I figured would never settle down. He has always had the desire to see new lands and have new adventures. Peter, why don't you bring the family around for supper tomorrow evening? We can tell each other tall tales of the old days and have a good laugh."

Uncle Peter readily agreed. We said our farewells and moved back to the wagon where we told the family the story of our conversation.

The next day was full of activity. For the first time since we had left St. Joseph we needed to battle with the oxen to shoe them. Unlike the horses I had seen shod in Tennessee, an ox could not stand on its own with just three legs, so when one person was shoeing the ox another person needed to balance the ox so it would not fall down. An ox that lies down is in real danger of having one of its stomachs crush its other stomach. All day, we worked carefully with our oxen. As much as I wanted to go sit and listen to more stories of Jim Bridger, I knew that my obligations to my family compelled me to stay and wrestle with the oxen who had worked so hard to move our family so far west. We cared for them because ignoring their shoes could lead to our being stranded on the road with footsore oxen.

At suppertime, Father gathered the family and we hurried back to Jim Bridger's cabin. There, we found Jim and his Shoshone wife. She was an attractive woman who was a true princess, being the daughter of a chief. She had beautiful black hair that hung straight over her shoulders. Jim Bridger sat on the front porch rocking in his rocking chair while she worked on the evening meal. The hospitality of this family made us feel welcome and civilized after endless meals eaten outside in the dust and the bugs. Mrs. Bridger played with Bitsy, who particularly enjoyed having a roof over her head for supper.

The food tasted better than any of our standard camp fare of the last days and we ate like there would be no food tomorrow. Finally, when we had devoured all of the available food, we backed our chairs away from the table. Mr. Bridger lit his pipe, blew the smoke into the air above his head, and sighed the contented sigh of a man whose stomach is filled with good food.

I looked at him. Curiosity overcame me and I was the one who broke the silence. "Mr. Bridger", I asked, "you mentioned today that I was younger than you were when you killed your first buffalo. When did you come out west?"

Jim Bridger fixed me with his eyes. He looked at me like an equal, not like a nosy child and that made me feel special. "Jeremiah", he said with a friendly smile, "if you have time, I would love to tell you that story. First of all, though, I want to hear your story about the buffalo."

When I realized that there would be no story from him until I told mine, I shyly began to tell the story of our buffalo hunt. I mentioned how I rode into the herd, steering the horse with my legs while I leaned over and shot the buffalo. As I became more comfortable telling it I became more excited and started to describe the hunt in more detail. Finally, when the story was over, I noticed that all of the people surrounding me were listening intensely.

Jim Bridger leaned back in his chair. "Jeremiah, you have a future as a storyteller. That was told like the best of any mountain man. Let me tell you the story of when I first came out here. I was a seventeen-year-old boy living with my folks in Missouri. One day, I saw an advertisement in a newspaper posted by a great man, General William Ashley, asking for one hundred enterprising young men to ascend the Missouri River to its source and work there for two or three years. Since my life on the farm lacked the excitement I desired, I joined his group of adventurers and I have never regretted it for a minute. This group had some of the greatest men I have ever met. Jim Beckwourth, Tom Fitzpatric, William Sublette and the best of us all, Jedediah Smith. We joined and had some of the greatest adventures. I was the youngest of that group but I was determined that I would become as good as any of those men.

"Old Jedediah Smith, he's dead now at the hands of the Comanche. He was the man who gave me my name Old Gabe. Jedediah was a religious man and he used to read the Bible sitting around the campfire. One day, he was listening to me tell some story, as is my habit, and he thought I sounded just like the angel Gabriel himself spreading the word of God. He called me Old Gabe and that name has stuck with me ever since.

"Anyway, one time, when we were up north around Yellowstone, one of our men, Hugh Glass, stumbled between a grizzly bear and its cub. Nothing is meaner than a mother bear who thinks you are threatening her cub. This bear attacked Hugh and he could not defend himself. He was mauled so horribly that by the time that bear was done with him, it would not be clear if you did not know better that he was a man and that he was still alive. General Ashley looked at Hugh and decided if he was not dead he would be dead soon. So, General Ashley asked for volunteers to stay with him until he was dead.

"Hugh was a good man. He had been a sailor when he was younger and decided to try his hand going west. Some men thought he was a pirate but no one really knew for sure. I felt very sorry for him because he had not really intended to do anything wrong and decided that I would wait with him until he died. John Fitzgerald and I stayed behind to bury poor Hugh. The only problem we had was that Hugh just would not die. We waited with him one day, then two days, and onto a week and he kept hanging on more dead than alive.

"Finally, one day, he would not wake up and we thought he was surely about to die. We had seen signs that we were in Arikaree Indian nation with their hostile braves all around. Much to my shame, we thought we were about to be attacked and killed, so we wrapped him up in his robe and laid him beside the almost finished grave and we took off to rejoin the main group with General Ashley.

"Well, the amazing part of this story is that Hugh Glass just would not die. He woke up and found himself alone and he started to crawl on his hands and knees. He lay his back over a rotten log and let the maggots eat his flesh to keep himself from becoming infected. He crawled or dragged himself over the roughest terrain you can imagine for two hundred miles thinking all the time how he was going to kill John Fitzgerald and me when he finally caught up with us.

"He made it to Fort Kiowa, the nearest trading post. The people there could not believe he made it. He rested that winter and let his body heal. Once he was healthy, he decided to kill John and me. He tracked down John and found out that John was in the army. To kill him would mean that the army would surely hang him, so he decided to leave John alone and take his revenge on me. He finally caught up with me and he could have killed me easily but for some reason he looked at me and realized that I was still as much a boy as I am a man and he forgave me. I have been around people who claim to be Christian all of my life and I have never seen more forgiveness than I did with that man, who had every reason in the world to strike me dead."

I sat in absolute wonder of this man who could tell stories better than anyone I had ever met. I had not realized so much of the evening had passed. I looked over and Bitsy had fallen sound asleep on Miss Spencer's lap. Father stood up and told us we needed to head back to the wagon and put Bitsy to bed. I thanked Mr. Bridger for the dinner and the stories and reluctantly turned and walked back to our wagon. I fell asleep that evening dreaming of crawling over the dry land for hundreds of miles and was thankful that my feet would carry me that distance.

I awoke the next morning to the smell of bacon frying over the fire. We gathered the oxen and started to move out from the green campsite back into our surrounding desert. As we started to head north for the trail, I was aware of a horse riding alongside our train. I glanced to the side and to my surprise, I saw our host, Jim Bridger, riding alongside. He waved for us to stop something we did with great effort. He dismounted, handed the reins of his horse to Uncle Peter, and walked over to me.

"Young Mr. Symons, I needed to see you before you left on the rest of the journey. I knew that any relative of Tenderfoot Pete

WEST TO THE SUN

would turn into a mountain man, but you have moved into our ranks younger than most. Before you left and headed for the rest of your journey, I wanted to give you a gift. Here, young buffalo slayer, is a strand of grizzly bear teeth that I want you to wear around your neck. It will bring you neither good luck, nor bad luck, but it will let you know that I regard you as a true comrade and mountain man. Now, take care of that precious sister of yours."

With these words, he waved at my uncle, ran his hand through Bitsy's hair, mounted his horse, and rode back to the fort. I looked after him, a great man who thought I belonged to the men I admired so much. I smiled, looked west and began my march with an additional lightness in my step.

CHAPTER 16

CLOVER CREEK

Marching from Fort Bridger, we reached the Muddy River. Hearing the name of the river made us hold the river in anticipatory contempt, yet, when we arrived at its banks, we saw not a mud hole but instead a clean flowing river, which refreshed us greatly from our morning travel. Names were misleading. We drank the cool water, splashed it over our heads, and then proceeded beyond the banks of the river and urged our newly shod oxen to move up the hill surrounding the river.

As we climbed the hills, it struck me how dry the land looked. The sagebrush grew here and sustained the antelopes that bounced along the prairie, but this brush would not sustain people for long. Uncle Peter grabbed his rifle and went hunting, desperate to supplement our diet. Our hearts sagged, though, when he returned to us near the end of the day, unsuccessful in his hunt. Defeated, we ate our evening bacon. I resolved silently that once we reached Oregon, no strip of bacon would ever voluntarily cross my lips.

The next morning, we loaded the wagons and started our dusty march. In this dry land, even if the wind did not whip the dirt onto us, dirt fastened to us, stirred by the feet of the walking people and the working oxen. Every opportunity we had on the trail, we tried to wash the clothes but it was impossible in this environment of constant dust to feel truly clean.

At noon, I saw a clear pool of water that I knew would be our resting place. I was not alone in this assumption, for the lead wagons started steering themselves in the direction of the water, led by the prospect of refreshment for man and beast at the time of the noonday heat. Sensing this end to our labor for the morning, I felt relaxed.

Suddenly, Captain Watkins rode to the front of the wagons yelling for the train to keep moving. Inside, I felt upset, as I knew that for no good reason, Captain Watkins was deciding to extend our struggles for the morning. My eyes flashed an angry look his direction. If he were walking on sore feet then he would not extend our journey. Then, I could hear what he was telling our wagons. "The water is bad at this place. It is alkaline. You can tell by the white powder surrounding it. If you drink this water, you will become very sick. More important, the oxen, if they drink this water, could die. Come along, we must break at a different location."

Nature had cruelly deceived us. Sadly, we left this false paradise. We urged our animals forward, away from the poisoned water. While I was disappointed at making another dry camp for the midday break, it was certainly better for all of us, man and oxen alike, to be dry and alive than to take our fill of soothing poison.

These were hard days. The late July sun beat down on us and caused sweat to pour off our bodies. Some of the rivers we passed in the preceding month had less water than our bodies during these days. The lack of fresh meat caused mealtime to become as much of a chore as the rest of our days labor. Bacon, bread, and beans; beans, bread and bacon caused our stomachs to long for some change of any type. We tried to supplement our diet with the edible plants that Miss Spencer identified along the way, but the taste of yucca, while providing variety, did not cause any of us to rejoice come mealtime. Uncle Peter reassured us that there were people who had it much worse than we did. Robert Stuart's Astorian party was delayed in the mountain snow and ate tree bark and shoe leather for sustenance; while this did not change my vow to live without bacon once I reached Oregon, it did cause me to be somewhat grateful that I had sufficient bacon for the day.

Finally, when we thought the world had turned into a place that consisted solely of shades of tan and gray, we came into the blissfully green Bear River Valley. This river watered a basin surrounded by the Bear Mountains, which promised the opportunity for fresh food. Berries were abundant; the juicy flavor of the currants never tasted better than to the train whose life had been solely reliant on bacon, beans, and bread since Fort Bridger. Fish, while not eager to sample our bait, at least occasionally graced our menu.

The first evening we entered into this sweet basin, Miss Spencer sent the children of our group out on a hunt for the black currants that grew so plentifully. Eagerly, we attacked this chore, since we knew that for every berry that made its way back to the wagon, we would devour three. When we could hold no more of the berries in either our pails or our stomachs, we returned our treasure to the waiting Miss Spencer. There, she looked at our berry-stained teeth and smiled, as she emptied all of the remaining fruit into a bowl. Taking the berries, she ground them into a pulp, strained the juice into a separate container, and poured milk, eggs and flour into the bowl with the currant pulp. Carefully, she mixed these items together and then cooked them slowly over the fire. The scent of the concoction kept us close to the fire, as if she were preparing the nectar of the gods and if we failed to keep close, we would miss the life-altering moment.

When we could not contain our excitement over a treat any longer, Miss Spencer called us together. There, she carefully spooned out the precious pudding to the waiting people. While the portion per person was small, the pleasure this unexpected sweet caused lingered in our minds and stomachs long after the last morsel passed our lips. When I lay down under my wagon, my stomach was happy and sleep came quickly.

This sleep did not last long. Mr. Elliott woke the camp relatively early in the night with loud screams that sent tremors down our spines. Scurrying from our beds, we all ran to find the problem. Immediately, we saw the difficulty. While Mr. Elliott was lying in his tent for the evening, a rattlesnake had joined him and bit him twice in the leg before Mr. Elliott and family were able to escape the creature. Quickly, Dr. Woods sprang into action. He propped Mr. Elliott against a wagon wheel. Then, he seized a knife and slit a parallel cut into his leg. With a degree of urgency that I had rarely seen from the good doctor, he started to suck on Mr. Elliott's leg. With each suck, he would take blood, mixed with the venom, into his own mouth and spit it on the ground. Finally, Dr. Woods stopped sucking on the leg.

The doctor turned to the concerned Mrs. Elliott and spoke in a quiet, reassuring tone. "Give our good banker all the fluids he can drink. Let him sleep in the wagon and keep his body raised above his leg. He has a very good chance of surviving."

Turning to the rest of us, he cautioned us: "Be careful where you pitch your tent. We have had enough excitement for this journey with snakes. We do not want anyone else to fall victim to these western menaces."

I slept the remainder of the evening lightly, half attempting to sleep and half imagining that every noise created by the wind was a snake seeking to seize onto my leg. When morning finally arrived, we awoke, relieved to find that Mr. Elliott, while not healthy, did not appear to be on a path towards imminent death.

The next day we arrived at the Thomas Fork of the Bear River. Captain Watkins warned us that this river, while not the most imposing of our trip, was one of the most dangerous we would cross. Captain Watkins suggested an unusual means of crossing this river. We would remove our wagon wheels, caulk our wagons, and convert them from prairie schooners crossing the land into water schooners that would float across the river. Our livestock needed to swim across the river, guided by men on horseback.

We spent most of the morning in preparation for the crossing. We carefully applied the sealant to our wagons, moved them to the banks of the river, and removed the wheels. Finally, we pushed our newly formed boats into the water. We held our breath as the boats sank into the water and then righted themselves and began to float slowly on the water. We carefully steered them across to the other side of the river. There, we reattached the wheels and converted them back into wagons.

While this crossing was enough adventure for the day, our rejoicing at the safe crossing ended when we focused on what awaited us on the other side of the river. Stretching in front of us was a steep, high hill demanding more from us than any other hill we had passed thus far on the journey. When I asked its name, Uncle Peter simply smiled and said that the trappers had run out of good names and just called this the Big Hill. He confirmed my fears when he told me that this was the hill with the largest incline since we had left Missouri. I felt my shoulders slump, as I knew the hard work we all would face in climbing this hill.

Uncle Peter laughed as he saw my discouraged form. "Come on, Jeremy," he called, "last one to Peg Leg Smith's store at the top of the hill needs to buy candy for the other one."

I did not know Peg Leg Smith. The competitive challenge had been issued and I was determined that I would not owe Uncle Peter the small price of a candy stick. I snapped the long whip in front of Bob and Todd and let them know that fresh grass awaited them at the top of the hill. With this encouragement, the strong muscles of the oxen strained to pull the wagon to the top of the hill. Each step required encouragement as the animals' thigh muscles rippled against their skin as they tried to move up the incline. Step after step they moved the entire hot afternoon, pulling our belongings up the entire length of the hill. Finally, as the sun was starting its decline we reached the top and moved off the trail to camp for the evening.

While the struggle of the journey shoved the thoughts of my wager from my immediate thoughts, once I reached the top, I looked into the distance and saw a small trading post. Guessing that I would find Peg Leg Smith there, I unhitched our oxen, started to whistle a casual tune, and then walked, slowly at first, in the direction of the building. Then, as I felt I had placed enough distance between the wagon train and myself so that I would not be noticed, I started to walk more quickly and then broke into a run. As I moved towards the shack, I heard the unmistakable sound of horses' hooves galloping my direction.

"I'm coming for you, Jeremiah Symons," yelled Uncle Peter. "You are going to owe me the candy. You cannot outrun my horse and me."

These words moved more urgency to my feet. I ran harder and yet could almost feel the breath of Uncle Peter's panting horse on the back of my neck. Faster I ran. Closer the horse came until we were running side by side in our race for the porch of the trading post. Finally, at the last second, I pulled ahead and fell, half panting and totally out of energy, onto the front porch. I heard Uncle Peter laugh as he pulled his horse to a stop and hopped off the animal.

"You won this time but wait until the next race," my uncle said, extending his right hand to pull me to my feet while slapping me on the back with his other hand.

Laughing, we burst into the trading post, walking to the sales counter. "I owe this boy some candy. He won our race fair and square."

Hobbling over to the counter was a man who had to be Peg Leg Smith. The man had one good leg and a wooden leg that he used with amazing grace. He hopped up on to a stool, thumped his wooden leg and laughed: "I am not sure either one of you could beat me in my youth, but right now I think you could give me a good race." Grasping a handful of peppermint candy sticks, he handed them to me and accepted the payment from my uncle.

Then, as we were about to leave, he noticed the necklace of grizzly teeth that hung loosely around my neck. "Why do you have bear teeth around your neck," he inquired.

"These are a gift from my good friend Jim Bridger," I responded. Mr. Bridger's easy hospitality had made me feel like I was his close companion even though I had only spent one evening in his presence. I ran my fingers over the uneven bear teeth and smiled at the memory.

Peg Leg laughed. "Anyone who calls Jim Bridger a friend is welcome in this store. He is a good man and one of the best of the mountain men." Then, massaging his leg, he looked at us and continued: "I guess you are kind of curious to hear about how I went from being Thomas Smith to Peg Leg Smith."

I eagerly nodded and he began his story. "One year, when I was new to the west, I was traveling with two other mountain men, trying to reach Oregon. We started our travels at the wrong time of the year. When we reached the Wind River Mountains, a late autumn snowstorm trapped us. We were convinced we would not make it much further that year and we needed to find shelter.

"We made camp and soon found a group of Blackfeet natives who helped us and treated us like we were brothers. They shared their food and their understanding and helped us survive the winter when they had no reason to do so other than the kindness in their hearts.

"One day, we found that our new hosts were at war with the Crow tribe. Since the Blackfeet had been so kind to us, we felt we had no choice but join them in their war party. Near the headwaters of the Platte River, we met a much larger party of Crows. While we knew the battle was dangerous, we attacked. We fought all day with the Crows and when the battle was over, my two friends were dead and I had been badly wounded in the knee.

"The Blackfeet tried their best to cure my leg. They chanted all sorts of incantations and used all of their herbal medicines, but the leg became infected. I knew there was only one way for me to live. I told them to take a bullet mold and make it red-hot. Then, I took a leather strap between my teeth, and with my sharp hunter's knife, sawed my leg off above the infected wound. I slapped the red-hot bullet mold onto my artery to stop the bleeding. I passed out from the pain, but when I awoke I knew that I would live.

"I fashioned a good wooden leg out of the trees available in the area. My Blackfeet brethren were impressed with my bravery; they gave me one of their women to be my wife. For the last twenty years,

I have lived part of each year with these people. I miss my old leg, but I have learned that if you concentrate and make adjustments, you can do anything, even walk around and ride a horse with one leg. It's only a disability if you let it become one."

I wanted to stay and hear more of this man's life, but more customers came into the store. Uncle Peter and I returned to our wagon in some wonderment over the courage of a man who could saw his own leg off to preserve his life.

The next morning we saw that as hard as the trip up Big Hill had been, the descent would be more difficult. The steepness of the hill required us to lash ropes to trees and slowly let the wagon down, inch by inch, foot by foot, with all of us straining on ropes to keep the wagons from crashing down the hill. It took all of the strength of the party to keep the wagons from tipping over and sending all of their earthly possessions skipping below to level ground.

Once we reached the bottom of the Big Hill, Senator Richardson decreed that this was enough work for the day and we would camp at Clover Creek, the settlement at the bottom of our latest obstacle. Gladly, we took the rest of the day to tend to our clothing, inspect our wagon wheels, and seek fresh fish and game for the meal of the day.

Early the next morning, Uncle Peter shook me awake. He whispered, "My horse is missing."

Uncle Peter and I stumbled out from under our wagon and found our way to Captain Watkins. We explained the situation to him and he readily agreed to provide the two of us with horses to follow the thief. We told him to push forward with the wagon train and we would return with the thief in order to face justice. Loaded with rifles, water, and hardtack, we proceeded out of the camp in the early morning gray light. Peter rode silently, seeking to keep his eyes on the trail. Each bent twig, disturbed branch, and overturned rock told his experienced eyes something I would have ignored. Finally, after riding for most of the morning, we approached a small stream lined with trees. Uncle Peter gestured that I needed to be quiet.

We dismounted, tied the horses to the low branches of the cottonwood trees, and slowly started to advance to a figure sleeping beside the brook next to Uncle Peter's horse. Uncle Peter gestured for me to seize his horse. Uncle Peter cocked his weapon and on silent feet strode over to where the man lay sleeping. As I seized the reins of the horse, Uncle Peter placed the barrel of his weapon squarely on the cheek of the sleeping man.

The sleeping man awoke from his nap. I was amazed as I saw that the sleeping man was our own Senator Richardson. Uncle Peter showed no sign of surprise. Instead, he told me to search the saddlebags hanging from the horse. I undid the saddlebags and pulled out a handful of paper money that was larger than any pile I had seen in my life. Uncle Peter nodded and said, "This is the money we all handed him to handle the remaining ferryboat crossings."

Roughly, he jerked Senator Richardson to his feet and tied his hands behind him. The senator started to protest, but Uncle Peter was in no mood to hear a speech. He pointed the gun at the senator and instructed him not to say a word and pushed the sizable man onto the horse. We rode back toward the trail with me following the senator and Uncle Peter leading the horse by firmly holding the bridle.

At noon, we reunited with the wagon train. The rest of our party knew that Senator Richardson was the culprit when they awoke and found his wagon empty. When Senator Richardson rode into their midst, the people reacted with rage. The realization that all of the money had accompanied Senator Richardson and his stolen horse caused people to spend the morning dreaming all types of punishment for the felon. Evidently, most of these punishments involved high branches and short ropes; mercy was not a Christian virtue in great abundance when our people thought of the ferryboat passage money our leader had embezzled.

When the senator arrived in the middle of our noontime corral, the men surged forward and pulled him off his horse. They shoved him down next to one of the wagons and made all manner of threats to him. Finally, Captain Watkins seized control of the situation and forced everyone to move away from the shaken senator. "We are not going to lynch this man. We are going to give him a fair trial and then we will decide on a reasonable punishment for him."

The men continued to grumble about ropes and necktie parties, but they listened to Captain Watkins. While the senator tried to come up with an excuse for his theft, the people were not inclined to listen to him. All of the evidence they needed was the money in the saddlebags of the stolen horse. Quickly, the question of guilt or innocence disappeared. In its place, the debate became one relating to the appropriate punishment for the criminal.

While there were people who still wanted to hang Senator Richardson, once people received their money from the saddlebags and started to discuss the concept of actually taking his life, there was reluctance. Back East, there were well-developed courts, open prisons, and a system of laws that people could rely upon. Here, we needed to make our own rules. After debating tar and feathers and other homemade punishments, we decided on something simple.

Dr. Woods, the most educated man in our midst, wrote a letter describing the senator's crimes. Then, we tied the thief to a tree along the side of the trail with the letter fastened to his shirt. We left him with a canteen filled with water. Perhaps someone would take him into a wagon train, but it would not be us. We knew that with his talents for empty speeches, he could convince someone to untie him; we also knew that with our letter no one would ever trust him with money again.

Our wagons moved forward. The senator yelled curses after us but slowly, the cries were lost in the distance and were drowned by the steady squeaks of the constantly turning wagon wheels.

CHAPTER 17

GOLD FEVER

Once we left behind the senator's shouts, we noticed the land around us. Oregon might be the ultimate goal, but could the Promised Land hundreds of miles further along this trail be more enticing than the lush valleys surrounding us?

We camped that evening under the trees beside a small stream and convened a meeting of the men. Captain Watkins began by pointing out the obvious changes in our train. We had started from St. Joseph with twenty-two wagons. After the refusal of Mrs. Parker to continue West, the wagons that had left us for the shortcut of the Greenwood Cutoff and the expulsion of Senator Richardson, we were reduced to fourteen wagons. Governing a wagon train became easier as it became smaller, but Captain Watkins wanted to avoid making decisions by committee.

Since our first two leaders had failed us, no one volunteered for control. Captain Watkins stared at all of us. "We have tried to act like we are the constitutional convention of these United States for too long. I am tired of elections." Staring at Father, our white-haired guide continued, "I am going to discuss what needs to happen from now on with Jedediah Symons. He will tell you what I am going to do. If you decide you want to follow me to Oregon, then you will listen to him. If you decide you know enough to reach Oregon without my guidance, then I wish you Godspeed and you can proceed at your own pace and at your own risk."

Father objected to this imposition of responsibility. Captain Watkins stared at him in a manner that let Father know this was a command and not a request. The men nodded their assent and started to stand and leave the meeting. Before we could leave, Josiah Braun, the father of little Amy Braun, who died from her injuries along the Platte River, stood and spoke:

"Friends. My wife, Elizabeth and I have made a decision. You may not know this but we are expecting a baby and the road is particularly difficult for her to endure. We are farm folk, not world travelers or great explorers. We will prosper wherever the land is rich and the soil is deep. We have looked at this valley and have decided that this is enough. We wish you all the best that God may provide, but tomorrow, when you move toward Oregon, I will start building a cabin by this creek."

This shocked us. We never thought anyone would voluntarily stop short of the goal. As a group, we attempted to change Mr. Braun's mind, but the look on his face told us that his decision was final.

The next morning when we left our camp, Mr. and Mrs. Braun waved at us and wished us well. We returned their wishes with equally positive remarks, while silently wondering whether we were foolish for proceeding or they were lacking in courage for staying. Perhaps neither or both sentiments were true.

Traveling along the trail, we noticed changes in the surrounding environment. A foul odor pervaded the land. Miss Spencer noticed the sour look on my face as I tried to block out the stench. She laughed. "These are sulfur springs, Jeremiah. They smell horrible.

Just plug your nose and walk."

The country surrounding this area amazed us with its wonderful sights. Water bubbled to the surface in a sickly red color, more like blood than water. Hot springs sprayed from the ground, squirting from the surface, surprising all of our senses. Finally, we discovered clearer springs of bubbling water.

Captain Watkins stopped our small band. Addressing the children of the wagon train, he told us, "Go gather as many raspberries as you can find. If you resist the temptation to eat these berries, you will enjoy a treat that you will never forget."

With these words of encouragement, we ran with our pails to find as many of the raspberries growing along the streams of water coursing by the trail. While we may not have fully obeyed his command to carry and not eat the raspberries, we soon returned with ample fruit. Gathering the fruit, Captain Watkins instructed the women of the train to grind the berries and capture all of the juice. While the women performed this task, the men dipped buckets in the soda springs.

Captain Watkins poured the fresh juice into the buckets of soda water and mixed them with a healthy dose of sugar. Stirring the concoction, he labored as if he were a chef cooking a world-famous prized dish from a recipe with numerous intricate steps and secret ingredients. Finally, when satisfied with the drink, he summoned the rest of the wagon train to his creation. There, he poured the red liquid into our cups. We timidly sipped at the strange drink, before realizing that this was a unique treat. The sweetness of the drink caused us to want to gulp the liquid down, while the bubbles from the water made us exercise caution in the drink. In my entire life, I had never drunk anything like the bubbly mixture Captain Watkins prepared for us. It was truly a sad moment when we realized that all of this raspberry soda was gone.

Pushing west from the soda springs, we noticed that the soil had changed into a black, rocky substance. Father observed that this was lava soil, deposited hundreds of years ago when neighboring volcanoes had exploded, depositing the boiling liquid for miles. The wonders of this area of the country increased with each turn of the wagon wheel.

Marching through these lava fields, one day we saw in the distance a white glistening structure. The sun beat down on it and reflected the light from its walls to us. Captain Watkins urged us forward toward the structure. "Hurry, lads," he called. "We will camp at Fort Hall tonight."

Obediently, we drove forward towards the glistening fort. As I marched, Uncle Peter told me the story of this facility, which rivaled Fort Laramie in its adobe construction.

"In 1832, Nathaniel Wyeth decided he could make a fortune in the west. He brought mountains of trading goods and descended on the trappers' annual rendezvous. The men who had spent all year in the mountains would surely buy his goods for the prices he wanted. Using the proceeds of these goods, he would travel on the Columbia River to the Pacific Ocean, build a fishery, and make a fortune shipping salmon to the Sandwich Islands far in the ocean.

"This plan failed. When he arrived at the rendezvous, no one bought his goods. Left with no money, Wyeth decided that he could still prosper if he built a permanent fort with a store. He built Fort Hall and started to trade. Shortly after, his dream of shipping fish to far islands died and he decided to leave. He sold his fort to the British and departed.

"The British ran this fort for years. Once settlers started to travel west, the British would always convince them that the land west of Fort Hall was so rugged that they could not travel with their wagons. Each year, they would park the prior year's wagons alongside Fort Hall and use them as silent testaments that no wagon could travel along the trail from here.

"This changed when Marcus and Narcissa Whitman, the missionaries to the natives, wrote letters East convincing people that while the trail was rugged, people could bring wagons to the Willamette Valley. Once word reached the East that men and women could bundle their possessions into wagons and travel all of the way to the lush lands of Oregon, people became more willing to make the journey than when they were forced to unload everything and place them on the backs of mules to travel the last hundreds of miles.

"Fort Hall became the last really large trading post on the trail. The Union Jack announces that the fort is British, although most of the people traveling here are Americans. For years, there was always competition between the British and the Americans over the beaver trade, but now that people do not want beaver hats, this competition has become far more peaceful."

We continued to march towards the fort. As the sun sank into the horizon, we reached the plains surrounding the fort and started our fires for the evening. Captain Watkins and Father sat on a stone near our wagon and discussed their plans for the next day. They nodded their heads and Father made an announcement to the people:

"We have been working very hard since Fort Bridger. The wagons need attention and the animals need rest. We will spend tomorrow at the fort and then we will start on the trail again. Captain Watkins tells me that the trail just west of here is very rugged. Make sure that you tend to your equipment and animals. Captain Watkins and my brother are heading out tomorrow morning to find some game for us and we will have a feast tomorrow night to celebrate our arrival this far.

While I wanted to go hunting with Uncle Peter, I was also relieved when I learned that I would spend the next day tending to our animals and exploring the fort. When the sun first peeked above the horizon, I opened my eyes to see Uncle Peter mount his horse, rifle in hand. Miss Spencer reached up to him, patted his hand, and handed him a package of hardtack and bacon. Then, she waved, as they rode out of our camp with Captain Watkins in search of fresh game for the bacon-weary travelers.

I spent the morning checking the harnesses and oxen yokes for tiny flaws that could prove dangerous. When we were convinced that this essential equipment was still in good condition, we inspected the oxen shoes to ensure they also showed no signs of unusual wear. Finally, when all of our work was properly finished, Father led Miss Spencer, Bitsy and me into the fort. Captain Watkins warned our entire wagon train that only emergency needs should be bought at the fort since the prices for supplies were so high. Still, we wanted to go into the fort and see people from the different wagon trains.

In the middle of the fort, a crowd surrounded a man making an impassioned speech to a group of spectators. We stopped and joined the group to listen to him. He was a smallish man with gray whiskers and he spoke in an excited manner that demanded our attention.

"I tell you, I have seen it with my own eyes. I have come back from California and am heading back East to gather my brothers and have all of us will become rich with gold. They are pulling gold nuggets out of streams in California with so little work that a man can wake up in the morning, start his breakfast fire, and put on the coffee. Then that man can pan for gold and by the time the coffee is fully brewed he will have gathered enough gold to let him live like a king for the remainder of his life."

"I have heard of a man who has developed a lotion that lets gold dust stick to the skin. I am told there are people who spread this lotion over their bodies and roll down hills. By the time they reach the bottom of the hill, enough gold dust has stuck to them to let them stop working for the rest of their life."

People began to murmur their disbelief. Some stories sound too impressive to be true. The speaker, though, shook his head at the doubters.

"I know there are those of you who do not believe me. I have seen the gold, though, and I can tell you that anyone who heads to California will become rich beyond their wildest dreams. Some of you may wish to continue to Oregon. I applaud your willingness to work hard and barely make a living. For you, continue towards your goal. If you want to become rich for yourselves and your families, you need to abandon Oregon and head to California."

The crowd buzzed with excitement. I saw a number of the people from our wagon train approach the speaker and continue the discussion after we left. We wandered through the fort, observing the people and listening to the conversations between strangers. Thinking about the conversation about California riches, I knew, deep down, that while easy riches would appeal to some individuals, they would not interest a man like Father who believed there was virtue in the act of hard work without concerns as to whether it led to extensive riches.

After spending the afternoon engaged in wandering through the fort, we returned to our wagons to find Captain Watkins and Uncle Peter roasting two large mule deer over a fire. Uncle Peter smiled at me and said "Venison for supper tonight. Of course, if you would prefer to dine on bacon, we can cook it for you."

I shook my head violently at this thought. I knew that no meal would taste worse than another meal of fried bacon and beans.

To work off the feast, the boys organized jumping contests. We had found a huge, bloated oxen belly that had been lying at the side of the camp. The boys shouted challenges and we finally agreed that we would use the belly as a target over which we would leap.

For a while, the jumping was uneventful. Then, Josiah Torrance, eager to regain his standing with Emily and Allison Elliott which had been damaged in his unsuccessful war over buffalo chips, announced that we little children did not impress him with our abilities. He had won many contests of athletic skill back in Ohio and he would show us his athletic abilities.

He stood back a long way from the target and began to sprint towards the belly. He launched his body forward in a leap, soaring through the air and stretching forward. Then, the unthinkable happened. He landed, short of the target, stumbled and fell to the ground. When he stood up, instead of a boy's face, the bloated belly covered his head. Somehow, he had managed to shove his whole head into the bloated belly.

The group was stunned at the sight. The Elliott girls turned away, embarrassed that their hero had fallen short in his efforts. He ran in circles, screaming into his head covering. We heard his muffled screams continue until his younger brother managed to stop his running and pull the stomach off his brother's head. Josiah ran toward a bucket of water and dumped it onto his head to remove from his face the traces of the oxen stomach. Laughter followed him, with people crying and falling on the ground from the howls directed at the young braggart.

Shortly after this episode, I crawled into my bed under the wagon to the sounds of Mr. O'Donnell and Uncle Peter playing camp songs. I snuggled myself deep into my buffalo robe and fell asleep.

Leaving Fort Hall, we traveled alongside our new companion, the Snake River. The Snake River was significantly different from our previous watery companions. While the Platte River flowed cautiously on its journey to the sea in a manner that was deferential to rock barriers, the Snake made it clear that it respected no such obstacles. Instead of altering its path to skirt the stony cliffs and boundaries, the Snake fought its way through and over the lava rocks. This created steep canyons that made the Snake less accessible than the Platte or Sweetwater rivers to travelers on foot.

Just as the river appeared harder, so did the trail. It became tighter, rockier, and harder to travel. Each step became a strategic decision as we tried to wind our way over the hard, unfriendly trail. The second day from Fort Hall we passed a series of rapids where a torrent of water violently shot forward in the river and fell fifty feet. Uncle Peter told me that these were the American Falls, named after an early group of American trappers who tried to run their boats through the rapids and died. Stories of this type made me respect and fear the power of the Snake.

Finally, we reached the Raft River. Using rough rafts constructed from remnants of prior rafts and wood that lined the stream, we crossed the river, moving our wagons to the top of the bluff overlooking the little stream. We circled our wagons and penned the animals into the middle. Then, Captain Watkins and Father called for a meeting of all of the people of the wagon train.

When the people gathered outside of the wagon circle, Father started to speak. "Captain Watkins tells me that this is a very important place on the trail. I know some of you have dreamed of the gold of California. Others dream of the good land and mild climate of our Oregon destination. This is the final decision point. Those of you who wish to pursue golden dreams need to head south from this bluff, while the rest of us continue west to Oregon.

"It will make me sad to see friends of mine head away from me. I am continuing our journey to Oregon. For us, easy money is a dream that always extends beyond the rainbow and eludes capture. Our dream is good farmland and a life sustained for generations. I do not criticize those of you who want to head south towards California. I hope that your dreams come true and that gold is as easy to find as those storytellers spoke about at Fort Hall. We need to know, though, who is heading to California and who is moving to Oregon."

After Father finished speaking, the people looked at one another, deep in thought and waiting for someone to speak. Finally, Mr. O'Donnell spoke: "Jedediah, I do not deny that the gold fields have a special allure for me. The question we have been discussing as a group is what our good friend Captain Watkins is going to do. We need a guide and I am reluctant to take my family alone through the deserts on the way to my fortune without a good man to guide us."

Several people nodded at his comments. Eyes shifted to Captain Watkins. He finally spoke:

"I agreed to take this group west. I always planned to end this journey in Oregon. Not having a family to protect, I really do not care if I journey to Oregon or California. Whichever destination the majority of you choose, I will lead. For the remainder of you, I will provide you as much instruction as I can to whoever you select as a leader, but I need to fulfill my contract with as many of you as

I can. When you reach my age, keeping your word becomes more important than riches."

The people of our group spent the next hour discussing the merits of Oregon opposed to the riches of California. Finally, Father asked each family for their decision. We found that eight of our families wanted to head to California and only five wanted to continue to Oregon. I found out sadly the O'Donnell twins would leave me the following morning.

That evening was a sad time of farewells. We spent most of the evening retelling the stories of the adventures we lived on the trail. We laughed again at the battle of the buffalo chips that we won over the lazy Torrance brothers. That evening, I slept in the tent with my friends, although most of the night was spent talking and not sleeping.

When morning came, we crawled out of the tent. Captain Watkins came over to our family fire and sat down on the ground as we cooked breakfast. Father gave him a cup of coffee and the older man enjoyed the strong liquid, passing his mouth and warming his body. Finally, Uncle Peter spoke:

"Israel, this is farewell for now. You are a good man and I will miss your company. I was unfair in St. Joseph. I thought that I could not trust you. You have proven yourself a good man, a good comrade, and a good friend. I am so glad we have spent these months together."

Father murmured his assent to these sentiments. "God bless you, Israel Watkins."

Captain Watkins smiled. "I know that when I was younger I was a scoundrel. One day, I was lying in wait to rob a man who was carrying the payroll for a mining company. As I waited there among the trees by the side of the road, I stopped thinking about the robbery and started thinking about my mother, who always told me stories about Jesus when I was a young boy. These stories came back to me and I realized guiltily that my life would please neither my mother nor the Lord. I simply wanted to change my life. I waved my hand at the payroll guard and let him go on his business. From that point forward, I have always tried to live in a way pleasing to my mother and Jesus. I may not always succeed, but I try."

Father smiled. "Be safe, brother. We will see you again, if not in this life then when we all camp in Glory together."

We shook hands and said our good-byes. For the last time, we left the campsite, some of us heading west and others south. I said my final farewells to the O'Donnells and started to walk with the oxen. As the wagons started rolling in their separate directions, Uncle Peter jumped off his horse, handed his reins to me, and began playing his guitar as loudly as he could. From the southbound train, I heard the strains of a violin as I saw Mr. O'Donnell playing his violin. I realized that they were playing the same tune, the lilting notes of the jaunty Irish drinking song, "Garryowen." The song reverberated back and forth, bouncing off the surrounding hills. They played this song passionately and aggressively. They danced energetically as they played with legs kicked out violently from side to side. Finally, Mr. O'Donnell moved to the top of a high hill, waved his bow from side to side over his head in salute, turned and was gone.

CHAPTER 18
THREE ISLANDS CROSSING

Our small wagon train continued along the canyons surrounding the Snake River. An air of sadness accompanied our trek as we realized that the friends we had made over the course of the last months had departed from our life, perhaps forever. Finally, at Uncle Peter's direction, we stopped for lunch and turned the oxen loose to find good forage. Father looked at the small group of people remaining and summoned all of us together for a meeting.

There were only five wagons remaining in our group. The small circle formed by the wagons was pathetic compared to how large the corral had been when we left St. Joseph with more than twenty wagons. I looked around the circle at the remaining people: Major Smith and his wife, the Torrance family with their obnoxious boys, the banker Mr. Elliott with his silent wife and silly daughters, kindly Doctor Woods and his family, and us. We would continue forward, hundreds of miles over desert, mountains, and rivers with these few companions. Looking at them made me feel lonely again for the people I had left behind in Tennessee and the people who had started on the trail who would not travel with me again.

WEST TO THE SUN

Father spoke. "We started so many miles ago with a large number of people and slowly, our large group has been whittled down to this little band. Yet, we are all here, we are all healthy, and we all share the same dream of life in Oregon. I miss the people who have left us along the way, probably more than any of you can imagine. We have two choices. Either we can wallow in our sorrow over absent friends or we can pick up and move on toward our goal, together. It will not be easy the rest of the way and our small size will mean that we all need to work together to cross the obstacles that remain. I know that with the guidance of Peter, who has been west many times, and the protection of our Lord, who created the obstacles in our way, we will make it all the way to our new home. So, let's commit to share our burdens and our assets cheerfully to make this journey as safe and pleasant as possible."

For Father this was a lengthy speech. It worked, though, as each person committed themselves to the small group. I noticed that when a leader expressed confidence, people responded in kind. Father's confidence spread through the group and we were more cheerful as we moved away along the river.

The Snake River was not a friendly traveling companion. Moving along the side of the river, we heard the constant rapids of the water, but the cliffs barred us from seeing the actual river. Once we decided to camp for the evening, we needed to wind our way down a lengthy trail along the side of the cliffs to reach the water. Then, we needed to trace our steps back to the top of the cliff, winding back and forth along its sharp face. While carrying the water was not as hard work as manually guiding the wagons down steep hills, it still surpassed the labor of my wars with the weeds at our home farm.

That night, I heard a new lullaby. Beyond the cliff face, out of sight of our group, the Snake River sang a powerful song to us. Over the rocks, the powerful river raced through the narrow canyon, dancing over the boulders that resided in the middle of the riverbed, crashing with music that constantly reminded us of the power beyond the cliffs. The constancy of the river lulled me into a deep rest.

The next day we reached Rock Springs. Looking down at the little stream, we knew that while the water was not wide, it was fast-flowing, and the steep cliffs surrounding it made this a portion of water that we did not wish to approach. Uncle Peter told us he would ride along the banks of this stream and find a suitable place for us to ford. He urged the rest of our group to take advantage of the opportunity to mend clothes and make wagon repairs while he found the best trail.

Bitsy could not bear the rest in an inactive state. She wandered through the camp, seeking playmates but finding no one willing to leave the chores to entertain her kitten and herself. Finally, Miss Spencer, seeing the potential difficulty posed by a bored child and a hyperactive kitten, asked the Elliott girls to take the two active souls to gather herbs to supplement our diet. I knew that the herbs were an excuse to let Bitsy expend the energy outside of the narrow confines of our wagon train.

After we completed our chores, we decided to rest until Uncle Peter returned. I climbed down to the banks of the inhospitable Rock Springs and waded in, allowing the cold, rushing water to make my perpetually sore feet feel better. Once my feet were cooled and my body relaxed, I climbed up towards our wagon. I saw the Elliott girls wandering into the camp with a pot of greens, but without either Bitsy or Sally.

Miss Spencer saw them coming and rushed to meet them.

"Where is Bitsy?" I heard her question the girls.

"She was tired, so we sent her back to the wagons on her own. She is here, isn't she?"

Miss Spencer did not respond. She ran back to the wagons, found my father, and quickly explained the situation to him. He dropped the work he was doing on the wagons immediately and ran to the now frightened Elliott girls. He asked them, in a tone that I had heard far too often when I neglected the weeds, to describe where they had gone with my sister. When the reply came, unsteadily, that the girls had sent Bitsy back to the wagon train because she was tired, my father turned and raised the alarm with the remainder of the wagon train.

Quickly, everyone sprang into action. Search parties were organized and people volunteered for assignments as to which direction they should search. We left the now crying Elliott girls with their parents at the wagons to make sure that none of the animals wandered too far away. The rest of us all began a desperate search, along the side of the stream, through the desert away from the water, and along the cliffs of the Snake River to see if we could find the little girl, wandering along in the inhospitable countryside with her little kitten.

While I tried to control my thoughts, I could not help but imagine how my sister must feel, so little and alone in the middle of a country that was so large and unfriendly to little creatures. Was she hurt? Was she hungry? Was she afraid of the distances and the uncertainty of not seeing the family who loved her? All of these issues must grip her heart.

The usual time for the noonday meal came and left and no one stopped the search to eat. "Bitsy", I called, walking along the streambed, until my throat was raw with the effort. The longer she was missing the more morbid my thoughts became. What if she had fallen into the water and drowned? What if hostile Indians or fierce animals had attacked her? With every passing step, with every moment of absence, panic rose in my heart and tears in my eyes. I had already lost my mother. Would it be possible that our desires to move towards the sun would deprive us of the companionship of another of our loved ones? Panic seized my thoughts and played cruel games with my mind.

Finally, having expended all of my energy in the search for Bitsy, I stopped alongside the bank of the stream, winded from exertion and frustrated at the unprofitable nature of the work. "Oh Lord," I prayed. "We have worked so hard and tried to please You in all of our ways. We have thought that we sensed Your will sending us out to this country. Already, Mother died. We have lost good friends. Lord, it is too much to take little Bitsy from us. Help us, God, because You control every good and bad situation and if it is Your will, You can show us where to look to find my sister."

Peace filled my heart following my simple prayer of desperation. I did not know whether my sister would be found or not, but I knew, at that moment, that I was not alone in my concern. I also felt like my labor was not solitary. I continued looking for her with renewed energy. I continued combing the side of the creek, calling her name and wandering up and down the stream

Afternoon turned to evening. The heat of the day started to recede. Finally, in the distance, I heard gunshots beckoning to me. I knew that we had always used a rifle shot in the air to signal the beginning of our journeys and the times for breaks. I followed the sound of the shots and made my way back to our familiar wagons. There, in the middle of our little circle, was Uncle Peter, holding a tired and obviously very frightened Bitsy, who was cuddling a sleeping Sally very close to her. Standing over his shoulder was a family of natives who were obviously very concerned with Bitsy.

People came running from every direction. We all rushed and hugged Bitsy, expressing our happiness at seeing her. The events of the day had worn down her constitution and the surrounding attention just caused her to cry. Finally, Father lifted her into his strong arms and tenderly held her close to him until the sobs subsided and she slowly fell into a needed slumber. Father gently placed her into her bed and then he returned to the center of the group.

"Peter, we missed you today. How did you find Bitsy?" Father asked.

"Actually, Jedediah, I did not find her. We have these good people to thank for the finding of her. I was riding back from the ford of Rock Spring and I found them taking care of her along the bank of the stream. She had fallen among the brush and nearly been swept into the stream about a mile from here. These people were taking care of her cuts. She was very afraid. I was able to convince them that I was part of her family. We rode back here together because I knew that they wanted to make sure she was going to be cared for and because I know you want to reward them amply for saving Bitsy."

"Can you speak to them, Peter?" Father asked.

"Yes", came the response. "They are Nez Perce and I spent a little time in their area."

"Tell them I insist that they stay for a meal with us. We do not have anything fancy, but that which we have we will share with them. I cannot thank them enough. I am reminded of another father who had great joy when his child, who wandered away, became lost and was found."

Uncle Peter relayed the message and our guests gladly agreed to spend an evening with the grateful travelers. The family consisted of an older, gray-haired man, his daughter and son-in-law, who were young, attractive adults, and their two children who were a girl about the age of Bitsy and an infant boy. I wished I could have spoken directly with them because I was curious as to their life in this place. They clearly possessed little that we could covet, yet, their manner spoke of their dignity and not poverty.

What a night! The entire wagon group opened their remaining stores and put together a feast of fried chicken, ham, bacon, beans, rice and bread. Our guests contributed dried fish and quamash. Quamash was a beautiful purple flower whose roots the women pit roasted. Like women everywhere, when we responded favorably to their contributions, they were pleased.

After we all had eaten our fill, we sat around the fire. Father presented the woman of the group with a beautiful shawl that Mother had especially valued. He told them, through Uncle Peter, that this would help her stay warmer when the summer suns gave way to the cooler temperatures. This pleased both the recipient of the gift but also the men who surrounded her and showed the reflected happiness from their loved one.

Uncle Peter played his guitar for our guests. They enjoyed the tunes greatly. Then, the older Nez Perce man sang some songs in his language. Even though I understood none of the words, I understood the emotions conveyed by the song. Finally, when we finished our concerts, we each bedded down in our camps.

The next morning, we prepared to say our farewells to the new friends who had saved so much for us. Bitsy whispered to Father and he nodded his head in agreement. The two of them walked from our fire to the camp of the Nez Perce family. Shyly, Bitsy walked to the little girl and extended her hand to her. In the little hand was her constant companion, the corncob doll Suzy. Bitsy nodded to the girl and extended Suzy to her. Without a word, the girl smiled and gladly grasped the doll. With that final gift, we started on our day's journey.

Before the adventures of the previous day, Uncle Peter had explored the banks of the Rock Creek. He found that we needed to travel eight miles before the sides of Rock Creek would allow us to cross it. That day was spent driving to the ford, crossing the creek and then angling our way back to the canyons surrounding the Snake River. We did not make tremendous westward progress that day but we had placed a difficult obstacle behind us.

Traveling along the Snake River remained a mystery to us. We could hear, but not see, the pounding of a mighty river. The day after we rejoined the Snake, it revealed one wonderful spectacle to us. Across the river from us, we observed that on a single green cliff, fourteen waterfalls emerged. Two of them came the traditional way, over the top. The remainder of the waterfalls exploded from the sides of cliff, compelled to seek the open air from the underground streams that had previously confined them. The power of the sight caused us to hold our breath and gawk at the wonder. As we moved past along the endless road west, I thought about all of the wonders that we had seen on this journey. If Oregon proved to be half as wondrous as the spectacles along the trail, my brain would never lack for excitement.

There was not time to reflect. The days were shortening noticeably and this reminded us of the compulsion to move quickly. We knew, without ever saying a word aloud, that we had more mountains to cross and the later in the season we were the more likely, we were to face snow. While the traveler in us wanted to stay and fully learn about the wonders of waterfalls shooting from the sides of the cliff, we had no choice but to put our heads down and urge our oxen to move forward.

The next morning, Uncle Peter woke Father and me a long time before the dawn would break. Initially, I protested. Then, as my eyes focused on his figure, I realized that he was holding our fishing gear. Never wishing to miss an opportunity to do battle with swimming animals, I climbed out from under the bed and quickly grabbed the fishing pole.

Uncle Peter spoke quietly to ensure that he would not wake our sleeping companions. "I am going to show you a real treat today. You have never tasted anything until you grill salmon. Be prepared to work. They are bigger than the fish to which you are accustomed."

Always interested in a new taste treat, I hurried down the trail toward the water. Father, while better at masking his excitement, also moved more briskly than he typically did. If Uncle Peter thought that salmon were worth a predawn adventure, how could we resist?

Our bait in the river awoke the fish. Perhaps they knew they were invited to breakfast, but did not understand that their role was to be that of main course and not honored guest. I dropped my line into the fast, cold waters of the Snake River. Almost immediately, I felt the familiar tug on the line that let me know there was a fish wanting to be my breakfast. I felt faint disappointment when I saw that instead of salmon, I had snagged only a battling cutthroat trout. Any disappointment was wiped away when I remembered that the only alternative was another breakfast of bacon, bread and beans. The fish wanted to fight and battle before I pulled it safely to shore.

Father and I each felt some disappointment at catching so many fish simply because they were not the right type. Uncle Peter though only caught a few fish but one of them was a large salmon that would provide me with a new taste sensation.

Breakfast that morning cheered the entire wagon. Everyone who wanted to avoid the continuous bacon diet was able to eat trout for breakfast. Rubbed in cornmeal, the trout tasted better than I remembered. The mystery of the morning was Uncle Peter, who insisted on preparing the salmon on his own fire, away from the rest of us. He laughed when I questioned him about this and simply told me that salmon did not look like any other fish and he did not want me to make any decision about it on sight alone. Once the fish was cooked, Peter brought us over a healthy portion of salmon. I noticed, much to my shock, that the meat was a shade of pink that I had never before seen in any of my meat. Yet, since Uncle Peter swore by the flavor of the fish, I felt compelled to try it and I truly loved it.

Continuing along the river, we finally came to a place where the river burst out of the canyons surrounding it. Seeing the Snake River in all of its power was startling. Never before in my life had I seen any clearer water. The river ran so fast that the mere knowledge that we would eventually have to cross the river scared me.

Finally, Uncle Peter stopped our column at a place where the river appeared to stretch before us for miles across. I was surprised when he announced, "This is where the trail crosses the river. I know it looks like the river goes on forever. Do not look at the width of the river, focus instead on the three islands in the midst of the river. We will cross from island to island and use them to help us make it across the river. The first channels we will cross just like any other river. The last channel though is very deep. We will cross the river from the last island by tying the wagons together and floating them to the other side.

As Uncle Peter indicated, the first channels were quite easy to cross. Once we reached the final island, we crossed it and prepared the train for crossing. Each family secured their belongings, removed the wheels, and applied the pitch necessary to convert the wagons into floating boats. Father gave me the job of gathering the livestock and preparing them for the crossing. To the Torrance brothers he gave the job of chaining together our five wagons. The plan was to float the boats across and then convert them back to wagons once we reached the other side.

We moved our floating wagons into the fast-moving river. The river rose to a depth that threatened to swamp the boats, but the pitch held and our wagons floated. Halfway across the river disaster struck. The last wagon in the train, belonging to the Elliott family, broke away from the other four and tipped over. The girls screamed out of fear for their lives. Quickly, Uncle Peter steered his horse to the wagon and stopped it from drifting downriver. With the help of Mr. Elliott who had dived away from the wagon, they managed to tip the wagon back to floating. Unfortunately, the river water drenched everything the Elliotts owned. Uncle Peter helped guide the unhooked floating wagon toward the shore and finally all five wagons reached safety.

Mr. Elliott was furious. He immediately started yelling at the Torrance boys, who had failed to chain his wagon properly to the line of wagons. This led to the river tipping their boat over. Fortunately, while the people were thoroughly drenched, there were no injuries. Their foodstuffs were not so fortunate. The flour and cornmeal were thoroughly drenched and would no longer be usable. This would cause a great deal of difficulty for them.

Father intervened in the argument between Mr. Elliott and the Torrance boys. "We need to pull together. Josiah," my father said as he put his hand on the angry man's shoulder, "we will not be successful by continuing with this grudge no matter how justified it may be. I know that the boys were negligent in hooking the wagons. But, we all should have checked their work more carefully.

"Right now, we are in the middle of a wilderness. We need to pull together as a family. Whatever foodstuffs are lost because of this accident, we will all share with you. Either we all will make Oregon or none of us will. I fully intend to make it there and be your neighbor for the rest of our lives."

The other members of our group murmured their agreement. We might not be large in numbers, but we all agreed that we were in this endeavor together. We were about to see how well we had all learned our childhood lessons on sharing.

CHAPTER 19

MALHEUR RIVER

This near disaster sobered our group. We had heard for the entire journey how dangerous it was to travel over the hills and through the rivers, but until we had actually seen a wagon tip over in a rushing river, the stories of danger were no more real to us than stories of man-eating giants, fire-breathing dragons, and other mythical creatures. As much as the Elliott sisters irritated us with their careless ways, the reality that they could have drowned in the Snake River made the journey troublesome.

That evening, we camped alongside the river and tried to prepare ourselves for the next portion of our travels. Uncle Peter warned us that the next phase of travels would bring us more challenges about water, since we needed to leave the river and move quickly across dry, sagebrush-ridden land. We spent the remainder of our time by the Snake, fishing, washing clothes, and allowing the Elliott wagon to dry thoroughly. The damage to the wagon was worse than we had initially hoped. The food, other than the bacon, had suffered serious damage. The river also damaged the spare clothing they intended to use once they reached Oregon City. These losses would challenge the rest of us throughout the remainder of our journey and would damage the ballroom aspirations of the Elliott sisters.

WEST TO THE SUN

Warnings of desert crossing and the reality of desert crossings are two very different things. I understood heat. I understood dust. I understood the feeling that comes when the lips crack and the tongue sticks to the roof of one's mouth. I did not, however, understand a desert at this time of our journey could become a place of death. The more we walked down the trail, the more I noticed that the carcasses of animals became more frequent.

Once we traveled a full morning away from the river, the trail became a clear graveyard of horses, mules and cattle. The months of work, combined with the incessant heat and the lack of moisture, had made animal after animal fall over, unable to proceed. Then, once they died, the natural rotting process took over. A stench, unlike anything I had ever smelled, covered the land. The ladies tried to block it by covering their noses and only breathing into their handkerchiefs. This only minimally spared their noses from the all-encompassing smell. The only creatures happy in this desert mortuary were the vultures who circled above the carnage, confused only by having to choose between so many available meals.

I will remember many evenings on our journey for the rest of my life. The first evening away from the Snake River will be the only night I remember because the smell of the territory invaded our camp and kept us from a deep sleep. Uncle Peter tried to make jokes about the area, but humor in the midst of constant reminders of death did not amuse us. We clung, however, to the positive thought that none of the livestock on which our lives depended showed any signs of expiring.

Morning came none too soon. We left this area of death eagerly and moved forward at first light to the west. We had barely begun our journey when we passed another amazing sight. Alongside our trail, we noticed that bubbling out of the ground were springs of hot water. The land we had traveled contained watery wonders of which I had never dreamed. Doctor Woods noticed my curiosity and started talking to me:

"Jeremiah, hot springs occur naturally in a number of different locations. There are people who swear that they possess great medicinal value. By bathing in the hot springs, circulation is improved and the increased body temperature prevents illness from taking hold of the body. There are entire groups of people who try to cure any number of diseases with these waters. I am not sure they do much good, but I am also sure that taking the waters does no harm. I think for us, though, what ails us can be best be cured by making twenty miles' progress today."

I nodded my head vigorously. Every day showed me new adventures. The one adventure I wanted to avoid by moving forward was trying to pass through a winter blizzard in a covered wagon. Some other time in my life, I might indulge in soaking in a hot spring, but not today.

We moved ahead past the dry wasteland. Caring for the oxen was the most important job we did during this time. If I went thirsty so Todd could drink his fill, then that was a price we all would gladly pay. Still, the heat and dryness of the territory bothered me.

Late in the afternoon of the day we found the hot springs, we received another reminder of the dangers faced by people traveling on the trail. Alongside our trail, we saw a wagon smoldering from a recent fire. Lying by the wagon was a young man, with a bloody cloth crudely wrapped around his head. Upon seeing this, Father ordered the wagons to stop. Doctor Woods stopped his wagon, grabbed his medical bag and hurried to the injured man.

Father walked to the other side of the wagon and emerged, pale and shaking his head. He walked to our wagons and told us: "We

WEST TO THE SUN

need to dig a grave. There is a young woman dead on the other side of the wagon. It is a violent scene."

Sadly, we all grabbed the shovels. We had seen far too many of these lonely graves on our journey. Uncle Peter selected a location away from the trail so that wagons would not trample the isolated grave. Uncle Peter and Mr. Torrance began digging while I gathered the rocks that would mark the resting place and discourage wild animals from feasting on the dead body.

Each of the women of the wagon train took a cup of cool water to the injured man. After our women poured enough water into him, the man started to cough and gag. Although this was an unhealthy noise, it did let us know that he was still alive.

Once Doctor Woods finished his examination, he told my father that the man had suffered a bad concussion, but that he would live. The man needed rest; the one commodity the trail did not provide in any reasonable measure.

We decided to stop at the site of this incident for the evening. We finished the woman's grave. When the man was sufficiently alert, we asked him his name and the name of his deceased companion.

In a pain-slurred voice, he responded, "I am John Bayard from the Hudson Valley in New York." He choked a tear and continued, "The woman is my beloved wife Martha. We have traveled this far on our journey to Oregon where my brother lives. I fear now that I may never be reunited with him this side of eternity."

"Nonsense", Father replied. "Our doctor says that you simply need to regain your strength, but that you will surely live. As for your traveling, you will join our wagon train and we will nurse you back to health. I seem to remember a Biblical story where robbers along a trail beset a man. I believe that our Lord commanded that we show our Christianity by binding wounds and providing sustenance to our fellow man. We intend to do so with you."

The man smiled in a forced manner that let us know he was in serious pain. "It is fitting that you refer to that story. Yesterday, we were traveling down the trail. My wife had become terribly ill and the larger group of wagons abandoned us out of fear that the illness would infect the entire train. Once my wife felt like she could endure the bumping of the travel, I began to move along the trail. Around midday yesterday, a group of men on horseback joined us and began to ride alongside.

"I freely admit that I did not like their looks. They were a rough group, but I also was weary of traveling alone, since my wife provided me little company as she slept most of the day. We rode together and the time passed quickly. Once we reached this spot, the leader of their group produced a pistol and told me they had decided that they could make better use of my possessions. Then, he hit me with the pistol several times on my head until I passed out. When I awoke, my wagon was burning, the mules were missing, and the foodstuffs that we needed for our journey to Oregon were either stolen or burnt.

"Most tragically of all, when I awoke, I found they had murdered dear Martha. Those men decided that it was not enough to deprive me of my property but they also shot my poor, sickly wife. I crawled to where you found me, waiting for death to come along and take me. Fortunately, brother, you have come along before I died."

Showing more tenderness than I knew he possessed, my father patted Mr. Bayard on the hand. Softly he spoke "I know what you are feeling John. By the banks of the Green River, I buried my wife and I thought my heart. We will nurse you back to health, John and perhaps you can find a measure of happiness once we reach the treasures of Oregon."

That evening was a somber time. Indians, wild animals, and diseases had concerned us previously. Tonight, a new fear occupied our minds. Robbers! How could a group so small protect our possessions from armed men with the will to steal our possessions? Once we buried Mrs. Bayard and Mr. Bayard climbed to a bed in Major Smith's wagon, Father asked everyone to meet by the campfire.

Father spoke quietly. "I have heard from some of you that you do not believe we have the supplies to care for Mr. Bayard, who joins us without resource. I admit that I also question the wisdom of adding to our body. I cannot look at my children and tell them to follow the beliefs I teach if I let this man suffer and die alongside the road. I believe that since he joined our company in such a terrible way, we do not have the right to turn him away."

I noticed that all of the people around the fire nodded agreement, although some of them did so cheerfully and others did so out of a sense of obligation. Father continued speaking:

"I know that we have another problem we must address. We have not taken enough precautions to protect our assets from those who would steal from us. I propose that we have one of our men stay awake all night to watch against any harm that might come. Once Mr. Bayard recovers, we will have seven men with this group. This means that we will all have one sleepless night a week. Better that than we awake refreshed without our food or livestock. The young men," pointing to the Torrance brothers and me, "can help drive the oxen if you need rest during the day following a night of guard duty."

Following our discussion, a group of us explored the abandoned wagon, looking for anything that could help the wagon train continue on its journey. Scraps of metal, spare parts for the wagons, food, and clothing: all of these assisted us in traveling and we scavenged everything we could use from the burnt hulk of the Bayard wagon.

We continued our travel west. Mr. Bayard proved to be an amenable companion, quick with a witty comment and willing to assist in any task that needed completion. Even those of our company who only reluctantly allowed him to join soon agreed that adding him to our crew was fortunate. Each day he became stronger and before long, he took his turn watching the livestock, hunting for fresh meat, and guarding our wagons.

The desolate landscape gave way to more inviting surroundings when we found a break in the bluffs leading down to the Boise Valley. This valley promised us sufficient fresh grass for our oxen and enough water to allow us to drink our fill. Conservation may be a virtue and waste may be a sin, but to live in forced deprivation of water did not render us virtuous. To reach this valley we needed to descend another steep decline, but seeing the green of the valley inspired us to move quickly. Our near disaster crossing the river caused us to perform our jobs in moving the wagons down steep declines with more care than usual. We knew what carelessness could do and we were determined that nothing would cause us to tip our wagons and spill our supplies.

Each night we assigned a different man to guard us. We rotated this responsibility among the various men. The night Major Smith took his turn, we all went to sleep and expected a night of quiet rest. A loud gunshot and the roars of pain from our major cruelly interrupted our sleep when the moon was at its brightest.

We all awoke abruptly. The men came running with their guns in hand, since we thought our wagon train was under attack. The major rolled on the ground holding his left leg while he bellowed in pain. Finally, when we calmed him down, we fortunately found a different story entirely.

Major Smith told us that as he walked the perimeter of the wagon train making sure that there were no intruders, he did not see a hole in the ground. He stepped into the hole, stumbled to the ground and his rifle discharged. The shot hit him in the leg and caused him to feel both incredible physical pain but also the intense emotional pain of clumsiness that led to the injury.

Doctor Woods directed us to move the Major into the light. I held a lantern over the wound, which the doctor examined carefully. Doctor Woods smiled at him reassuringly and told him that the shot had gone straight through his leg without hitting any of his bones. Carefully, the doctor cleaned the wound and wrapped the leg in bandages. Then, we moved Major Smith back to his wagon and let him sleep in an embarrassed slumber for the remainder of the night.

Uncle Peter and I stood guard for the rest of the night. Uncle Peter shook his head. "Jeremiah," he said, "I wish things like this were unusual. In my experience, though, I have seen as many people seriously injured by accidents as I have seen people become seriously ill with disease. People need to be cautious especially when they handle rifles."

The next morning we watched Major Smith and Mr. Bayard make breakfast and do their chores together. Mr. Bayard had no strength following his injuries; Major Smith had no mobility following his wound but somehow, by working together they made their breakfast and cared for their oxen. Sometimes, I guess, a team works not because of its strengths but instead in spite of their respective weaknesses.

Our wagons moved down the valley toward Fort Boise. Since

the disaster at Three Islands Crossing, together with the addition of Mr. Bayard, we needed to buy additional supplies. The night before we arrived at Fort Boise, Uncle Peter described the history of this Fort Boise while we all sat around the campfire.

"When Nathaniel Wyeth built Fort Hall in 1832, the Hudson Bay Company panicked. The beaver trade was still profitable enough that they did not want any competition for the pelts. One of their leaders, Thomas McKay, found a site close to this fort and built his own fort for the Hudson Bay Company to encourage Indians and mountain men to trade here instead of at Fort Hall. Once Nathaniel Wyeth sold Fort Hall to the Hudson Bay Company, there was no longer a competitive need for Mr. McKay to stay here, but the company decided that there was enough distance between the two forts to allow them both to thrive. Then, when the beaver trade slowed and people started heading west, the company decided to make money by outfitting Oregon-bound travelers.

"In 1835, Mr. McKay turned the fort over to a French Canadian trader named Francois Payette. To make the fort profitable, Monsieur Payette knew he needed workers but he did not have enough of his colleagues willing to follow him here. Payette found a new source of labor that amazes me to this day. Instead of trying to staff the fort with Canadians, he instead went to the Sandwich Islands in the South Pacific and convinced men to leave their paradise and come join him at this wilderness fort.

"This was a fantastic business decision. Instead of showing signs of homesickness, the people from the islands developed a reputation for treating all of the people who came to the fort like kings. Monsieur Payette is gone from the fort now, but his workers and their reputation remains."

The next morning we saw the stockade clearly needed repair.

We did not care about its state of disrepair, as long as the fort would allow us to buy flour and cornmeal.

Once we resupplied at the fort, we met our old friend, the Snake River. To cross the Snake we used the help of some Shoshones who helped us navigate the river that had cost us so much earlier. Since Fort Boise was the last major supply post on the way to Oregon City, leaving it behind made us feel as if we were rapidly approaching our destination.

We traveled along the banks of the clear Snake River for several days after Fort Boise. Finally, we reached a river with the unfortunate name, Malheur River. Miss Spencer told me that Malheur meant misfortune in French. Evidently, according to Uncle Peter, the Canadian fur trader Donald Mackenzie stored his cache of beaver pelts along the banks of this river. A native found this cache and stole them. Mackenzie told this story to some of his younger colleagues, one of whom named the river misfortune in his honor.

Uncle Peter continued his story with a cautionary tale. "I have heard that in recent years Stephen Meek led a wagon train along this river to find a shortcut to Oregon City. Meek was a fine mountain man, one of the first to claim land at Oregon City. This time, though, his luck deserted him.

"Meek led his group through the Malheur Mountains that rise to the west. Wandering around in the mountains, the wagon train ran out of water. By the time they escaped the mountains and found water, two dozen people had died from thirst. People who survived this expedition started a legend that they had found so much gold that they could have filled blue buckets with the nuggets. Who knows if the nuggets were gold or if the minds delirious with thirst invented the story?"

Once we crossed the Malheur River, Bitsy began to worry us.

Miss Spencer prepared dinner for our group. While it was no better than our typical fare, it was no worse either. Bitsy refused to eat. Her stomach hurt, she claimed, and the smell of the food made her stomach upset. We hugged her affectionately that night and tucked her into bed. Then, when she refused to eat breakfast, Father scolded her lightly for being an obstinate child. At the noonday break, without any prodding from an adult, she crawled into her bed and fell asleep with Sally. She repeated this pattern the next day and Father promptly summoned Doctor Woods to examine her.

Doctor Woods carefully poked and prodded at Bitsy. He spoke gently to her, then kissed her on the forehead and left our wagon. Once outside, he spoke to us in a concerned fashion. "She is a very sick little girl. The diet of this trip could make even the strongest person sick. Food to her is unappealing; part of this is in her digestive tract, which cannot handle the dry bacon and beans. A bigger part of this is in her head. The food does not taste like her mother's cooking and she simply does not want to eat anymore. I hope that her mind will overcome her digestion and she will decide that food of any type is better than starvation, but I have seen some people, mostly the elderly, decide that they no longer want to eat or to live. I think that Bitsy's mind is making that decision."

We prayed that evening, individually and as a family. We loved the little girl immensely. To be so close to our end goal and lose one of our loved ones would be too cruel a fate.

CHAPTER 20

DOE CANYON

Illness scared us. We had known too many people who had died on the trail and seen too many graves along the way to make us comfortable that our loved one would always recover. I thought of my mother, who had been ill for a very short time before we buried her along the banks of the Green River. Surely, the same thing would not happen with little Bitsy, but deep inside, my soul a silent voice told me to prepare myself to leave another loved one behind.

I slept fitfully. I was tired, but my spirit was so troubled that when I closed my eyes, only the weakest form of rest arrived. When Father woke us that morning, my body was tired beyond measure. I stumbled out from under the wagon to the familiar camp smell of bacon and coffee. As I walked to the water bucket to wash my face and invigorate my soul, I nearly stepped on a recently killed rabbit. This still warm rabbit lay outside the back of our wagon.

Uncle Peter saw the rabbit as soon as I did. He picked it up and examined it carefully. He said aloud, "What is this? I wonder if Bitsy would eat fresh meat today. There is only one way to know."

With these words, he cleaned the rabbit and cooked it. Miss Spencer took the fresh rabbit and without telling Bitsy what it was, she managed to convince her to eat some of the fresh meat. Doctor

Woods watched this approvingly. "Every bite she eats", the good doctor said, "brings her closer to good health."

That day we continued traveling alongside the clear waters of the Snake River. Our hopes that Bitsy would recover from her malady quickly disappeared at lunch, when she announced that even the sight of our dry camp food made her want to vomit. We debated whether we should force-feed her, but Doctor Woods assured us that the rabbit would help her throughout this day. Due to this advice, when the same situation arose at our evening meal, we kissed her and put her to bed. We were concerned, though, since we could not count on rabbits falling from heaven much like manna did on the children of Israel of old.

My tired body fell asleep easier that evening. I woke the next morning, stumbled to the water bucket, and once again nearly stepped on a still warm, dead rabbit. Uncle Peter saw it at the same time, laughed and told me, "I guess we know what to do with this meat falling from the sky."

Uncle Peter cooked the rabbit. Miss Spencer took the rabbit into the wagon, together with some of our bread. Bitsy ate all of the fresh meat eagerly and even ate some of the bread. We felt better after this meal, thinking that as long as mysterious rabbits appeared, Bitsy would live until we reached Oregon.

In the middle of that morning, we arrived at Farewell Bend. At this point, our traveling companion, the Snake River, continued powerfully through a tight, intimidating canyon, but we veered away from its inhospitality. The beauty of the river was undeniable, but our home lay a different direction from it and so we simply waved at it, and as the name of the place implied, we bid the river farewell and headed overland away from the clear water.

Bitsy's appetite remained disconcerting. At our noonday meal, she ate a little bread, but still professed that the remainder of the food made her ill. This scene repeated itself in the evening and once again, a very concerned family placed her in bed.

The next morning, Uncle Peter shook me awake when it was still dark. "I have to see what's happening, Jeremiah," he said. "Let's see if there is another rabbit presented as a gift for Bitsy and if so, from where the rabbits are coming."

I forced my eyes open. As much as I wanted to sleep, I also was very curious since the only food Bitsy ate came from an unknown location. We sat and watched, battling the urge to fall asleep. Finally, our patience in waiting was rewarded.

Walking in from the bushes surrounding our camp, with a rabbit firmly in her mouth, was Bitsy's own kitten, Sally. We watched as Sally dropped the rabbit by the back of the wagon, licked herself clean, and hopped up into the wagon and curled up next to Bitsy's sleeping form.

I stared at Uncle Peter, with my jaw wide open, and found that our looks were identical. Uncle Peter woke Father and explained to him that the little kitten whose life Bitsy had spared along the bank of the creek so long ago had somehow sensed that she needed to preserve the life of the little girl. Father silently shook his head, as if he could not believe us, or even if he could believe us, he could not believe the love of the little kitten who knew that her owner was in trouble.

That morning, Father held Bitsy in his arms as she ate the rabbit. I could not hear what he was saying to her, but I know that he was telling her the story of the little kitten who loved her so much that she hunted for her each morning. I also know he assured her that as much as the little kitten loved her, that her family loved her even more and wanted her to live. While I could not hear the precise words, I know they had the desired effect for from that time forward, Bitsy started to show more signs of surviving life on the trail. Bitsy ate full meals that day. The kitten must have observed this and processed the knowledge that recovery was occurring because the next morning no rabbits appeared at the back of our wagon.

Traveling away from the Snake River, we followed the Burnt River through the Burnt River Canyon. Days became noticeably shorter, reminding us of the approach of autumn with the possibility of early snows that could attack us in the Blue Mountains short of our ultimate goal of the Willamette Valley and the lush land we sought. While the days remained warm and dry, the mornings served as a constant reminder of the approach of the end of summer. The fires felt better on our bodies than any fire we had previously. The morning water was brisker and on occasion, we needed to break a thick layer of ice before we actually could drink. Captain Watkins had warned us during our earlier times along the Platte River of the need for speed. These warnings reverberated in our ears as we continued onward, on the long journey towards our new homes.

Along the way, I had heard from many people mention of a group of travelers in a train called the Donner party. When people spoke of the Donner party, they spoke in hushed tones, much as children sleeping in dark rooms speak of the monsters that lurk around the corner. Finally, one evening along the Burnt Canyon, I heard another reference to the Donner party from a tremulous Mrs. Elliott. Once she left, I turned to Uncle Peter and asked him who the Donner party was and why people spoke of them in such tones of terror.

Uncle Peter sighed and then spoke to our family group. "I know you have heard rumors of the story and I have not wanted to tell you of these unfortunate people since our own experience

WEST TO THE SUN

is most assuredly different from theirs. The Donner party traveled to California two years ago. They traveled too slowly, took some wrong turns along the way, and followed bad advice as they tried to blaze a new shortcut through the mountains around the Great Salt Lake. The delay cost them three fateful weeks.

"With all of their delays, they tried to cross the Sierra Nevada Mountains into California in late October. That was much too late to cross the mountains. Blizzards trapped them and kept them from moving forward or back. They sent a small group ahead to California for relief. Before the relief party could reach them through the incredible snows, they ran out of food. Lacking any other food, they ate all of their animals, boiled the oxen hides to sustain themselves, and finally they started to cannibalize their dead comrades in order to sustain life. Out of the eighty-seven people who started with the Donner party, nearly half of them died. It is a gruesome, terrible story that people tell themselves when they want to ponder the worst thoughts imaginable."

What a horrible story! I knew Uncle Peter was right in his caution that we were nowhere near the risk of these people since the mountains we needed to cross were not as high as the Sierra Nevada Mountains, but the story made me want to walk faster as we continued along the trail toward the Blue Mountains.

Following a difficult journey along the Burnt River, we reached Flagstaff Hill. The trail in this area was strewn with rocks and littered with the dead bones of livestock that had journeyed this far but lacked the strength to continue. Sage plants reached the height of our shoulder and cut at us when they brushed against our shirts. The climb to Flagstaff Hill demanded great exertion but we gained a hopeful view beyond from the summit of the hill. Ahead of us stood the Blue Mountains. We needed to cross these mountains, drive beyond them, and reach our destination. While the mountains looked formidable, hope still filled my heart and for the first time since we left St. Joseph, I allowed myself to dream of a life where I would sleep in a bed and not on the ground underneath a wagon.

Beyond Flagstaff Hill, we continued our journey closer to our home. We descended a steep hill that demanded all of our skill. This labor was rewarded, though as we entered the most wondrous valley. Unlike the usual valleys that possessed irregular shapes, this valley was perfectly round and surrounded by the most wonderful forest of evergreen trees. I watched Father examine the dirt, taking soil into his hands and letting it fall through his fingers to the ground.

Father turned to Uncle Peter. "I cannot imagine how wonderful the Willamette Valley must be if settlers are passing up this good, lush territory. If we had not promised to lead this group to the Willamette, then I would be tempted to stay here for the rest of my life."

Uncle Peter nodded. "This is wonderful territory, Jeddie. I think we would do well in the Grande Ronde Valley. However, the land to which we are heading will surpass this ground tremendously. We need to keep moving forward and we need to do it quickly."

Father nodded. We paused only briefly to allow us to pick as many berries as we could carry. All of our group, but most certainly the Torrance family, had been showing signs of trouble with their diets. The lack of fresh fruit had left them with bleeding gums, which Doctor Woods had indicted was a sign of scurvy. While we lacked the ability to gather citrus fruits as sailors of old did in the South Pacific, the doctor assured us that any fruit would help us in balancing the diet. It did not hurt us that this medical cure tasted wonderful.

Following our berry hunting expedition, we moved across this fertile, tree-lined valley until we reached the river cutting through the valley. While we had crossed rivers far more challenging than this one, such as the Snake River at Three Islands Crossing or the Thomas Fork of the Bear River, the Grande Ronde River was not one with which we wanted to gamble. At the river crossing, a group of Cayuse Indians offered to help us across.

At times like these, I learned to appreciate money. With our would-be guides at the Grande Ronde, the concept of paper money or even gold dust meant nothing. Only through using Uncle Peter as a translator and negotiator were we able to come to an agreement, trading bacon and clothing for a safe crossing of the river. Happily, we closed the transaction with a supper of smoked salmon that the Cayuse offered us.

Crossing the river, we began the climb to the Blue Mountains. These mountains stretched in front of us, presenting a solid barrier to our future home. Uncle Peter told me that before 1843, there was no road through these mountains. Then, Marcus Whitman led a wagon train through to his mission on the other side, creating the road.

Climbing this mountain, I began to wonder if perhaps Doctor Whitman had not claimed too much credit for the road. The path was narrow and twisted, always upward, back and forth across the mountains. For a number of days, we urged our tired oxen onward to the peak. Slipping and sliding on the rocky road, our friends complied, stepping always forward as we ascended the mountains.

Trouble struck in an unusual manner. As we were continuing our climb, late one afternoon, one of the oxen pulling the Major's wagon stepped into a hole. Even over the squeaking of the wagon wheels, we heard the snap as the poor animal's leg broke and it fell down. The sudden stop of the oxen caused the wagon to lurch violently to one side. We ran to the wagon and using all of our strength managed to keep it from tumbling back down the mountain.

Major Smith knew what he needed to do. He cocked his rifle and shot the poor, suffering creature who had worked so hard to bring the Major this far on the trail. Uncle Peter announced that we needed to stop at this point for the evening and have a proper funeral for the ox.

A funeral for an ox? I loved Bob, Bill, Todd, and the rest of our friends as much as any creature, but this affection did not make me want to say any particular prayers over this animal. At Uncle Peter's instruction, the Torrance boys and I went and gathered as much wood as we could possibly carry. When we returned from our chore, I could see that what Uncle Peter had in mind was more a funeral feast than a sad time of prayer. Just as the group stopped and feasted on the buffalo, we were going to enjoy as much meat as we could eat due to the death of the oxen.

Unlike the prior feast though, this meal had a sad tinge to it. Losing an ox was dangerous, since without their strength we would not be able to continue west. The men spoke about it and decided to share the remaining animals among our five wagons so that the Major would not bear the entire burden of the loss. Once we decided on sharing the burden of the loss, we enjoyed roasting and feasting on the dead ox with more enjoyment, music, dancing, and storytelling.

We continued up the Blue Mountains. The temperature was cold and the skies opened in a miserable rain. This was not a strong rain that would produce fear due to a storm, but a slow, steady, cold rain that beat against our faces and robbed our souls of energy. Up the moist slopes we continued, crossing Emigrant Spring and refreshing our water supply for the dry land that would follow. Once we finally reached the top of the trail, looking out to the northwest, we saw the Cascade Mountain range, reaching high into the sky. We knew we would skirt these mountains and that knowledge made us extremely happy since they appeared to be a fierce opponent for us to battle so late in our travels.

Once we began our descent from the peak, we remembered how difficult a job the decline could be. We used our ropes and chains, lowering ourselves slowly to the floor below. Moving too fast could lead to total disaster if the wagons broke free and crashed into kindling on the rocks below.

Following our decline, we made it to a canyon alongside the Unadilla River. Father called our small group together and told us, "We have made a very difficult journey in the last week. Crossing these mountains has not been easy on our machines, our animals, or us. For the next day, we will rest, work on repairs on our wagons, and let our animals graze. If you are done with your chores, you can go hunting. I understand that this canyon is sometimes called Doe Canyon, because so many deer, elk, and pronghorn live in this area."

These were wonderful words. The last days had been so tiresome. The last leg of the journey, without my old friends the O'Donnell twins, was simply hard work. A hunt could enliven my heart once again.

That night at dinner, I asked Father if I could go hunting. Father smiled and told me that I could go hunting only if I agreed to take Uncle Peter with me. A day of hunting with Uncle Peter certainly appealed to me and that night I crawled into my buffalo robe with a great sense of anticipation.

The morning sun rose brightly. We ate breakfast and hiked

into the canyon. It was a pleasant late summer day that did not either cause us to sweat or shiver. We watched carefully for any of the animals who we hoped would provide us with the food that would supplement our diet. Ever since the disaster at Three Islands Crossing, we were aware that our food supplies had been shrinking. Uncle Peter warned us that there were pioneers who traveled the last miles of the trail with little more than a biscuit and a piece of bacon each day. Others showed up in Oregon City with so little that instead of rushing to their new farmlands, they begged food to survive the winter. Every berry we picked, every fish we caught, or animal we hunted kept us further from that fate.

During our hike into the canyon, a high-pitched squeal startled me. I glanced at Uncle Peter, who smiled. "Elk," he said. "This is their mating time of year and these bugling sounds are how they attract each other. It is amazing that an animal so powerful has such a high, whining noise. Do not make a mistake because of their timid voices. These animals are magnificent."

With that word, we split up and went on different paths. Previously, Uncle Peter told me that elk were the most wonderful-looking animals. Their legs extend feet off the ground, making them much taller than a deer. The legs were thin, but powerful. Elk acted in a way that spoke of pride in their size. The multiple shades of brown added a beauty to their being.

Notwithstanding that beauty, I knew that a single elk could feed our wagon train for several days. Each day we avoided using our food supply would protect us from becoming starving beggars at the end of our journey. I ground my teeth together. I carefully walked along the trail, keeping my eyes trained on the bushes around me. Determination filled my body and motivated me to hunt as if my life depended on the outcome, which indeed it may.

WEST TO THE SUN

Slowly I advanced. Finally, ahead of me I noticed movement in the bushes. My hands started to sweat. My heart raced inside of me and the dryness in my mouth caused me to want to spit on the ground but also to realize that no spittle would ever form. I knelt to one knee and watched as an animal, beautiful in its majesty, emerged. It walked slowly, confidently, as if it knew its size precluded any but the fiercest animal from advancing against it. I smiled. I knew I was that fierce animal who would conquer it.

I pulled my rifle carefully into firing position. I focused my eyes on the animal's midsection. I cocked the rifle and twitched my finger on the trigger.

Just as I was about to pull the trigger, a small, awkward younger elk walked from the other side of my target. I blinked. I realized at that moment that the larger animal was a mother. I thought about my own mother and the way I felt when Father told me, she had died. No creature should feel that sorrow because of me, I resolved. A tear welled in my eye. I pointed the rifle into the air and fired. The elk pair looked at me and trotted off confidently to the other side of the trail, into the bushes and out of sight.

Uncle Peter came to me. I looked at the ground and said, "I missed."

He smiled at me, placed his hand on my shoulder, and whispered, "I saw. I would have missed also." We stood there silently without moving for a minute, each lost in our own thoughts and then we moved on, seeking other targets.

CHAPTER 21
BARLOW ROAD

On the remainder of our hunt, we each shot a mule deer buck. We struggled, but successfully managed to return to the wagon train. Venison brought smiles to everyone's faces as they realized that we would not suffer with nothing but bacon for a time. We roasted one deer on the open fire, and butchered the other, salted the meat, and stored it for future use.

Around the fire that evening, the people wanted to talk more than they wanted to dance. When Uncle Peter lowered his guitar and came to me, I looked at him and asked him about the wagon ruts I had seen on the other side of the river. Usually, on the trail, wagon ruts appeared only on one side of a river since people wanted to follow the easier path.

Uncle Peter nodded. "Good observation, Jeremiah. Until last year, the trail ran on both sides of the river. People on the other side of the river went to the Whitman Mission. People on this side of the river took a shortcut to the Columbia River. Since the Whitman family died and the mission was destroyed, there is no longer any reason to go to the Whitman Mission and the other side of the river is unused."

I asked Uncle Peter one more question. "What happened to the Whitmans?

"It is a sad story," he said. "Marcus and Narcissa Whitman were missionaries who came to this part of the country to work with the natives. Narcissa was the first white woman to make the trip through South Pass to Oregon on this trail. They settled about forty miles north of here and started to work with the native people. They told people about Jesus and tried to help people in the area grow more food to take care of them.

"As more settlers came to the Willamette Valley, people used the mission as a place to restock their food and to rest. Doctor and Mrs. Whitman viewed hospitality as part of their Christian duty and so they always welcomed and restocked the wagon trains for the last leg of the journey. Sometimes, their generosity caused them to provide too much food and they wound up having short rations. These people gladly suffered a lack of food if it meant that their generosity helped other people make it to their new home.

"Last year, one of the wagon trains stopped at the mission. Some children had measles and the children at the mission became sick. Doctor Whitman tried to cure the children. With the white children, his efforts were successful. With the Cayuse children, though, the medicine did not work and they died. Seeing this, some of the Cayuse people thought that Dr. Whitman had poisoned the Cayuse children and decided to take revenge. One night, some of the Cayuse attacked the mission and killed the Whitman family and some of the people staying with them."

I interrupted this story. "That is horrible. How could anyone do something like this?"

Father, who had been listening to the story, replied, "Be careful Jeremiah of making bold statements until you think about the issue from all peoples' perspective. Think about how you would feel if you were a Cayuse parent who had seen the white children survive the disease and yet you held your dead baby. We have a certain ability to fight this disease; the Cayuse do not. They could assume, though, that the medicine provided by Doctor Whitman was poison. If I thought someone poisoned you or Bitsy, I might be tempted to murder, especially if I did not believe in God. It is best, though, that we hate no one since it can blind us to both logic and God's love."

I silently thought about this story. The Whitman family had accomplished so much in their life, but this accomplishment did not give them the peaceful end to their existence. Perhaps whenever people came together without understanding one another, there would always be the prospect of tragedy and bloodshed.

The next morning we continued along the Unadilla River. The countryside was sparse, brown and uninviting. Deep down I knew that this was not the Willamette Valley, but still, I hoped there would be a major change in the scenery when we finally reached this valley. Any of the dry lands along the way could have offered us this barren territory. Surely, Oregon would offer us more than this grassland.

Fortunately, as we approached the Columbia River, brush became more plentiful to serve as kindling for our fires. It was in this area that Miss Spencer had one of her most memorable adventures.

One morning while most of the men were fishing, hunting and otherwise trying to supplement our food, Miss Spencer found her own manner of supplementing food. Since Miss Spencer had developed a skeptical attitude about our promises to bring fresh meat for the morning meal, she was preparing the bacon for another breakfast. Suddenly, out of the bushes a fierce black bear with an appetite for bacon approached our wagon. Miss Spencer grabbed a broom and tried to whisk the hungry animal away from our breakfast. The bear continued onward, toward our precious food supply. Without thinking, she dropped the broom, grabbed a rifle, cocked it, and fired. The animal fell where it had been killed by a single gunshot.

Hearing the gunshot, we dropped our fishing poles and ran back to the wagons. We found Miss Spencer standing over her dead bear with a triumphant look of puzzled victory. When we burst into the circle of our wagons, she looked at us and asked, "Why did you need to leave the camp to find meat? Meat found us."

With those words, the entire party started laughing. We listened to Miss Spencer tell the story and then returned to the river, gathered our fishing tackle, and came back to the camp where we began the difficult task of butchering the bear and taking the bearskin for a souvenir that Miss Spencer could pass through to her future children and grandchildren. Generations from this time, her descendants would try to imagine the fierce woman who killed bears. Certainly, the mental image would differ from reality since no future generation would conjure the picture of a petite woman like Miss Spencer when they thought of their bear-killing ancestor.

Traveling west became more challenging. While we wanted to keep the same schedule of travel, the available daylight diminished the later into September it became. One day, we wanted to travel twenty miles. While we showed the same amount of energy we previously had shown, by the time we reached our camping place, the only fuel we could find for our fire were green, moist cedar limbs. These limbs refused to burn, instead smoldering uselessly. Supper proved cold, tasteless, and unfulfilling.

We moved on from that place of hunger early the next morning. Our goal that day was to reach the John Day River. While walking, Uncle Peter told us the story behind the name of the river.

"Back in the fall of 1811, at the time Fort Astoria was being built, one of the men of the overland expedition was John Day. Day wound up running into a band of natives that meant him no good. They captured him. Instead of killing him though, they took all of his clothing and let him wander around this wasteland naked. Another group of natives saw him and took mercy on him. They gave him food and clothing and let him spend the winter living with them.

"The next spring, he traveled west through the Columbia River Valley until he finally arrived at Astoria, where Robert Stuart, his commander, determined that his adventures had driven him slightly mad. When Stuart began his overland journey to the east, he took Day with him as an act of mercy. Partway through the journey, Day decided he would prefer to stay here, where he remained a solitary and slightly insane figure until he finally died."

This story convinced me that while I might admire mountain men, the lifestyle away from other humans could drive a man crazy. Perhaps it was better to know one and to hear stories about them than actually to become one.

Crossing the John Day River challenged us. The evening before, we had received a steady rain. The added moisture caused the river to rise. We needed to call upon all of the skill developed over countless crossings to make it across this time. We were too far along in our journey to allow a river to spoil our remaining food. Carefully, we picked our way across the river and gladly reached the opposite shore without adventure.

Beyond the river, we moved into the continuing terrain of the Columbia Plateau. The plants had a look of autumn about them; the green colors of spring were a distant memory and had been replaced with the brown that spoke of preparation for the coming winter. Boredom overtook the company. We knew one another's favorite stories so well by the time we had walked nearly two thousand miles together, that we spoke not so much to have other people listen as to pass the time.

Our next watery obstacle was the Deschutes River, which, stretched in front of us about a day and a half after we left the John Day River. Facing us beyond the ford of the river was a large hill that we climbed only by pushing our animals hard to make the climb. Previously, we had climbed other hills with less difficulty. The weariness of the animals, brought on by hundreds of miles of exertion, made the challenges greater than they would have been had we faced them at the beginning of our journey.

By noon of the following day, we reached The Dalles. This community bordered on the Columbia River of which we had heard so much. Once we cared for our animals properly, I wandered through the town and walked to the edge of the cliffs overlooking the river.

What an amazing river! The Columbia River demonstrated total power. The water ran quickly and the waves on it and the whirlpools generated by it told me that was not a river upon which we would ever gladly float. Some of the streams we crossed, I could have thrown a rock from bank to bank. This river, if I launched a rock with a catapult, I could not have reached even the middle. Silently, I vowed that I would respect this river always and never try to engage it in a struggle unnecessarily.

Walking back through town, I saw countless wagons and families waiting their turn to board rafts that would take them down the powerful Columbia. The town itself was unimpressive. The amount of traffic had reduced the streets to bottomless, irregular pits of mud, from which animals would need to exert themselves greatly to move the wagons. I felt that I needed to stay out of the streets since the mud could swallow me whole.

As I walked past the wagons, I listened to the conversations of the people. I heard that some of them had been waiting for days going on into weeks for a ride. The longer the wait the more desperation etched on their faces. I knew that soon, this pained look might be plastered on my face.

Returning to our campsite, I heard the men discussing our options. Uncle Peter was speaking "The trail directly west ends here. The territory overlooking the Columbia River is too difficult for wagon travel. Until the last few years, the only way to reach the Willamette Valley was to float down the Columbia River on rafts. This journey was expensive and dangerous. In this river, there are rapids and whirlpools that can suck a raft in and never release it. Many people have died on this river and for those who survive the journey is terrifying.

"One family, the Applegates tried to float down the river and lost one of their rafts, which cost several lives, including some of their children, the age of Jeremiah. At that time, they decided that the Columbia River should not be risked in a journey to Oregon City, so Mr. Applegate created another route to the Willamette Valley. His road would have kept us with our California travelers much longer and passed us into the valley from the south. This journey is so long that there is really no reason to take the road.

"Another alternative is to take the Barlow Road. A few years ago, Samuel Barlow was so disgusted by the danger and the cost of the journey on the river that he received permission from the territory to build a road through the woods and mountains to Oregon City. The road is narrow and rough, but it will take us to Oregon City. One of my friends once told me that if you choose to go on the river, you will wish that you had taken the road, but if you take the road, you will wish you went on the river."

The men discussed this report. While the thought of difficult road passages appealed to none of us, the prospect of drowning in the dangerous Columbia River also lacked appeal to us. Finally, after much debate, we agreed that we would spend a day outside of The Dalles, provision ourselves for the remainder of the journey, and then start our trip on the Barlow Road to Oregon City.

Once we stopped, we looked at our provisions and made a list of items we needed. Food topped our list; the supply of flour and cornmeal had reached a low enough point that if we did not buy some more, then the entire party would need to be placed on half rations of flour. The bacon supply was sufficient, since we had managed to supplement our meat with the deer that Uncle Peter and I had killed at Doe Canyon and some of the salted bear meat from the animal Miss Spencer killed in our camp. Our clothing showed signs of wear, but we should be able to make it to our new home without wardrobe trouble. Armed with this knowledge, we went into town the next day, with Miss Spencer riding Uncle Peter's horse and the rest of us walking alongside.

That evening, we found much to our disappointment that another of our companions would leave us. After our evening meal, Mr. Bayard walked over to our campfire. He sat down on a log along the fire with a pensive look on his face. Clearly, he was thinking thoughts we knew he wanted to share with us. Knowing that it is easier to continue a conversation than start one, Father spoke, "You look like you have something on your mind, John. Speak freely. You are among friends."

Mr. Bayard nodded. Softly, he said, "Jedediah, you truly saved my life. Most men would have abandoned me for dead alongside the trail with my fallen wife. What is more, your kindness has given me at least a reason to continue living and I will never thank you enough. In town today, I met a man and he has offered me the opportunity to share a ride down the Columbia River with him tomorrow morning. I believe that for a man who has lost everything and everyone on this trail, it is important to reach my destination and start to rebuild my life as soon as I can. So, tomorrow morning, when you and your wonderful family start on the Barlow Road, I will begin my journey down the Columbia River."

Father smiled and warmly clapped Mr. Bayard on the back. "Godspeed, John Bayard," he said. "I cannot argue with you on your decision, even though the decision would be the wrong one for me to make with my family. I hope that the Lord leads you safely to a happy place. This trail has been cruel to you. We know, though the Scriptures teach that the Lord never places a burden on a man that he cannot bear. You are truly a good man, John Bayard and we will keep you in our prayers. When we each reach the Willamette Valley, we all will take it as a personal insult if you do not seek us out to let us know how the journey ended."

We all said farewell to Mr. Bayard. I would miss him as a good companion who had joined us under tragic circumstances. I could not fault him for his desire to end his travels. I knew that we were just over one hundred miles away from Oregon City and I, too could not wait for these miles to be completed.

The next morning, we watched as Mr. Bayard loaded his few surviving possessions onto his back and walked into town. Once he was out of sight, we turned south and started to work our way to the Barlow Road. To travel on the Barlow Road, we paid a toll of five dollars per wagon and ten cents for every milk cow, ox, and horse. We gladly paid the toll, knowing that it was less expensive than the river route and presented us with less danger.

Traveling the Barlow Road, I remembered Uncle Peter's cautionary words that those who chose to travel on the road would soon wish they had gone by river. We were no exception. The trail was wide enough only for a single wagon to pass and the road was slippery with rocks and dirt that tested our ability to climb the steep grades. We possessed little strength. The knowledge that home was waiting just a hundred miles away gave us hope that we would soon arrive at our new lives, but this hope was not accompanied by a needed infusion of strength into our tired muscles.

The Barlow Road trapped us among the trees, much like a prisoner trapped in the close enclosure of a tight jail cell. Unlike the trail by the Platte River, where if we felt constrained by other travelers, we could spread out until there was sufficient room for all travelers, there was room for only one wagon to pass at any time. If there was a disaster ahead, then all traffic would stop and we would remain fixed in place until the obstacle cleared.

Moving through the Tygh Valley, we again crossed the Deschutes River. We started heading west along the White River. We traveled through the thick, jungle-like forests, which sunlight only occasionally penetrated. The forest supplied the fuel for our camping fires and the river supplied us with the needed water. With the food we had conserved on our journey, we felt we would soon be able to reach our new homes.

On the fourth day traveling on the Barlow Trail, we crossed Barlow Pass. From this place, we saw Mount Hood, which was even more magnificent in sight than in my imagination. Snow covered its peak and reminded us of the need for speed, as we wanted to have a roof over our heads before the cold rains or snow of winter fell on us. Still, we stared at this mountain for the longest moment.

Uncle Peter told us the legend of the creation of this mountain. The Multnomah tribe believed that the Great Spirit had two sons who fell in love with the same maiden. To win the heart of the maiden, the boys went to war, destroying forests and villages. Seeing this destruction, the Great Spirit destroyed both sons and the maiden. Regretting his rash action, the Great Spirit built three mountains memorializing the three lovers. Mount Hood was one of these mountains.

I knew this story was only a legend. Regardless, I appreciated that we would soon call home a territory with this incredible mountain.

CHAPTER 22
OREGON CITY

We continued along the narrow, rocky way through the dark forests of Oregon. We drove our tired oxen forward, using the coaxing of a man with his friend and not the tone of a man abusing an animal. These creatures had served us so well since the time we purchased them in Tennessee. When people spoke of my family, I thought of the loyal, hardworking oxen as much as I did my human relatives. Not even Uncle Peter spoke of Todd as roast beef anymore; the toil of nearly two thousand miles had grudgingly won Uncle Peter's loyalty and respect.

Once we left Barlow Pass, we continued our travels to Laurel Hill. Reaching the top of Laurel Hill, we stood amazed as the road led down the sheer face of the cliff. Looking at the decline, Father shook his head and whistled. "That must be a sixty-degree decline. We are going to need to do some work to pass down this cliff."

The men examined the slope. Clearly, the oxen could not lead us down the hill. We unhitched the oxen and walked them, back and forth down the face of the cliff. Then, attaching ropes to the wagons, we slowly lowered the wagons down the cliff. Unlike other hills, the angles caused us to see the wagons as being airborne, dangling over disaster as we pulled them off of the top of the hill down to the road waiting below.

I moved through the remainder of the Barlow Road as if my head were in a dense, impenetrable fog. After the adventure at Laurel Hill, we walked for three more days to reach Oregon City. Mechanically, I went through the motions of our daily life. We awoke, ate our breakfast, hitched the oxen, and marched. Oddly, we lacked energy due to the two thousand miles of marching, but we were also energized by the knowledge that our new home was less than a hundred miles away. Therefore, we walked, thinking less about the journey and more about the destination.

Once we crossed the final toll station of the Barlow Road, I guessed that even the oxen felt excitement. I looked around and saw, for the first time in the longest time, large hardwood trees where the leaves showed some sign of the autumnal colors. Looking around us, I decided that if this were what my new home would look like, then I would surely never leave.

We stopped our wagons just shy of Oregon City. We camped once again, as we had done so many times. This was different, though, because we knew we would be parting soon. While all of us would live in the same valley, never again would we all work together to cross a river or climb a hill. We had spent so much of our lives together in the last several months and they had become a part of me.

We spoke of our plans for the coming days. Father planned to visit the land office the next day. Then, following a day or two of shopping in the community for things we had left behind in Tennessee, we would head to our new farmland. Others expressed the same desire. We did not want to rush good-byes, but the thought of reaching new land, building our new homes, and sleeping inside appealed to all of us.

Uncle Peter rode into town that evening before supper and returned with a man wearing a white collar around his neck. The man looked sternly at all of us, with a frown on his face that spoke of nothing other than he was an important personage who demanded our respect.

Uncle Peter called for all of us to gather around our family fire. "Friends," Uncle Peter said in a cheerful tone, "I want to introduce you to a new friend of mine. This is Reverend William Geary, a duly licensed minister of the Methodist Church. I mention this because, friends, there is going to be a wedding. I have asked lovely Sarah Spencer to marry me and she has honored me by saying yes. The two of us discussed whether we should wait until civilization for the wedding, but we both agreed that we would rather be married in God's good outdoors with our comrades than to marry each other in a church building full of strangers. So, the last party of this trip will be our marriage."

I nearly fell over with surprise. Every person in the party whooped their excitement. The men rushed to congratulate Uncle Peter while the women devoted their attention to preparing Miss Spencer for the best wedding possible in this rustic surrounding. We prepared the couple for the ceremony and, finally, Mrs. Elliott announced that the bride was ready.

Uncle Peter stood by the fire with Father and me. Out of the wagon, assisted by the other women, stepped Miss Spencer clothed in an ivory dress owned by Mrs. Torrance. Miss Spencer walked holding Bitsy by the hand. While the fit of the dress was imperfect, the look on Uncle Peter's face spoke volumes about her beauty.

Reverend Geary directed traffic and made sure the couple stood at the appropriate places. All of our comrades stood around the fire that served as a church altar. I ran my hand through my hair, hoping that the cowlick that had stood upright for the better part of two thousand miles would finally lie down. Finally, the Reverend began speaking and ended my hair war.

"Ladies and gentlemen. We are gathered in God's good outdoors to take part in the most time-honored celebration of the human family, uniting a woman and a man in marriage. This is a living testament to their love. We remind them that they are performing an act of complete faith, each in the other; that the heart of their marriage will be the relationship they create and its devotion to our Lord."

The reverend turned to Uncle Peter. "Peter Symons, will you receive Sarah Spencer as your wife? Will you pledge to her your love, faith, and tenderness, cherishing her with a husband's loyalty and devotion?"

Peter turned and smiled softly at his bride and quietly said, "I will."

Reverend Geary then gently asked Miss Spencer, "Sarah Spencer, will you receive Peter Symons as your husband? Will you pledge to him your love, faith and tenderness, cherishing him with a wife's loyalty and devotion?"

Through tears of joy, Miss Spencer smiled and whispered, "I will."

Reverend Geary then had them join hands and kiss. He announced to us that in as much as there were no objections to the union, they were husband and wife. We applauded and rushed the couple whose smiles told me all I needed to know of their joy. As happy as I was for the two of them, I was equally pleased for me since I knew that being a married man, Uncle Peter would no longer disappear from us to undergo distant adventures. I thought he would be a part of my daily life for as long as I remained in Oregon.

The celebration continued most of the night. We ate the last of our special foods and we sang and danced in happiness. As the darkness advanced, we moved our wagon away from the rest of the group so the young couple could spend their first night as a married couple in rustic privacy. Once they went to the wagon, though, the entire group grabbed metal plates and sticks and interrupted their time together with the noise made by hitting the plates hard with the sticks. We ran around the wagon, causing them to come out and join us until finally Father decided that his brother and sister-in-law were entitled to some marital happiness, and sent us away from them.

The events of the day excited me so much that I did not sleep well that night. When morning arrived, we ate breakfast quickly, cared for the animals, and finally awoke the happy newlyweds. Once they joined us, we immediately started to head into town. Oregon City was where our new life would begin; fortunately, our life would not revolve around Oregon City. Like The Dalles, deep, rut-filled mud covered the streets. The city consisted of possibly a hundred houses, two churches, two saloons, and two blacksmiths. All of this mattered little to us as we cared mostly about arriving at the land office.

Under the laws of Oregon, a married man was entitled to six hundred forty acres of land and an unmarried man received three hundred twenty acres. My heart beat in excitement at the thought of coming home. This land was so beautiful and even I, who was just an unskilled boy, could see that this land was better than the bottomland we had left behind us.

Before we left Tennessee, we all agreed that we would try to have adjoining farms and whatever division the state might put on it, the family would share the land evenly. In examining the land records, we placed a claim for nine hundred sixty acres of farmland thirty miles south of town. Smiling, we left the land office, feeling much closer to home.

Miss Spencer, now my Aunt Sarah, was shopping for supplies while we took care of the land. I noticed that Uncle Peter looked for her when we left the office and upon finding her, his face lit with an unlimited joy. Father visited a blacksmith and ordered the plows our farms needed. He then visited a mill and bought more flour and some seed necessary to help start our crops next year. Finally, after we ate our noonday meal in town with a very joyful Reverend Geary and his wife, we returned to the wagon.

That night, Father called our group together for one last time. "Friends, this is our last evening together. Tomorrow, we head to our new farm and start building a home in this fine valley. We have worked so hard together. We have experienced joy and sorrow, none of which would mean as much without the companionship of good friends. I hope that you may become my neighbors south of town and we may continue to grow deeper friendships in the days ahead. If our paths do not cross again, let me say that I have loved everyone of you and hope to see you throughout eternity. Be good, prosper as families and love God."

With this talk, Father went one by one to each person in the wagon train, shook hands, embraced and bid a final farewell. We all followed suit and realized that for all of the petty irritations of the trip, close bonds existed between all of us, bonds built of tears, laughter and sweat. We spent that evening in sweet reminiscence both of the people who sat around the fire currently, but also the people who had begun our journey and no longer were with us.

It rained the next morning as we pulled out of camp, a solitary wagon heading to an unknown home. Father brought the detailed legal descriptions of the land of our claim. We moved down the road, with each turn of the wheel adding expectation to our homecoming.

At noon of the second day, we crossed a small stream cutting through a stand of tall trees dramatically painted with autumnal leaves of the brightest red, orange, and yellow. We drove to the top of the hill and Father then turned the wagon to the west off the road and stopped. He jumped off the wagon seat, spread his arms around him and said simply, "Look at this land. This is our home."

Home! What a beautiful word. The five of us gathered in a close circle, held one another's hands and said a sweet prayer of thanksgiving. The rain fell, but the moisture landing on the good dirt on which we stood gave us hope of a fruitful time coming.

EPILOGUE
HOME

We worked all winter, cutting trees and building two beautiful log homes for our families and laying out the fields that would sustain us in the coming years. Trees that would cool us in the summer and protect us from the winds of the winter surrounded the cabins. In the main room of our cabin was a fireplace on which we placed the candlesticks that Mother had secreted away against Uncle Peter's advice when she packed our wagon so many months ago. Next to the fireplace sat her rocker on which rested a prized quilt that she had made as a newlywed. In the coming days, Father would frequently touch this quilt gently and develop a look on his face that was neither smile nor frown, but which told us that his thoughts were located a long distance and time away from us.

The first night I spent in the loft above the main floor of our cabin, I thought much and slept little. I smiled when my hand touched the grizzly teeth that Jim Bridger gave me. I remembered the adventures of the trail: the buffalo hunt, the fears of Indian attacks and the struggles across rivers and up hills. I thought of the sounds of the trail, from the constant squeaking of the wheels to the roar of the prairie winds or the high-pitched squeal of the elk. As I lay in my loft, I thought about the O'Donnell twins, Billy

Hollis, and Captain Watkins, friends who affected my life greatly but each of whom I probably would never see again. I thought of my precious mother lying in a grave along the banks of the Green River. She would have loved this fertile, beautiful valley.

I thought of other family members. My silent father who I had learned to love instead of merely fear over the miles together. Uncle Peter, now a married man, who taught me so much about survival and life on the trail. Aunt Sarah and Bitsy, each of whom taught me in their own ways about life, love, and determination. I loved my family and the good God who brought us to this place.

Downstairs, I heard the sleepy purring of Sally, no doubt dreaming of rabbit hunts and nearby mice. In the distance, a coyote called for companionship. The rain fell gently against the solid roof. I sighed, a sound of sweet contentment. The trail would always be a part of me, but now I was home.

Finally, home!